The Lynx

IN THE SAME COLLECTION

By Michel Corday
The Eternal Flame

By André Couvreur
The Necessary Evil
Caresco, Superman;
The Exploits of Professor Tornada (3 vols.)

The Lynx

by
Michel Corday & André Couvreur

Translated, annotated and introduced by
Brian Stableford

A Black Coat Press Book

Introduction

Le Lynx by Michel Corday and André Couvreur, here translated as *The Lynx*, was first published by Pierre Lafitte in 1911. It had the unusual privilege of an English translation, published in America by Dillingham in 1913 as *The Inner Man*, but that version is extremely rare and almost impossible to find; even Everett Bleiler, the great bibliographer of American imaginative fiction, never managed to lay his hands on a copy; thus, the present translation seemed a worthwhile endeavor.

The novel is notable within the history of French *roman scientifique* as a significant extended treatment of the notion of telepathy, and it represents a point in the evolution of the genre in which it had become both possible and expectable to combine a serious *conte philosophique*, attempting to address an interesting question regarding the desirability of a hypothetical alteration of human nature, in the context of a suspenseful thriller in which a powerful and clever arch-villain must somehow be thwarted, although the odds are heavily stacked in his favor.

It was not the first time that the philosophical aspects of the "thought-reading" had been addressed in French fiction; the first extensive treatment was carried out by Delphine de Girardin in *Le Lorgnon* (1832; tr. as "The Lorgnon" in the Black Coat Press edition of *Balzac's Cane*)[1], but Madame de Girardin had approached the theme more prudently, in the context of a mild social satire and a relatively conventional love story. Her

---

[1] ISBN 978-1-61227-368-6.

thought-reading device, although given a slight pseudo-scientific gloss, was essentially magical, and thus of intrinsically arbitrary and strictly limited existence; the one featured in *Le Lynx*, by contrast, is the product of scientific discovery, invested with a much more forceful hypothetical reality, capable of being reproduced indefinitely and gifted to the entire human race. That sharpens the philosophical question markedly, and it is also worth nothing that it changes the love story element of its more complex plot considerably. Like *Le Lorgnon*, *Le Lynx* is orientated toward a problematic "happy ending" seemingly difficult of attainment, but it calls the assumed "happiness" of the ending into question in a far more brutal, and far more intriguing, fashion than its pioneering predecessor.

Both of the authors who collaborated in the writing of *Le Lynx* had written previous *contes philosophiques* within the genre of *roman scientifique*, although both were better known at that point in time for naturalistic fiction; both of them were also to go on to write more works of a similar nature. Couvreur must certainly be reckoned one of the key contributors to the genre, especially to the sector of it that Maurice Renard called "scientific marvel fiction," and although Corday's contributions to the same sector of the genre were fewer in number and lighter in literary ambition, they were by no means insignificant. There were other pairs of writers who worked in tandem within the genre but they were mostly pedestrian producers of formularistic works; the exceptions all appear to be instances in which an experienced and artful writer—Jules Verne and Théo Varlet are the most conspicuous examples—revised a manuscript produced by someone else, without any preliminary association. Corday and Couvreur certainly did not require anyone to revise their work, and must surely have planned and executed the writing of *Le Lynx* in close collaboration, discussing every element of it even if they took turns at writing particular sections. It represents, therefore, the most interesting marriage of minds within the genre.

According to the Bibliothèque Nationale catalogue, Michel Corday was born in 1869, although other sources record the date as 1870. He was educated at the Collège Chaptal and the École Polytechnique. He is best known today because he edited the final collection of works left unpublished at his death by his friend Anatole France, *Pages inédites d'Anatole France* [Unpublished Pages by Anatole France] (1925), and also wrote a memoir of the author, *Anatole France, d'après ses confidences et ses souvenirs* [Anatole France, in accordance with his confidences and memories] (1927). The latter helped pave the way for Corday to achieve considerable success thereafter with two further biographically-based works, *La Vie amoureuse de Diderot* [Diderot's Love Life] (1928), focusing on the private life of the great Encyclopedist, and *Charlotte Corday* (1929), about his most famous namesake, the assassin who stabbed the Revolutionary leader Marat in his bath.

Prior to that late success, Corday had enjoyed a long career, when he was moderately well-known as a writer of light popular fiction, mostly in a sentimental vein. His first novel, however, had been the more intensely earnest *Le Cancer* [Cancer] (1894), written when that diagnosis was still relatively unfamiliar and the mere word first began to engender a quasi-superstitious terror, thus afflicting the luckless protagonist with the status of a modern leper. It was presumably that novel, which has something in common with André Couvreur's early work, that attracted his eventual collaborator's admiring attention. *Intérieurs d'officiers* [Officers' Home Lives] (1894) set a pattern that was to become more typical of Corday's endeavors, however, and was followed by *Femmes d'officiers* [Officers' Wives] (1895), *Jeunes mariés* [Young Couples] (1896) and *Coeurs de soldats* [Soldiers' Hearts] (1897).

Mon petit mari, Ma petite femme [My Dear Husband, My Dear Wife] (1899) was probably Corday's most successful novel, and in the early years of the twentieth century he became a regular contributor to the new generation of middlebrow magazines that sprang up in that period, including *Touche à Tout*, which serialized several of his novels and numerous shorter pieces, and *Je Sais Tout*. He continued to publish steadily, save for the expectable interruption by the Great War, when he worked as a civil servant—an experience that served to instill him with an ardent pacifism—until his death in 1937.

Corday's first significant venture into *roman scientifique* was the striking novelette "Le Mystérieux Dajan-Phinn" (1908 in *Je Sais Tout*; tr. as "The Mysterious Dajan-Phinn" in the Black Coat Press anthology *The World above the World*),[2] about the difficulties a reclusive scientist has in persuading his skeptical colleagues that he has created an artificial human being. *Le Lynx* was his second. Among his post-war works, the satire *En Tricogne, un an chez les Tricons, roman très contemporain* [In Tricogne, a Year among the Tricons: An Exceedingly Contemporary Novel] (1926) also has an inevitable fantastic element, but his most significant

---

[2] ISBN 978-1-61227-002-9.

8

contributions to *roman scientifique* were *La Flamme éternelle* (1931; tr. as the title story of the Black Coat Press edition of *The Eternal Flame and Other Stories*),[3] about the discovery of a new source of power, and its sequel, describing a bold experiment in induced pacifism, *Ciel Rose* (1933; tr. as "Pink Sky" in the same collection).

André Couvreur was born in 1863 at Seclin in the Nord; his baptismal name was actually Achille-Émile-Henri Couvreur, but he signed his early literary works, all of which were intended for the theater, "A. Chils," adapting his Christian name. The first production that was staged, in Lille in 1885, appears to have been a farce entitled *Ipéca et Cuana*. It is difficult to determine whether any others were produced prior to *Le Secret de Polichinelle* [The Secret of Polichinelle], a satirical play in verse staged in 1893, which appeared in print in the same year under the extended pseudonym of "André Chils." The author retained the André when he began to use his own surname instead of the improvisation

By the time *Le Secret de Polichinelle* was produced, Couvreur had qualified as a physician, receiving his degree in 1892—slightly belatedly, perhaps because he had been pursuing his literary ambitions in parallel with his studies. His father and older brother were both doctors, and he had doubtless been encouraged to follow in their footsteps, perhaps a trifle reluctantly, but it must have been obvious by 1892 that medicine offered him far better opportunities to make a living than literature, and he presumably made a firm commitment to establish a steady income when he married, in 1893. He never

---

[3] ISBN 978-1-61227-189-7.

surrendered his literary ambitions, however, and when his novels began to appear he was quick to become an active member of the Societé des Gens de Lettres as well as maintaining his medical endeavors; it was probably through that organization that he met and befriended Corday.

The 1890s was a good time to begin writing novels set in the world of medical practice, which was becoming a fashionable literary topic, aided by the abundant publicity given to the medical advances it was hoped that intensive scientific research—like that carried out at the Institut Pasteur, founded in 1887—might soon produce. Corday caused something of a sensation with *Le Cancer*, which broke new literary ground in its consideration of the psychological and social effects experienced by its protagonist after receiving the diagnosis of his condition, and Léon Daudet caused a sensation of a different kind in the same year with his scathing satire on the medical profession in general and surgeons in particular, *Les Morticoles* [a slang term for doctors, approximately decodable as "death-sowers"].

Couvreur's first novel was *Le Mal nécessaire* (1899; tr. as *The Necessary Evil*),[4] a scathing account of a brilliant but morally irresponsible surgeon, Armand Caresco, who has something in common with the villain of *Le Lynx*, Dr. Castillan, although the latter is more of a caricature, as befits his more luridly melodramatic context. *Le Mal nécessaire* was advertized as the first volume of a trilogy collectively entitled *Les Dangers sociaux* [Social Dangers], and was soon followed by two thematic sequels *Les Mancenilles* [a noun improvised from the toxic plant *Hippomane mancenilla*] (1900) and

---

[4] Black Coat Press, IUSBN 978-1-61227-253-5.

La Source fatale [The Fatal Source] (1901), the former dealing with the threat posed by syphilis and the nexus of infection maintained by the prostitutes of Paris, and the second with the perils of alcohol abuse.

After completing his first trilogy Couvreur began a second, collectively entitled *La Famille* [The Family], with *La Force du sang* [The Strength of the Blood] (1902) and *La Graine* [The Seed] (1903). Before writing the third volume, however, he digressed into fiction of a very different sort by producing a futuristic sequel to *Le Mal nécessaire* featuring the same protagonist: *Caresco, surhomme, ou le voyage en Eucrasie: Conte humain* (1904; tr. as *Caresco, Superman; or, A Voyage to Eucrasia*)[5] —a rare example of a boldly fantastic sequel to a grimly naturalistic work. In *Caresco, surhomme*, which is set in the mid-twentieth century, Caresco, now immensely rich and equipped with numerous advanced technologies, has acquired a heavily-defended private island where he has establish a utopia of sorts, in which surgically-enhanced beauty is almost universal, free love is assisted by elaborate aphrodisiac technologies, and he is worshiped as a Dionysian demigod.

Although Couvreur did go on to complete his second trilogy with *Le Fruit* (1906), the core of his subsequent literary work consisted of a series of scientific marvel stories dealing with potential developments in biotechnology, all credited to one Professor Tornada. Tornada began his career in *Une Invasion de macrobes* (1909 in the literary supplement of *L'Illustration*, reprinted in book form, in a revised version, 1910; tr. as "An Invasion of Macrobes" in the first of the three vol-

---

[5] Black Coat Press, ISBN 978-1-61227-254-2.

umes of *The Adventures of Professor Tornada*)[6]. It was the publisher of the book version of that novella, Pierre Lafitte, for whom Couvreur and Corday then wrote *Le Lynx*. Both stories appear to have been deliberate attempts at popular melodrama, presumably reflecting the relative lack of success of *Caresco surhomme* (for all its ambition and spectacular brilliance) and his later naturalistic novels.

Presumably the experiment in question was not deemed a success either; although *Une Invasion de macrobes* was reprinted several times in the course of the century, *Le Lynx* was not, and became almost as hard to find as *The Inner Man*. When Professor Tornada returned after the interval of the Great War (in spite of the inconvenience of dying at the end of the first novella), he was a markedly different character, having combined Caresco's surgical skills with his original biochemical expertise, in order to figure mercurially in a series of extended *contes philosophiques*, in which melodrama, although by no means eliminated, took a back seat by comparison with satirical and sentimental issues. All the later novellas in the series appeared in the periodical *Oeuvres Libres*, only the first of them, *L'Androgyne* (1922; tr. as "The Androgyne") being reprinted in book form, the publisher of that volume, Albin Michel, apparently having pulled out of a four-book contract to issue more.

The subsequent stories in the Tornada sequence were "Le Valseur phosphorescent" (1923; tr. as "The Phosphorescent Waltzer"), "Les Mémoires d'un immortel (1924; tr. as "The Memoirs of an Immortal"),

---

[6] Black Coat Press, ISBNs 978-1-61227 -279-5, -280-1 & 281-8.

"Le Biocole" (1927; tr. as "The Biocole") and "Le Cas de baronne Sasoitsu" (1939; tr. as "The Case of Baronne Sasoitsu). The last-named is of particular interest in relation to the present volume in that it reiterates the speculative motif of *Le Lynx*, again in the context of a crime story in which an innocent man is famed for a seemingly-perfect murder, and subjects the central philosophical issue to a re-examination that might be reckoned considerably more cynical.

Le Lynx is not the best of Couvreur's scientific marvel stories, by any means, but it has a more complex plot than any of the others, which adds an extra measure of suspense to the story, and it is as challenging as any of the others in the problematic rhetoric of its conclusion. The ending tacitly invites the reader to make an assessment of an evaluation of the key philosophical question offered by a character whose entitlement to issue such an evaluation is dubious in the extreme, thus making the problem even more convoluted than it is in essence. It is, in consequence, a story well worth reading and well worth weighing with all due care in the scales of approval, no matter how the balance might eventually tip in the reader's mind.

This translation as made from a copy of the Lafitte edition kindly loaned to me by Marc Madouraud; I am extremely grateful for his kindness in making a very rare text available for a new translation.

Brian Stableford

THE LYNX

PART ONE

I

In the clear night, Gabriel Mirande made out the white walls of the village and, above the foliage of the square, the brown silhouette of the church and the bell-tower. The young scientist was alone, absolutely alone, on the road that traversed the fields, linking the railway station to Chaligny. Nothing was alive, nothing was moving in the nocturnal countryside save for the scintillating stars swarming in the summer sky.

Sometimes, a perfume passed through the calm air, the odors of ripe crops, trodden grass and warm earth; and Mirande shivered as if it were a caress. Since his departure from Paris his senses seemed to have been refined and sharpened under the empire of an abnormal nervous tension. Perhaps he owed that to the excessive emotions that had assailed him recently, perhaps to the stimulant injection that his master, Brion, had given him in advance.

He penetrated into the village, where his footsteps resonated between the closed facades. Everyone was asleep. Only one window remained illuminated, on the first floor of the inn. From time to time, as he passed by, a dog barked in a courtyard; and, incapable of mastering his nervousness, he started every time, his spine chilled by a frisson, although all the houses were familiar to him in the village where he had been born.

Mirande passed under the linden trees of the square, whose flowers embalmed the night. Then he pushed a gate, which grated sadly. He was in the cemetery, whose graves were grouped together, in accordance with the ancient custom, around the church.

That path was very familiar to him, alas. He and his sister Jeanne had still been children when they had escorted their father and their mother, at a short interval, to that nearby mound, shaded by yews and florid with roses. The names on the crosses, already half-effaced by time, and the steles reminded him of the faces of friends...

This time, however, it was before a freshly-filled grave that he intended to meditate first. Three days...for three days Simone Castillan had been buried in Chaligny cemetery. He knew the family tomb well, a large and heavy stone almost level with the ground, in a quiet corner, under large aspens. In the shadow increased by the screen of foliage he made out the bouquets, wreaths and sprays that strewed the stone, whose flowers, still fresh, were shining, as if they had retained the light in their corollas.

Standing there, head bowed, he sank into a dolorous meditation. He wept for the adored friend of his childhood and youth, for all the love and all the poetry of his life.

How he had loved her! She had always appeared to him prestigious, distant, almost divine. Already, when he was no more than a village schoolboy, a little peasant, thin and timid, he had contemplated her with a kind of veneration through the railings of the noble estate where she lived on the bank of the Yonne. And later, when a tutelary hand had raised him above his condition, when he returned to Chatigny on leave in the tunic of a collegian, he had experienced, in crossing Simone's path, in going past her dwelling, the same religious hesitation.

Perhaps he would never have addressed a word to her without his sister Jeanne, whose hard life under the patronage of Sens had not eroded either her valor or her enthusiasm. The two girls, doubtless seduced by the contrast in their nature, had acquired a mutual amity. Simone's parents, who were reputed in the village to be proud, dared not deprive their daughter of that playmate, and the beautiful domain had been opened to the ecstatic little Mirande.

Those vacations… they remained for him the intervals of light, the blue gaps in the somber wall of the boarding-school. Innocent days, fishing expeditions, picnics on the grass, escapes into the woods, in which his timidity melted, in which Jeanne's laughter rang out, and the well-behaved and careful Simone became animated.

The years at the lycée had gone by, gray and similar, but crowned by those sunlit vacations. And it was during one of those returns to the village that he had found, instead of an indecisive adolescent, a complete young woman that he hesitated to recognize. He had just entered Brion's laboratory as an assistant. Henceforth, their childish camaraderie was over, Mirande no longer dared go into the beautiful domain. Before Simone, his hands clenched, his gait stiffened; he lost his ease and his simplicity; he had become conscious of loving her.

For nothing in the world, however, would he have risked the confession, so afraid was he of appearing to covet the young woman's fortune. Rich at present, she would become even more so in future. He possessed nothing. And even if he had unmasked himself, even if she had loved him, she was too submissive to tradition, to obedient to her family, to rebel without suffering.

Unaware even whether she retained her tender childhood amity, therefore, he had nourished a secret and desperate passion for her until the day when she had married, in accordance with the rules of society. She had married Doctor Castillan.

Who can tell whether his chagrin was not more bitter than day, on learning of Simone's marriage, than a year later, on learning of her death? The noblest love has terrible undercurrents of egotism. Who can tell whether it had been less cruel for him to know that she was lost to everyone than lost to him alone?

No more than he had had the courage to follow the nuptial cortege, had he had the courage to go to the funeral. When the ceremony was over, however, he took the first opportunity to go to Chatigny, where Simone had wanted to be buried.

A letter that he had received one morning from his notary had furnished him with a pretext for his departure. The same evening, when his work at the laboratory had finished, he had thrown himself into a train, even though the state of fever and weakness in which he had left his master, Brion, had caused him some anxiety.

In any case, trials appear to come in clusters to fall upon the prey they have chosen. At the moment when the health of his benefactor preoccupied him, when the death of Simone Castillan revived in him the melancholy of the past, Mirande was still under the influence of an implausible nightmare: his best friend, Henri Lacaze, his sister's fiancé, had been accused—and then, alas, convicted—of a crime of blood and money. The judgment that condemned him to forced labor for life had been pronounced only a few days before, Mirande could still hear his howls of innocence, and he could still see the gesture of savage violence with which he had threatened the tribunal and the jury.

But he reproached himself for an impiety for evoking before the dead woman memories that did not animate her. He would have liked to talk to her, to murmur all the words that he had not dared to pronounce to her. Now, she no longer belonged to anyone, either to her proud parents or to a husband. She had been returned to herself. He could allow his heart to expand.

Obedient less to the ritual custom than an instinctive need to draw nearer to the tomb, to incline even more deeply before her, he knelt down. His eyes closed and his head leaned forward, he savored the bitter sweetness of evoking and seeing again all those faces, all those Simones, all those portraits that his memory had made and fixed in the great light of childhood.

Suddenly, he raised his head again, his hands at his temples. Was it the night, the lugubrious location or the dolorous evocation? It seemed to him that he had heard someone speak.

Evidently, he had only been the victim of a hallucination, inasmuch as the voice had appeared somehow immaterial, as if it had been addressed directly to his mind, without striking his ear first.

Again, however, he perceived the subtle murmur...

Oh, this time he was certain of not being mistaken. He had heard the words distinctly: "I can't... where am I?"

For one second more he hesitated, refusing to formulate the thought. Then the truth dazzled him. It was her! She was not dead...

He leaned over, his forehead against the stone. Plaints reached him, in a neutral, distant tone, devoid of emphasis: "I'm stifling... where am I? Wait... I can't move... oh! That veil over my face..."

How, through so many obstacles, could he perceive those faint moans? He did not dwell on that. She was alive! She was alive...

She must have emerged a short while ago from a lethargic state. She was about to suffer the most atrocious martyrdom. But an attempt could still be made to snatch her from the torture before she succumbed to it. He would save her. He had no other goal henceforth, no other reason for being.

Springing to his feet, leaping over the mounds and the stones in order to take the shortest route, he reached the gate. In the square, the window of the inn was still illuminated. He ran to the door and found it locked. He attacked it with furious blows of his fist and his foot.

Finally, the casement opened. A shadow leaned out, grumbling.

Breathless, Mirande shouted: "Madame Castillan isn't dead. Come down quickly. I'll meet you in the cemetery."

For he had run toward the nearest aid, and the most prompt—but he needed other collaborators. Fortunately, he was guided by the extreme lucidity that reveals itself in certain people at critical moments. In his mind, a list was established, an itinerary drawn up. It was necessary to alert the mason, the gravedigger, the physician and the gamekeeper. Fortunately once again, he knew all the inhabitants of Chatigny and all the doors.

Alas, he ran into the torpor of the first sleep every-where. It seems that a leaden air weighs upon sleeping villages. Here, no one responded to his appeals; there, he collected only surly grunts, a suspicious interrogation. But that mild, discreet, reserved man would have bat-tered down walls that night, violated dwellings, and woken an entire town. He named himself, shouted the news, howled as if to tear his throat, doubled his blows upon the doors until his fists were bleeding.

His vehemence ended up prevailing. Before every house, listening at the closed shutters, he waited for the sound of heavy footsteps and the buzz of voices. And his attention was so prodigiously extended that he thought he could divine the meaning of the distant words. Here the annoyance of an abrupt awakening was brutally re-vealed, elsewhere the curiosity of such a rare event; on the one hand incredulity, or the hope and calculation of an unexpected gain—and also joy, the beautiful human joy of being able to snatch one of their fellows from death.

Having alerted all those aides, Mirande, without waiting for them, ran back to the cemetery. He wanted to counter the waiting by movement, by action, by thought, forget the flight of time, the precious minutes lost.

Oh, what if the help arrived too late…! What if the spark of life reanimated in that tomb were extinguished forever...

Simon must be suffering an abominable torture, since she had recovered consciousness. To be buried alive...who can tell whether the circumstance might not be more frequent than is generally believed? He recalled the audacious theories of Doisteau, a young surgeon he had known during a residency at the Brion laboratory. According to Doisteau, death was often only apparent.

An organism ought only to perish by falling apart. In many accidents, life was merely suspended. If it were definitively avoided, it was due to skillful intervention or fortunate hazard that it resumed its course. It was like an automobile stopped by the roadside; if one can find the source of the trouble and remedy it, it sets off again immediately—but if it is abandoned to itself, it degenerates, and soon falls into veritable death...

Gradually, however, the village was animated. From here and there, the click of a door and a heavy tread resounded.

Soon, a small squadron was gathered around the tomb. But what slowness, what laxity there still was in the work...

As time went by, Mirande lost his lucid calm. Feverishly, it seemed to him that he could still hear, in a kind of vertigo, the reflections that he had surprised among those men behind their closed shutters.

He could not stay inactive any longer, his hands inert, Perhaps his aid might not be useless. He took possession of a pickax and braced himself with the others to shift the massive stone.

Suddenly, while they were all uniting their efforts Mirande heard Simone again. She had recognized the horror of her situation.

"Buried...since when? Days? Hours? It's frightful...I'm doomed...help!"

He did not want to interrupt the labor of his companions, but, overwhelmed by horror and hope, to stimulate their zeal, he said: "She's speaking, She's alive. Come on, courage! Quickly, quickly..."

The innkeeper was there, the mason, the gamekeeper and the bellringer who served as the village gravedigger. The four men, while continuing to weigh in, cocked their ears. But soon they testified by their mime that they could not hear anything. Mirande shrugged his shoulders. Evidently, their senses were too crude and coarse to perceive that distant voice.

At that moment, the physician joined them. He was a corpulent old man, vigorous and jovial, whose experience and method Mirande appreciated, Out of breath from running, he demanded, in a tone that betrayed his incredulity: "Well, do you still believe you can hear something?"

Irritated by that secret resistance, Mirande replied, sharply: "Listen yourself!"

The doctor knelt down on the ground and ausculated the stone. Then he stood up.

"Nothing. Absolutely nothing. And yet, I have good hearing."

This time, Mirande was afraid. Was he really the victim of a hallucination? He would soon know. In fact, the stone, hoisted up wooden levers, finally gave way. It uncovered an obscure excavation, into which the mason lowered his lantern. A second stone, fitted with a ring and sealed around its perimeter, formed its bottom.

Mirande leaned over the opening, from which a cold draught emerged. He could still perceive the plaintive murmur, but with increasing difficulty. The voice seemed to be sinking into the earthy. It was weakening incessantly. Soon it faded away...

Had the unfortunate woman been resuscitated only to die? Or had she simply lost consciousness? Weak with impatience, Mirande urged the workers to hurry up. Fragments of stone flew away under the blows of the chisel, but now it seemed to him that even the zeal would remain futile, that the sepulcher would never be opened in time...

He sensed the effect of a sudden depression, doubtless provoked by anguish, fatigue, the troubled and cold hour that precedes dawn. Those men, whose most tenuous reflections he had penetrated a short while before, now seemed strange and distant to him.

A few early risers, alerted to the event, had joined the group of laborers. Some offered their services. Others, their hands behind their backs, looked on curiously. Mirande suffered from their presence. He would have liked to be able to finish the work on his own, far from those profane, almost hostile eyes.

Finally, the second stone was lifted. In the gray light of the imminent dawn, the coffin appeared. It was laid down on the grass. While agitated hands unscrewed the lid, Mirande stuck his ear to it.

No sound. Nothing. However, he was not mistaken; he really had heard plaints. Oh, the interminable seconds...! His own life could have been at stake and he would have been less anxious.

Lamentably, he pleaded: "Get ready, doctor. As soon as you can listen to her heart..."

The doctor acquiesced with a gesture, and got down on his knees. As soon as the shroud was uncovered he moved it out of the way over the breast and leaned over.

Almost immediately, he stood up again, his face brightening.

"She's alive."

Thus, in spite of the old physician's anticipations, the miracle had been realized. But the physician was too glad to have been mistaken to retain any resentment.

As for Mirande, he was dizzy with joy. But the excess of happiness rendered him his clarity of decision. The young woman's face retained all the appearances of death. It was important, above all not to allow that fragile flame to be extinguished, to reanimate it, and to transport the invalid to her home as quickly as possible.

Aided by the physician, he raised the poor inert head, and poured a few drops of cordial between the bloodless lips. Then, preceding the little group of porters, he ran to Simone's house. In the absence of their masters, the gardener and his wife were the only residents. For it was in Paris, where Monsieur Castillan was retained well before the season, that his young wife had almost died.

He found the two guardians awake, informed them of the prodigious adventure and the imminent arrival of their mistress, shook off their stupor and directed them. He anticipated the most scrupulous cares, going into the most minute detail, entirely absorbed by the work of salvation.

But a moment came when, in her brightly-lit bedroom, in the warmth and comfort of the bed, Simone, uttering a profound sigh, finally opened her eyes—and it was only at that moment that Gabriel Mirande became conscious of being a stranger in the house.

Simone was married...

Now, he had completed his task. He had returned his wife to Castillan. Nothing remained for him to do but cede his pace to that man. A flood of bitterness rose up against fate. What irony! To have saved her only to lose her again...

The best thing to do was to leave immediately. Simone, when she had come round completely, might perhaps be offended, by an instinct of modesty, to find him at her bedside. If he explained, how would he justify his presence at her tomb, during the night? Finally, what point was there is hearing words of gratitude, of mutual tenderness, since he was still bound to flee?

He took the physician to one side.

"She's saved, isn't she?"

"Certainly. It's evidently a case of catalepsy. She must have woken up at the moment when you heard her. Then she fainted again. But no organ is damaged."

"So you'll answer for her?" Mirande insisted.

"Yes, but why?"

"I'm leaving for Paris. I left Brion with a high temperature, very feverish. I'm anxious about his condition. I'm in a hurry to get back to him."

The old practitioner let a profound gaze fall upon Mirande. He was aware of the tender amity that united the two young people. Undoubtedly he was measuring the violence of an amour so umbrageous as to hide itself even from gratitude. But he did not betray his thought. He took the hands that were extended to him and shook them warmly.

"Go, then," he said. "Count on me."

Mirande contemplated one last time the sweet visage that was already tinted by the colors of life, amid the gilded hair spreading out over the pillow. Then he left.

Outside, he found one of those blue summer mornings, scintillating and pure, in which one would like to drink the fresh air like a liqueur. He went through the garden, which, from every path, behind every bench, in the midst of the hedges, the invisible statue of a memory loomed up for him.

Having reached the outbuildings, he went into the gardener's cottage.

"As soon as the post office opens, telephone Monsieur Castillan. I don't have time to wait. I'm catching the train."

He headed for the station along the bank of the Yonne, as much to cut the journey short as to avoid passing the cemetery. His haste to flee, to get away from the temptation of seeing Simone again, was so urgent that he neglected the ostensible purpose of his journey, his visit to the notary. The office would not be open yet, He would settle or having the money that was due to him sent the same day—a very small sum, alas: all that his sister and he had been able to procure by mortgaging the cottage and field that their parents had left them. It had cost them to borrow on their poor heritage, but the sacrifice was necessary. Incapable of believing, in spite of the evidence, in Lacaze's culpability, they had wanted to set forth in search of the truth. At the first step, they had perceived that, without the lever of money, all their efforts would be in vain. Without the few banknotes that he was about to receive, they would not even be able to remunerate the private detective they had charged with checking the work of the police.

On the platform of the station, where a bell was ringing, he sat down on a bench. He felt himself invaded by the great lassitude that had already descended upon him at the moment when he had ceased to hear Simone's plaints. He relived that prodigious night.

Now that he reviewed the events in their ensemble, one point seemed inexplicable to him. How, through so many obstacles, had he been able to perceive Simone's faint voice, when his companions could not hear it? Had the stimulant serum with which Brion had injected him he previous evening developed the acuity of his senses?

That mystery, his old master would surely be able to penetrate. His impatience to see him again increased. He decided to go to the laboratory as soon as he jumped down from the train. With a telegram sent on the way, he would inform Jeanne of the resurrection of her friend.

27

The memory of the singular events he had just traversed, and the apprehension of those that awaited him, whirled in his fatigued brain. And it was an impression of deliverance for him, as soon as he had thrown himself on to the banquette, to feel himself sinking into sleep.

II

"Hey there! Everyone's getting off..."

Shaken by a rude fist, Gabriel Mirande woke up. He perceived, with astonishment, the blue uniform of the crewman leaning over him, his numbered cap and his mocking smile. He found that he was lying down on the banquette in his empty compartment.

"Where am I, then?"

The man riposted with coarse laughter. Mirande sat up, and compressed his dolorous head, where the mechanism of thought was functioning awkwardly, with his hand. He looked out of the window. High walls loomed up in a dim light. In the distance, the architecture of a hall deployed its metallic arch against an expanse of sky. Porters were wheeling away baggage. It was Paris.

"Have to get off, I tell you. They're taking the train away."

"I'm going, I'm going..."

His mind troubled, his legs unsteady, he went out into the corridor of the carriage and jumped down on to the platform. In front of him, an employee was pushing a cart bearing an elongated black trunk, not unlike a coffin. A sudden association of ideas brought him back to reality.

It's true: last night...Simone...! Could I have dreamed it?

He turned his head to flee his memories, for he retained a frightful melancholy. In vain he congratulated himself for having saved the life that was most precious in his eyes, to have rendered life, and soon health, to Simone, to have created happiness. From that resurrection, another would profit. The flood of bitterness that had invaded him in the invalid's bedroom assailed him again. Oh, the appeasing certainty that death brings... To know that one can any longer possess someone who no longer exists...

But already his conscience was revolting against the odious thought.

"Exit this way!"

Yes, exit, escape to normal life, and no longer to think about anything but work. He handed over his ticket automatically, went past the collector, who sounded him with his gaze, and found himself outside.

A special atmosphere floats around railway stations. The fever and rush of departures collides with the lassitude of returns, much as opposed electric fluids must clash. Gradually, a sort of equilibrium, or rather an exchange, is established between the two currents, in which those who are going are calmed, and those who are coming restored.

All travelers, and even passers-by, have observed that ebb and flow, have felt themselves caught up in its eddies. This time, however, Gabriel Mirande, ordinarily to sensitive to the ambient environment, did not participate in it. He was unmoved by a woman who, at the moment of separating from her husband, placed her head on his shoulder and wept inexhaustibly. He was unamused by a group of Cook Agency tourists, English, German and Rumanians mixed together, under the guidance of their young gilt-capped cicerone, who were standing on the edge of the sidewalk, wide-eyed, waiting for their carriages. Neither did he savor the animation of the great boulevard, whose perspective was already encumbered with trams and automobiles, and whose high facades, in the vaporous azure, were opening their windows to the morning sunlight.

No, his rancor persisted, and that incomprehensible leaden hand weighted upon his brain. He took a few steps at random. Then, whipped by the fresh air, he was slightly reanimated.

What am I doing here? What about the boss?

Had he not decided to rejoin his old master, Brion, whom he had left ailing he previous evening, as rapidly as possible?

Planted on the sidewalk, he waited momentarily, hoping for an empty automobile taxi. As none appeared, he hailed a fiacre.

"15A Rue Méchain, Driver!"

"Rue Méchain?"

"Yes. It opens into the Rue Saint-Jacques, not far from the Observatoire."

"That's right," conceded the man, touching his forehead.

A violent appeal of the reins, an energetic crack of the whip, and the horse was already under way. But Mirande changed his mind.

"Call in at the Post Office first…the nearest one…"

Yes, decidedly, where was his head? He had promised to telegraph his sister as soon as he got off the train, to inform her of the resurrection of her childhood friend. Even though they had ceased to see one another after Simone's marriage to Doctor Castillan, Mirande anticipated Jeanne's joy on learning of the incredible event.

He went into the Post Office like a whirlwind, and scribbled the prodigious news in twenty words on a pneumatique form, leaving the details until later, when Brion's health permitted him to return to the communal nest. He wrote the address more carefully—

Mademoiselle Jeanne Mirande, 12 Rue Monge—and slipped the blue paper into a tube.

"Now, Rue Méchain, at the trot!"

His dear old master...

He was running to his bedside with a filial piety. He owed him, materially and morally, everything that one man can owe another. He had felt himself sustained by that benevolent hand since childhood.

Mirande remembered the epoch when the chemist, already in the glory of his laboratory discoveries, had arrived in Chatigny. To begin with, he had rented a kind of abandoned farm for a season—at the extremity of the village, because he was in search of isolation. Then, seduced by the green peace of the locale, and the tranquil charm of the banks of the Yonne, he had bought the house and the surrounding meadows. Gradually, demolishing and reconstructing, he had turned it into an eccentric dwelling.

Physically, Brion had then appeared to be a tall fellow, excessively hirsute and bearded, whose meager torso was carried obliquely on long legs. One saw him go past, always alone, not addressing a word to anyone, absorbed in thought. Dressed like a peasant in a blue blouse and shod in sturdy boots, defying the dust and the mud, with a long knotty stick in his hand, he wandered the fields and the woods. Sometimes he stopped, looked at the ground, and bent down over a plant, which he uprooted and enclosed carefully in a botanist's box maintained over his shoulders by two leather straps.

His appearance and his behavior had rendered him suspect in the locale. Strange lights with green, red and yellow flames were seen shining at night in one of the outbuildings of his domain. He was not far from being reckoned to have cabalistic powers; he was called "the sorcerer." It was claimed that he cast spells, and one day, he was held to be responsible for an epidemic that decimated whole flocks of sheep.

When it was learned, however, shortly thereafter, from journalists who had come to interview him, that he had just discovered a remedy for the disease in question, the suspicion in which he was held, while remaining just as superstitious, was transformed into consideration. He was still a sorcerer, but a good sorcerer.

Finally, when it was notorious that his science brought him money, that he invented serums for all sorts of maladies and that he had created an institute in Paris to rival Monsieur Pasteur's, he became a local glory. The cult of the peasant for wealth had accomplished the prodigy of turning the devil into a good God.

It was already a long time ago that Gabriel Mirande had acquired the scientist's amity. Aroused by their parents, who attributed the loss of their livestock to the sorcerer, the village children had gone to throw stones at the windows from which fantastic lights escaped. Young Gabriel did not share in that superstitious hatred. Several times, on crossing the stranger's path, he had received a smile in response to his tipping his hat, with the consequence that the evildoer no longer seemed so terrible to him as legend claimed. He even sensed an attraction toward him.

He therefore protested against the aggression of his comrades. His natural inclinations, a mysterious atavism of reserve, mildness and generous revolt, rendered the cowardice of the crowd odious to him. But when he saw that his tranquil counsels went unheeded, that two windows had just been smashed, he became suddenly enraged and put his fists in the service of reason.

Little Gabriel launched himself at the mob and, alone against ten, struck out wildly. He would inevitably have succumbed to the weight of numbers if an ally had not appeared to aid him. That reinforcement was the sorcerer himself, armed with his knotty stick. He had seen the whole scene. A few blows of the cudgel, well applied, quickly dispersed the young fanatics.

"So it's you who are protecting me, little fellow!" the sorcerer pronounced, in an astonishingly paternal voice. "Do you know that you've just rendered me a great service? You've just saved a culture of streptococcus whose flask a stone would certainly have broken. And well, they're precious to me, my streptococci."

Troubled, Gabriel had bravely raised his head to look at his ally. He received without quivering the cares of the bony hand that stroked his cheek. He glimpsed, beneath the terrifying aspect of the bushy eyebrows, the kindness of the gaze. The whole ensemble seduced him.

"You have an intelligent air about you. What's your name?"

"Gabriel Mirande."

"*Mirandum*,"[7] Brion emphasized, smiling.

Gabriel did not know whether he ought to smile too. *Mirandum* was a very enigmatic term to him, and smacked of magic. What if the man really was a sorcerer?

But the strange man had already continued: "Where are your parents, so that I can compliment them?"

Alas, Maman had been sleeping in the cemetery for three months, next to Papa, who had preceded her...

"Poor kid!" the sorcerer had murmured slowly.

---

[7] i.e. that which warrants wonder.

But he had not lost interest in his young defender. He had quickly judged him capable of more elevated studies that those of the communal school. His steps, supported by a favorable report from the schoolmaster, had soon earned him a bursary at the Lycée de Sens. Brion took responsibility for the accessory expenses. Of course! Gabriel would reimburse him later by assisting him in his work, in rendering him small services during the vacations. As for his Sister, Jeanne, at the same time, she had been confided to an orphanage kept by two charitable ladies—with the consequence that the two children, in order to climb that social step, to pass from the plow to the book, did not have to eat into their meager heritage, ownership the few fields that the hard labor of generations of ancestors had acquired for them.

After the baccalaureate, the headmaster of the Lycée would gladly have spurred him on to the École Normale, but Mirande asked for time to think, in order to consult his great friend, and Brion had riposted with a formal reproval.

He was hostile, with prejudice, to the overwork of the competitions, which, in his opinion, exhausted the brain, or at least entangled it with methods that the mind has difficulty escaping. He had found his independence; it had been fecund. It permitted him to launch himself into paths still unexplored by science, to succeed in biological discoveries on which his laboratory and his pupils lived.

He offered to associate Mirande with his research. And when the student raised the objection of the absence of resources, Brion replied that he would pay him a wage immediately, and that it would be sufficient for Jeanne to live in Paris with her brother.

Mirande accepted enthusiastically. To emerge from the scholarly cage, those captivating studies, under the direction of a master he venerated, was an enchantment. He put on the long white smock, took his place among the disciples in the vast luminous room continuous with the boss's private laboratory, where the chemical compounds and serums utilized by the new therapeutics were prepared. He was initiated into the troubling struggles of phagocytosis. He knew the benefit of vaccines, the power of toxins, their molecular groupings, and their radioactivity. And his wonderment increased further when Brion, setting him aside and taking the bridle off his audacious mind, drew him into the vast fields of hypothesis.

When his work was finished, Mirande went home on foot. It was his only daily exercise. Whether the ground was dry or the rain was steaming over the causeway, he always obtained a physical satisfaction from that movement, reminiscent of the vagabondage of his childhood.

Sometimes, there was a joyful surprise: his sister Jeanne was waiting at the door of the institute. He linked arms with her, with a protective affection, and they both set forth, musing and stopping in front of shop windows, deliberately extending the route in order to go past favorite displays. On fine some evenings they sometimes took the boat and went downstream as far as the shores of Billancourt or Meudon. There they ate in a small restaurant. It was their great enjoyment.

Most of the time, however, Gabriel went home alone. He hastened his steps, thinking that his little sister might worry if he were late. He anticipated an affectionate welcome, two arms that would knot around his neck, and the table laid, where good odorous soup would be served.

One evening, he had fallen into the arms that were extended toward him, weeping. Simone was getting married. Jeanne had guessed that immediately. With a tacit accord, they had never talked about a union they knew to be impossible. When he had withdrawn to his bedroom, however, his shoulders drawn in and his legs weak, like a poor man whom life had just run over, she re-read a hundred times, with a bitterness mingled with anger, the announcement that her brother had just read. She finally understood the long silence of her childhood friend.

They lived melancholy days in the little apartment in the Rue Monge. Jeanne continued to respect her brother's dolor. She knew that words would not have eased it. In any case, she was soon to know the alerts of amour herself.

That great clown Henri Lazaze, although his appearances were intermittent, was also affected by his friend's chagrin. At the whim of his adventurous life as an aviator, he exiled himself for weeks to Mourmelon, in order to perfect the helicoplane he had invented, reappearing thereafter, his expression exultant or despairing, according to the results he had obtained. And one evening, when he was dining with the Mirandes, he had squeezed Jeanne's hand violently, as she was about to escort him to the antechamber. Then, in his free language, he had said: "Excuse me, I don't know how to make phrases...but perhaps, Jeanne, in both putting ourselves into it, in association, we might arrive, all the same, at consoling poor Gabi. Does that suit? Eh? Does it?"

The request was a trifle nebulous, but it lit a flame in his steel-gray eyes. It was the abrupt explosion of a sympathy already old, and which she shared. She had consented, smiling.

"Later…wait…I'm not saying no. Now, he's still too sad."

She kept her secret for a long time, but it slipped out. One morning, a newspaper announced that the aviator Lacaze, departed to pilot his famous helicoplane at a meeting in Buenos Aires, had just succumbed to yellow fever. Jeanne had no sooner cast her eyes on that information than she fainted. When she woke up in her brother's arms, he smiled.

"Don't worry, my dear, it's false news. Look at this other paper, which denies it. Henri has, indeed, been afflicted by yellow fever, but very slightly, to the point that he's already out of danger."

And as she sobbed, in a hectic nervous release, he scolded her gently: "And you were hiding that from me! You should rather have thought that if one thing might make me forget, it's your happiness."

A telegram was sent. The response was reassuring. In any case, Henri Lacaze soon returned. The sea voyage had already half-cured him. A season at Vichy completed his convalescence. When he was entirely reestablished, the engagement was announced. Alas, destiny does not rest when it has begun to strike, and poor Jeanne had to climb, in her turn, a calvary far crueler than the one that had driven her brother to despair.

All those events passed through Gabriel Mirandes memory with a cinematic intensity. The abnormal constriction of his brain had dissipated, leaving ideas their free play. He would have continued that return to life if the carriage had not turned into the Rue Méchain.

The sight of the little street, ordinarily dormant in its quietude, disturbed him with a presentiment. On the sidewalk, facing the Institut Brion, people were grouped in discreet discussion, as if before a funereal threshold. Faces were visible at the neighboring windows. Reporters clad in long sports coats, soft hats over their ears, were taking notes. An automobile drew away, carrying two people who were saluted with deep bows, doubtless physicians.

Mirande recognized, among the groups, present disciples of Brion, and others, who had quit the institute a long time ago, but who nevertheless remained attached to their former master. In the first rank, his attitude anxious, his hand tugging at his long Gallic moustache, he perceived Doisteau, the young surgeon whose operational skill and ingenuity were becoming legendary, and who had spent a residency at the Brion laboratory—and also the most reliable and surest of friends. He ran toward him.

"Doisteau! You here…the boss is in a bad way, then? When I left him yesterday evening though, he seemed relatively well. What's happened?"

The surgeon shook his head dolorously. "I've just asked that of the great colleagues who came out. Oh, science! They lose their Latin in it...or, rather, mask their ignorance. They pontificated about some vague infection, the nature of which they can't define, and which is complicating the poor condition of the heart, afflicted for a long time. The paralysis is increasing, the limbs growing cold, Oh, yes, science!"

"Have they any hope?"

"None."

Mirande made a gesture of desperate rage. "Can he still speak?"

"Yes, he's lucid. Just now he bade us all adieu, confiding his work to us. It was poignant! He's asked for

39

you several times. Go, my friend, quickly. He's in his laboratory, where he wanted to be transported."

A swift handshake, and Gabriel ran under the porch and traversed the bushy garden. At the back, the buildings of the institute loomed up, its chains of bricks and stone framing vast bay windows. It was an enchantment, that oasis, under the oblique smile of the sun, a corner of a wood in the heart of Paris. Mirande's sadness was increased, however, by the contrast between that exuberant nature and the imminent death-throes. Here, so much sap, there, mortal exhaustion! At the sight of the great oak spreading its branches over the lawn, he thought of the beautiful human tree, once so robust, so rich in fruits, which was collapsing...

He went past a vestry where his comrades' white smocks were hanging, climbed a few steps, opened a door and stopped, oppressed by emotion, on the threshold of the laboratory.

In spite of the penumbra of the great lowered blinds, he soon discerned the familiar décor, the alignment of shelves and bottles, and the vast bright porcelain fireplace, the mantelpiece of which was host to an entire population of instruments, retorts and Bunsen burners. In the middle of the room stood a table of translucent glass, covered with microscopes, ampoules, pipettes and a hundred flasks filled with tinted solutions. That display alone revealed an incessant labor, the continuous struggle of a brain for the triumph of human beings over the inertia or ambushes of matter. More moving still, however, was a group immobilized near the table: the physician and the faithful maidservant Catherine, leaning over the dying boss.

The boss! Was that really him under that mass of bedcovers? Was that really him, that great body collapsed on a divan and scarcely breathing, jerkily? Only the head was alive. It was opposing to the inertia of the torso and the limbs, amid the tangle of his gray hair and white beard, the acuity of a gaze that one might have thought rejuvenated on the brink of extinction. Oh, that gaze, still shining with creative power...!

And its intensity increased further when it alighted on Mirande.

"Finally...it's you! It's you, my child," Brion stammered, in a small and distant voice, pallid, vibrating between two tones, as if the vocal cords were unequally taut within the throat. Immediately, though, he turned his head toward his two guardians. "Leave us...I want to remain alone with Mirande...I have to talk to him...to him alone..."

The physician offered his further assistance with a gesture; and Catherine who did not seem to understand, leaned over to draw a bowl of hot water nearer to his feet.

Then he insisted: "Alone! Leave us alone!"

They obeyed, regretfully. Mirande reassured them with a sign. Then, when they had disappeared, he approached the scientist and held out his hands fervently.

The pitiable voice started speaking. "Closer, my child, closer. Oh, you did well to arrive! I feared...I have so much to tell you. I have to tell you something! You alone...for I've read in you...I've read...!"

"Master..."

"No, no, no futile effusions!" Brion protested. "We no longer have time. I can hardly breathe. The paralysis is rising...it's reaching the head...it won't stop. Notice my voice...can you hear me?"

"Quite clearly, Master."

"Let's talk, then..." But his face became suddenly anxious. "The door. If someone were to overhear..."

"Firmly shut," affirmed Gabriel, after having made sure.

"Let's talk, quickly. What did you do yesterday evening? What happened to you?"

"Oh, Master, let's only concern ourselves with you," Gabriel implored.

"I'm talking about me in talking about you," Brion insisted, enigmatically. Then, with slight impatience: "Tell me. What's happened since you left me?"

Mirande tried to describe his journey and he prodigious night in broad strokes. When he pronounced Simon's name for the first time, Brion interrupted him.

"You loved her," he said, softly.

"How do you know that?" said Mirande, alarmed.

But Brion reassured him with a pale smile. "What does it matter? I know. And you'll understand, shortly. Go on. Quickly."

As his story advanced, the old man's excitement increased. When he heard about the young woman's resurrection, an intense expression of triumph illuminated his face. Then, fatigued by the very excess of his joy, he murmured: "Unhoped for... unhoped for... prodigiously convincing. Yes, prodigiously..."

He returned a gaze shot through with victorious irony to his pupil. "You say that you heard Madame Castillan's voice?"

"Evidently."

"In spite of the obstacles? Those two sealed stones? The coffin? The voice of an exhausted woman, half-dead? When you can scarcely hear mine? Do you believe that?"

All the doubts that had assailed Mirande since dawn, and which he had wanted to submit to his old master, were imposed on his mind with a new form. All the implausibility of the adventure burst forth.

"And yet," he said, to himself. "How could I have divined it otherwise?"

Then he wanted to reassure himself, to bring the alarming problem back to the limits of the possible. He returned to the hypothesis that had already crossed his mind. Perhaps he was endowed, that night, with a particular hyperesthesia, in the same fashion as hysterics who can hear sounds at a distance that healthy ears cannot perceive.

"Master," he interrogated, "was I in my normal state? Was I not subject to an influence? Did I not have senses particularly stimulated by the injection that you gave me at the moment of my departure, under the pretext of giving me strength? Tell me, Master, is that it? What was in the serum that you injected into me?"

Again, Brion's visage was resplendent. Overcoming the embarrassment of his lips, he said: "Finally, you've guessed! Well, yes, I tested a formidable discovery on you. Forgive me. It was necessary, in order to convince you...but I dared not hope for such a decisive proof. I wanted to confide my secret to you before dying...to you, who, alone among all, are worthy to possess it...to you, the brave, the great heart that I've read so often..."

He fell silent. Would he have time to reveal his discovery? His effort had exhausted him. Imminent death revealed itself to him. His eyelids lowered over his dull gaze. His head tilted in the posture of deep sleep.

Fortunately, it was only a faint. Mirande seized a bottle of salts from the table and approached it to his master's face. The stimulation of the vapors soon reanimated him. His respiration resumed its jerky rhythm. And as he observed the anxiety of his pupil, he remembered, and he designated with his eyes, in the corner of the laboratory, a cupboard built into the wall near the chimney-breast.

"White cupboard...the key in my waistcoat, on the right," he pronounced.

Mirande parted the covers, rummaged in his master's pocket and took out a minuscule key with intricate teeth.

"Open..."

Mirande obeyed. The cupboard was armored like a strong-box.

"The box of ampoules...notebook beside..."

"I see them."

"Leave them. Close it...and keep the key...you alone...no one else!"

After having given the lock a double turn, the disciple put the key into his fob pocket and came back to take his place beside he old man.

"Listen now...closer... I've discovered a talisman without rival. It's the serum in the blue ampoule. In the notebook, the formula, the employment, my observations of myself..."

He stopped momentarily, like a wrestler gathering himself in order to launch himself triumphantly. Then, with a final contraction of all his facial muscles: "Whoever injects himself with that serum perceives the thoughts of another...as if he were hearing his voice...for some hours. One becomes a receiver...a wireless telegraph post...which vibrates to Hertzian waves... Only...the secret...keep the secret! At all costs! If not, they'll think you're mad... Keep the secret! It's my last will..."

But his tongue, in the grip of the paralysis that was reaching the superior nervous centers, was suddenly immobilized. He tried to emit a few more sounds: a futile struggle. His eyes filled with tears. Was that the confession of his impotence? A supreme adieu to the threads of his thought?

Then his energetic head, falling backwards, mingled its white wisps with the fringes of the cushions. A few contractions of the face; one last glimmer in the gaze, and that was the end of the great seeker.

III

Outside, Mirande wondered whether he was awake. Had he not dreamed that supreme conversation with Brion? Several times, he forced himself to take an interest in the spectacle of the street, in order to prove that he was alive, that he was walking in full reality.

He dared not even measure the extent of the power that he had obtained from his master. At the very most, he tried to assure himself of the very existence of the discovery, to convince himself that Brion had not been speaking in delirium.

Timidly, he invoked the experiment that he had made without knowing it, the previous night. Certainly, without a superhuman power, he would not have perceived Simone's feeble voice through so many obstacles. When he had thought he could hear the reflections of his aides and the physician, first behind the walls of their dwellings, and then over the tomb itself, he was glimpsing their thoughts without knowing it. And later, when Simone's voice had seemed to fade away, when he had felt so isolated from all those men, doubtless the action of the serum was wearing off. Yes, the prodigy explained everything. And that alone could explain everything...

He arrived at the Rue Monge. He ran up the five flights of steps swiftly, glad to find Jeanne again after so many unusual events, to be able to tell her in detail about Simone's resurrection. And at the same time for the first time, he regretted being bound by the master's will not to reveal Brion's prodigious discovery to his cherished confidante.

He searched the narrow lodgings. The bedroom door was ajar. Jeanne was sitting by the window, her elbows on the table, her head leaning forward, her hands lost in her brown hair. A letter was open before her eyes. In the large letters that cut across the page, Mirande recognized Lacaze's handwriting.

He deduced that she had been overwhelmed by a new blow, and put off until later telling her, carefully, about Brion's death.

He was not mistaken. Oh, the ferocious and touching egotism of love...

When he had drawn her out of her dolorous reverie with a kiss on the forehead, she scarcely had a few rapid and distracted words for her old childhood friend, miraculously saved. Immediately, her own chagrin took hold of her again, entirely.

"Henri informs me of his imminent departure for the Île de Ré," she said. "From there, he'll be sent to Guyana. Here, read it—it's atrocious."

He scanned the first page with a glance.

My darling, I've never addressed you as tu, *but I dare to do so today, for one can do that to the idol to whom one prays, whom one implores on one's knees. My darling, it's really the end this time. I'm going to leave for the Île de Ré, and from there to the prison colony. But you! You whom I adore, will you have the courage not to turn away from me, to remain faithful to the memories that bind us together? What does the shame matter to me, since I'm innocent? What does the unmerited punishment to which I shall be subjected matter, the torture of the odious contacts that await me? But to be separated from you, my darling! Oh, that torture is truly too cruel! Let them lacerate me, let them burn my flesh, but not tear me away from you, at the moment when my arms were about to envelop you! Do you understand what I'm losing? Do you understand that I'm hanging on to your phantom, desperately? Life without you, with the atrocious obsession that you might be subject to the abominable suspicion, that you might repudiate me, that you might reject my poor love, the only softening of my misery...of, if that's what awaits me, tell me. Let oblivion carry me away. It won't take long; I shall go toward death with such haste to finish with it...!*

Jeanne interrupted him. "Isn't it frightful? But I shall follow him. I shall marry him out there, as soon as I have permission to join him. For we can no longer save him. We'll never get to the bottom of it. Oh, we're too weak, you see..."

Too weak...

Suddenly, inspired by revolt and pity, Mirande glimpsed salvation. Why not employ the weapon that Brion had put in his hands, that divinatory faculty, in the struggle? By that means, he could acquire money, influence, everything that he lacked to vanquish human stupidity, indifference and malevolence. Too weak! Oh, they would cease to be...

He had to master himself, to invoke the august and sage will of his master, not to betray himself, not to cry out his hope and his confidence to the unfortunate Jeanne, who was isolated in the vision of a future sacrificed.

A ringing bell extracted them from their meditation. After negotiations in the antechamber, Francette, the maidservant, came in, familiar and abrupt.

"It's a man."

"What man?"

"I don't know. Tall, thin as a hundred nails, with a toothbrush moustache. He said that Monsieur was waiting for him. 'All right, then,' I said. 'You can wait there.' Because, these days, one never knows eh? Need to be careful."

She finished with a burst of laughter. A curious little individual, that Francette. In her, everything was contrast. Her nose, too large at the root, suddenly terminated in a malicious little point. Her milky complexion was dotted with red blotches. Behind lips that were too short, perfect teeth gleamed. The rude arc of her eyebrows sheltered a tender and meek gaze. The tumultuous flood of her coppery hair stopped short at her little straight collar. Finally, her short torso was planted on long legs with delicate ankles.

Was she pretty? Was she ugly? A mystery. But the ensemble was surprising, like a commonplace foodstuff that had been cleverly spiced.

Her language was as singular as her physical appearance. Free and frank, it was peppered with ludicrous images and argot. But in the two years that Francette had been in their service, Jeanne and her brother had become accustomed to her eccentricities.

In any case, how could they not be indulgent toward her? No devotion was comparable to hers. Since the day when the arrest of Lacaze had cast their abode into morning, Francette had consoled them ingenuously. She sustained their confidence with her naïve faith in the innocence of the accused. The rare glimmers of hope, reflected by her, suddenly took on a brighter radiance. Her spontaneous gaiety and her mischievous sallies held the most poignant anxieties in check.

And as, in those periods of crisis, Jeanne neglected the cares of the household, Francine had taken its direction. She defended its interests stubbornly. She reduced the pretentions of suppliers by using the familiar form of address. With a grimace, she obtained a good discount from the grocer, which she passed on to the purse of her employers. She washed, ironed and folded all the linen, polished the parquet, beat the carpets and found time to consult cookery books in order to concoct flavorsome dishes. When she understood that the household was short of money, that Lacaze's defense had exhausted its savings, she even refused her wages and declared flatly that she too would make sacrifices for the cause. How, after that, could they take her to task for her liberties of language and behavior? One does not reproach the sunlight for entering into a house.

Her good humor had only known one eclipse. That was at the moment of Simone's marriage. She had not been told about that intimate drama, but had doubtless divined it. At any rate, she had become unapproachable. She had been glimpsed in the kitchen maltreating the crockery and the pans, lavishing the most furious and crude insults on the oven. For a week, all the dishes were inedible. Then nature had regained the upper hand; again her laughter had rung out, and her face lit up the abode.

Thus, Mirande did not have the heart to scold Francette for having received an expected visitor in such a cavalier manner.

"That must be Monsieur Nitaud, the enquiry agent," he said to Jeanne.

"That's it—Nitaud; he told me his name," said the soubrette, laughing again. "I thought at first he said Nigaud."[8] Curiously, she added: "Is he the policeman? Is he good?"

---

[8] i.e., Simpleton

Nothing that was to do with the Lacaze affair left her indifferent. Mirande had to promise to inform her as to the policeman's talents. She then consented to introduce him to the drawing-room, this time in a manner full of deference.

Monsieur Nitaud corresponded well enough to the description that Francette had sketched. He was a tall man with an enigmatic quality. His astonishingly mobile eyes compelled attention immediately. One only discovered afterwards the extreme development of the forehead, the short gray hair and the hollow cheeks, united by a thin brown moustache—Francette's "toothbrush." Under the maroon suit, one divined a powerful musculature, a deceptive thinness.

"It is Monsieur Mirande to whom I have the honor…?"

"Indeed, Monsieur Nitaud. I wrote to you in order to confide a difficult investigation to you. I can't do better, it seems to me, than to address myself to the man who…"

With a gesture of his splayed fingers, the policeman rejected the compliment. He sat down, put down his soft hat and looked at Jeanne, whose presence he seemed to think superfluous.

"Mademoiselle is my sister," Gabriel explained. "I'd like her to be present during our conversation."

Nitaud nodded. "I'm listening, then."

Mirande collected himself, his hand on his forehead. Then he began: "You must know, Monsieur, about the Lacaze affair?"

"I do indeed, but superficially. I was away when it unfolded, in America, where I was operating on behalf of the Russian government. A matter of nihilists. Like everyone else, I've been brought up to date by the news-papers."

"From what you know, does the affair seem clear to you, cut and dried?"

"It seemed to me to be rather banal. Furthermore I'll admit that the work of the Prefecture of Police doesn't interest me much. I passed through it once, with the title of inspector, before setting up on my own ac-count...nothing serious...scamped work."

"It seemed to me, in fact," said Mirande, "that the police did not conduct it with enough zeal and above all, impartiality. They only sought to doom our unfortunate friend, and we don't believe him to be guilty."

"Oh, no, we can't believe it!" Jeanne added, ardent-ly. "Lacaze is innocent! It's therefore in you, Mon-sieur..."

For a second time, with a more impatient gesture, Monsieur Nitaud suspended the eulogy he anticipated. As positive in his questions as in his attitude, he interro-gated: "You'd like to have the verdict overturned, then?"

"That's our hope," Gabriel admitted.

"Were there faults of procedure?"

"There were, but not sufficient."

"You need new evidence, then—proof that the prosecution was mistaken on some point?"

"Yes, some discovery...I don't know...the small clue capable of casting doubt into the minds of new judges—for the jury of the Seine that condemned Lacaze had no doubt. The penalty of forced labor for life was pronounced unanimously."

"Oh, that's abominable!" Jeanne protested. "Henri, a heart so honest, so upright..."

With his keen gaze, Nitaud scrutinized the young woman. He seemed to divine her, for he shrugged his shoulders in a compassionate manner. Then, in a tone less curt, he went on: "Let's see…I'd like nothing better than to help you. It will be costly, of course. To recommence an investigation, find the witnesses, demolish the monument that the Prefecture has constructed, can't be done without money. It requires sleuths. It takes time. Have you thought about that?"

"All that we have—everything! We'll put it all at your disposal," Jeanne affirmed.

"Oh, Mademoiselle…arrangements are made…this is how I proceed. I make an approximate calculation. I'm furnished with an advance, and then I begin. I don't wring the client dry." He turned toward Gabriel. "Refresh my memory about the affair now—and don't be surprised if I insist on details. In our métier, a grain of dust can be important. First, tell me about Lacaze. What was he, that fellow? A friend, you say; how do you know him?"

With a rapid glance, Mirande exhorted his sister to be brave. It was necessary for them to relive the drama once more.

"I met Henri Lacaze at the Lycée de Sens, where we were fellow students," Gabriel declared. "He was then a turbulent child, even violent, who suffered from scholarly discipline, but he also had a remarkably intelligent mind and a generous heart, sensible to affection and reason. He scarcely worked except on the eve of the baccalaureate, but to general amazement, he passed more brilliantly than the hard workers. When we left the school, life separated us. I met him again six years later in Paris, where he'd become fanatical about aviation. He'd just invented the famous helicoplane, of which you've doubtless heard mention…"

Nitaud apologized for his ignorance. Progress moved so rapidly that the profane could not know about the helicoplane. In any case, in haste to continue his investigation usefully, he asked: "What kind of life? Bohemian?"

Embarrassed by the presence of his sister, Gabriel meditated his response. "Bohemian? Certainly he was subject to the enthusiasm of his comrades. One lives more intensely in that milieu, where one is not certain of being alive the following day. But he amused himself intermittently, like a man who works relentlessly and who relaxes from labor in pleasure."

"Debts?"

"Yes, debts. They were one of the charges in the accusation. Rather large debts, even. Debts that certainly resulted from his taste for largesse, his generosity and, it must be said, his recklessness. But debts, above all, imputable to the enormous expenses of a small factory that he had established for the manufacture of his helicoplanes. Perhaps he did not know how to impose practical direction, the surveillance that avoids wastage. In sum, his industry was the principal origin of his need for money."

"A liaison?"

This time, it was Jeanne who responded on her brother's behalf. She simply said: "We have been engaged for a year, Monsieur."

The policeman nodded. On that delicate point he resolved to interrogate Mirande one-to-one. Turning to the latter, he continued: "Monsieur Lacaze is violent, you said?"

"Yes, but a violence always inspired by a sentiment of justice, or truth..."

"For example?"

"For example, his attitude during the course of his trial, when he questioned the prosecutor and the judges, to the detriment of their indulgence. He employed regrettable terms that certainly contributed to indispose them. During the final hearing, he showed his fist to the advocate general."

"In truth, if he's innocent...," Nitaud said, by way of excuse. "But can't you cite me another instance from his private life—a quarrel in his factory?"

"He was adored by his workers. I don't see...oh, yes! I remember one adventure that comes to mind. It was at Issy-les-Moulineaux, the day of his departure for the Circuit de Nord. The aviation field was guarded militarily. Lacaze, having forgotten his card, wants to go through the cordon of troops anyway. A sub-officer stops him. Annoyed that his word is doubted, Lacaze insists, becoming heated, and one thing leading to another, finishes up by assaulting the sub-officer. The race committee had a good deal of trouble sorting the matter out—which characterizes Lacaze perfectly."

"Yes, I see..." The policeman pinched his chin, and then stroked his toothbrush moustache. "Let's pass on to the victim. A cousin of Monsieur Lacaze—a cousin with an inheritance, if my memory serves me right."

"Yes, Monsieur Gagny. An octogenarian."

"Did this Monsieur Gagny have other relatives?"

Mirande hesitated. Simone was also a cousin of old Gagny, who was, like her and Lacaze, originally from the environs of Sens, but he was reluctant to name her to the policeman. He resolved to do so, however.

"Yes, one of our friends, Madame Castillan.

Nitaud observed: "That lady, who similarly stands to inherit, must have benefited from Lacaze's departure, who, by virtue of his conviction, has lost his right to the succession?"

The dramatic events had fallen upon Mirande so rapidly that the observation in question had never crossed his mind. He made an evasive gesture. "It's possible."

But the policeman persisted: "Did the police look in that direction?"

This time, Mirande rebelled. "With what right and for what reason? The Court was not brushed by any such suspicion. In any case, Madame Castillan is rich herself, very rich, worthy of all respect. No, no, it's absolutely necessary to set that idea aside."

The policeman did not insist. "So be it. Let's pass on to the crime."

Gabriel prepared to recount it, but he was anxious about his sister's nervous condition. The evocation of the fatal night troubled him in advance.

"Do you want to leave us?" he asked.

But she stiffened herself, and refused with an imperious shake of the head. Gabriel had to resign himself.

"Monsieur Gagny," he replied to the policeman, "was killed in the town house he owned in the Avenue Raphael, at 22A. We know the house for having gone into it on the day that Lacaze introduced his fiancée to his cousin."

"How did he receive you?"

"Badly."

"For what reasons?"

"No reason. We were treated like everyone else, as importunate individuals. The old man lived wrapped up in himself, in sordid avarice."

"He was very rich, was he not?"

"His fortune was estimated at some ten millions."

"How had he acquired them?"

"By hoarding money avidly and subsisting meanly."

"That considerable fortune must have had an origin, however?"

"Yes, the paternal heritage and that of his wife, who died a long time ago. He had accumulated the interest for some fifty years—Monsieur Gagny was eight-three when he was murdered."

"The upkeep of the town house, though—the charges, the servants—represented expenses."

"I repeat Monsieur," Gabriel insisted, "that old Gagny was implausibly miserly. He did not travel, did not belong to any club and did not permit himself any pleasure. He wore his clothes until they were completely worn out, picked his own vegetables from his garden, transformed into a kitchen garden, supped on a morsel of cheese and a crust of bread. His entire staff consisted of two domestics; when the wife became infirm he even reduced her wages. An unattractive man, in truth."

"Why, then, did he live in a house in the Avenue Raphael? Why didn't he sell it in order to lodge in a maid's room on some sixth floor?"

"Because he had to accommodate some splendid furniture and a collection of rare paintings he inherited from his father. All those objects were acquiring value over time; keeping them was, therefore, a fashion of hoarding."

"In sum, a madman?"

"Yes a madman," Gabriel affirmed. "Possessed by gold. A sick man who must have been confined to bed the day he lent money to Lacaze."

Monsieur Nitaud started. "Ah! So Lacaze had borrowed money from him?"

"Yes, Monsieur—a trivial sum; five hundred francs to pay his workers, once, when he was in a hole. He had to beg to obtain them."

"If only he'd asked us for them!" Jeanne lamented. "We could have saved him from a step that perhaps served to doom him in the mind of the judges. But he was too proud…much too proud to address himself to us."

Monsieur Nitaud resumed teasing his moustache, His eyes fixed on the floor, he reflected. His brow furrowed. Assuredly, he had taken unfavorable note of the loan. He continued "I believe I remember that on the evening of the murder, Lacaze, who admitted it during the hearing, went to see Gagny again to ask for money?"

"Indeed," Mirande replied. "Lacaze requested, that evening, further assistance from his cousin. Harassed by his creditors, he needed ten thousand francs, under pain of bankruptcy. At eight o'clock he went to ring the bell at the gate of the garden that separates the house from the avenue."

"That's the vegetable garden you mentioned?"

"No, this garden is a kind of forecourt planted with trees. The kitchen garden is behind the house. It's separated from the Boulevard Suchet by another house. I stress that detail, which has some importance. So, Lacaze rang, and was introduced by Justin, the domestic. The conversation was calm at first, but then became animated to the point that Justin declared himself surprised by violent outbursts of voices. Lacaze withdrew proffering insults; he didn't try to hide that."

"What insults? Threats?"

"No—appreciations, in truth very vivid, of his cousin's avarice, but nothing that marked his intention of harming the old man. The gate was closed behind him by Justin, and locked with a double turn, as was customary. And he went away."

"To go where?"

"To Issy-les-Moulineaux, to undertake a night flight in his helicoplane."

"Well, that's an alibi!" exclaimed Nitaud.

"Which, unfortunately, couldn't be corroborated, for the helicoplane can take off at the discretion of its pilot alone. Numerous witnesses came forward to affirm that at the tribunal. Lacaze thus accomplished his nocturnal excursion alone."

"Alone—that's unfortunate," murmured the policeman. But he glimpsed the young woman's anxiety, and dissimulated his bad impression as best he could. "At what time did he return from his expedition?"

"About four o'clock in the morning."

"And the medical report estimated Gagny's time of death…?"

"At about two o'clock in the morning."

"Who discovered the crime?"

"Justin, the old domestic, when, as was his custom, he brought his master's breakfast. He immediately went to inform the Commissaire de Police of the occurrence, who preceded with the usual investigations."

"And what did they reveal?"

"Monsieur Gagny had died from a thrust to the heart delivered by a perforating instrument. He was lying at the foot of his bed, in a chemise, and did not seem to have offered any resistance. He had not even cried out, for the domestics affirmed that they had not heard anything. The sureness of the thrust, delivered exactly to the region of the heart, and accompanied by very little effusion of blood, seemed to indicate that the murderer possessed certain notions of anatomy, or that it was not his first murder. The instrument of the crime was found near the corpse: a commercial file with three faces, recently sharpened. It presented the particularity that it was stamped by a hot iron with an L."

"Lacaze's initial. Does your friend mark his instruments like that?"

"Yes."

"That file had been stolen from him!" Jeanne exclaimed, before even leaving the policeman time to reflect on that grave detail.

But Gabriel moderated her impulsion: "Wait—let me finish. Monsieur Nitaud needs to know everything." Then, addressing the stranger, he said: "In the room, moreover, there was no evidence that theft had been the motive or the crime. The writing-desk, full of title-deeds, was intact. None of the paintings was missing, or precious trinkets that might have been easily carried away. The coolness, the method, and if I might put it thus, the neatness of the act gave the impression that the murderer had been carrying out an order..."

"Naturally," Jeanne added, "the Court saw in the criminal's disinterest a further charge against my fiancé. It was claimed that only Henri had an interest in not stealing what he would inherit. But I ask you, Monsieur, would he not at least have simulated a break-in? Would he have made use of a weapon that could denounce him? Come on! A child would have thought twice about it."

Nitaud did not reply. He addressed Gabriel: "Was it perceived, the following day, that a file was missing from Lacaze's workshop?"

"There was no way of telling. There was such disorder in our friend's abode..."

"Leaving that implement near the body thus served the prosecution?"

"It spoke for itself. Its discovery was the examining magistrate's principal argument for arresting Lacaze. In addition, that magistrate gave evidence throughout the affair of a revolting partiality."

"Who was it?"

"Monsieur Dutoit."

At that name the policeman started. "Ah! It's Dutoit...I know the fellow. He's a complete idiot. I once had dealing with him, and it was in consequence of those difficulties that I had to resign. I admit that it's unfortunate that a man's fate might depend on an imbecile of that stripe."

This time, Jeanne was radiant.

"I'm not even sorry to find myself facing that individual again," Nitaud continued. "But let's pass on. Tell me how the prosecution explained the arrival and departure of the murderer."

"Behind the house, as I told you," Gabriel said, "there's a kitchen garden separated from the Boulevard Suchet by a property that's for rent. The criminal must have gone though that empty house, climbed over the boundary wall, come through the vegetable garden..."

"Without leaving any traces?"

"None. The soil was dry. Then he introduced himself into Gagny's house."

"How? Hadn't the door been locked?"

"Carefully barricaded, in fact, as were the windows. But there's another door leading to the basements. One gets to it by going down a few steps under the perron. The door is glazed and furnished with strong bars. Now, it was customary to leave the key inside the lock. The criminal broke the glass, cutting himself, as traces of blood were found on the door. He only had to put his hand through that opening to turn the key and draw the bolts. From then on he was inside the house and nothing was easier than to reach the floor where the victim's bedroom was."

"That denotes a certain knowledge of the location, at any rate," the policeman reflected. Then he added: "He cut himself, you say?"

Gabriel understood all the interest that the police had attached to that question. He was about to respond, but Jeanne got in ahead of him again.

"Once again, Henri was unfortunate. That same evening, during his nocturnal flight, while adjusting a metal fitment on his airplane, he cut his wrist."

"They must have searched for traces of that accident on the apparatus? The aviator's blood ought to have remained on the wire?"

"No, he'd wiped it away," she confessed, lowering her head in dejection.

An oppressive silence followed. Nitaud seemed inclined toward culpability. His lips formed a significant moue.

A clock chimed midnight. The policeman awoke from his meditation. "And no other indication in the house as to the identity of the criminal?"

"Nothing."

"Did they search for fingerprints on the doorknobs, the banisters and the bedroom furniture?"

"A search was made. They were contradictory. In any case, I repeat that the criminal didn't touch anything."

"And Henri Lacaze's fingerprints were found," Jeanne emphasized, "because he had visited his cousin a few hours previously."

Nitaud shook his head. The edifice established by the examining magistrate seemed solidly built. For once, his enemy Dutoit had been served by circumstances.

He summarized his thoughts without worrying about sparing his listeners: "Well, it doesn't look good for your friend. If he's innocent..."

"He is!" exclaimed Jeanne. "I swear on everything I hold most sacred in the world." She added, violently: "You believe it, don't you? Say that you believe it!"

"Evi...dently," stammered the policeman, "since you affirm it...and I'd like nothing better than to be convinced. But the law? The law can't be content with a young woman's oath...it requires evidence. Now, admit that our friend has not been able to furnish any...that, on the contrary, all the circumstances overwhelm him. Think, then: only one man had an interest in killing Gagny: him, the heir threatened with bankruptcy. And then, what do you expect? It's unfortunate that Lacaze argued with his cousin, that his alibi can't be established, that he injured himself that same night, that the murderer took nothing away...yes, he's truly unlucky!"

But he observed so much distress on the part of the two young people that he did not want to leave without offering them some hope.

As he picked up his hat, he said: "In sum, I don't have anything to encourage me in recommencing the investigation, except for your conviction. It's a little thin. But it's a stimulant all the same, for you seem to me to be worthy people. I shall, therefore, set to work and try to find something new."

He stood up, and unable this time to contain his rancor, raised a menacing index finger. "And if I can stick Dutoit's nose into a judiciary error, I'd gladly work for that result alone. For now, *au revoir*."

In spite of that sally, the policeman left them with a disappointing impression. Jeanne did not hide her despair. Sobbing, she threw herself into her brother's arms. He hugged her and consoled her.

Oh, how he would have liked to give her something more than banal words! How he would have liked to cry: "Hope! Be certain. We shall triumph. We were weak, it's true, we were blind—but now, thanks to Brion, we have Power, we have Light!"

PART TWO

I

In waves of dust and gusts of heat, in the racket of horns, sirens and clutch-releases, automobiles were returning to Dorville-sur-Mer after a day of races. In fits and starts they filed past the facades of hotels, cafés and restaurants aligned along the quay of the harbor. They maneuvered with a miraculous smoothness, avoiding scrapes and collisions that seemed inevitable. The light vehicles, profiled with the last possible intervals, slid between the more imposing limousines like sloops between the warships of a squadron. The sea breeze was agitating the bright veils that surrounded the faces of women. The declining sun illuminated sparks in the copper fittings of the hoods. Here and here, a correct carriage, or a cavalier leaping from his anxious horse, found themselves close to that stream of metal, and the sight of them seemed anachronistic.

Without missing anything of the file-past, Mirande, sitting on the terrace of a bar, lent an ear to the conversation of two young people sitting at the table alongside him. Well-informed about that luxurious troop, they were putting a name to each face, underlining it with a brutal comment, and mounting an assault of erudition.

Mirande was listening avidly. His village childhood and his studious youth had always kept him a long way from a society that inspired more fear than curiosity in him then. He had never witnessed one of the meetings that offer to the gaze a kind of cross-section of all notorieties. It had required the arrest of his friend Lacaze to constrain him to confront the milieux of influence where opinion is elaborated. He had attempted to interest newspapers, move judges, touch politicians, but very rapidly, after his first steps, he had been obliged to beat a retreat, so much did he sense that his was disarmed, alone and vanquished in advance.

He still experienced that distress of a timid child lost in a crowd, while his two neighbors continued to list the people who held, by virtue of their wealth, their talent or their employment, a thread of power. This time, however, he knew that the fear would not last. He was about to confront the struggle with confidence, fortified by a talisman that might give him victory.

Pressed to act, to help his friend in time, he had quickly perceived that in Paris, in summer, he would find closed doors everywhere. And he had chosen, to test his strength in a first contact, the resort of Dorville, where fashion was grouping, for a few days, a number of those he wanted to encounter.

Shortly after the policeman's visit, he had taken the train to the seaside. To Jeanne, surprised by that abrupt departure, he had naturally only revealed part of the truth, the hope of finding people out there useful to their cause.

He had not watched the races. Since Brion's serum only acted for a few hours, it was important to put himself under its influence at the most favorable moment. Mirande had deliberated his choice carefully. He waited for the evening.

He had perceived as soon as Lacaze was arrested that the power he lacked the most, the one for which he was most avid, was that of money: the money that would permit him to move quickly, to go far, to appear and to please; the money that stimulates zeal and reawakens dormant memories; the money that can open all doors and lips.

Those initial subsidies, Mirande had decided to seek in gambling. Certainly, the important role he occupied in the laboratory since Brion's death assured him of a small income, but he needed a round sum, quickly. No other procedure could procure it for him more rapidly or make better use of his faculty of divination. He did not hide from himself the incorrection of his conduct; he even suffered from it. Obviously, he possessed an unjust superiority over his adversaries. Without the necessary of helping Lacaze urgently, he would never have resolved to go to that extreme, but time was pressing. Furthermore, he would be enriching himself at the expense of people who had superfluous wealth at their disposal, and who did not seek gain at the green baize so much as excitement.

The casino at Dorville was renowned for its big bets. It was frequented by important lords. Who could tell whether Mirande might not have an opportunity to approach one, and subjugate him by his penetration? Thus, better than anywhere else at that time of year, he would advance at a stroke toward both influence and fortune.

Meanwhile, the stream of vehicles had almost dried up; the last automobiles were traveling at top speed. Already, dusk was falling. In a nearby restaurant, Mirande expedited his dinner distractedly. Solitude weighed upon him. He was used to eating with Jeanne, with the cheerful confidence that had animated her until Lacaze's arrest. Obliged to retreat within himself, he fell apprehension of the approaching ordeal growing as the hour advanced.

Outside, a moonlit night prolonged the day. Mirande went on to the wooden jetty that protected the harbor and separated it from the beach. The sea was high and calm. The plash of the waves was softly noisy in the framework supporting the platform. At the extremity, a green light shone at the summit of the semaphore.

Mirande sat down on a bench, facing the shore. Lights were scintillating all along the shore, amassing at Dorville in a compact constellation. All that could be heard was a distant orchestra. He felt alone, as absolutely alone as in a boat at sea.

He took out his watch. Nearly nine o'clock. According to Brion's notes, the serum took effect after an hour. The moment had come. He opened the case of the slender ampoule lying in its bed of cotton wool. It was a glass tube tapered at both ends, which contained a pink, slightly phosphorescent liquid.

Mirande broke one of the tips, and through the narrow opening introduced the extremity, formed as a hollow needle, of a Pravaz syringe. The small metal reservoir was filled up by a slow aspiration. Mirande rolled up his left sleeve in order to inject it into his forearm.

Just as he was about the insert the slender point into his skin, however, he was numbed by a vertigo. He doubted. Such a power, such a prodigy…it wasn't possible. Brion, already ill, on the threshold of death, perhaps delirious, had believed, in his fever, in the realization of his great dream, but...

But what about the notebook he had found next to the case of ampoules in the cupboard his mater had indicated to him? He had written those notes in full lucidity. The oldest dated back ten years. What strict logic there was in the account of the research, what entirely scientific precision in the mode of preparation...and the results of the experiments, reported with dry concision, those glances darted into the consciousness of others like thrusts of a scalpel into the core of the brain. Did not those words have the bitter flavor of truth, the odor of life?

Had he, Mirande, not proved the prodigious action without knowing it? Without it, how could he have perceived Simone's plaints through the stones of the tomb? Had he not been in a superhuman state that night? Had he not perceived the thoughts of the workers grouped round him?

No, no, doubt was not permissible. Once again, the implausible was true.

Resolutely, he introduced the hollow needle beneath the skin and injected himself with the dose of serum.

As soon as he had accomplished the decisive gesture, however, a revolution took place in his mind. One might have thought that his conscience, his intimate being, was protesting against that violation of natural laws, that the cells in which thought is elaborated were rebelling against that temeritous invasion.

His scruples had reawakened, and, full of a new vigor, were stifling the voices that had cried out to him to act.

He was gripped by the sharp sentiment of a profanation. He was about to violate the thought of others...and all the relationships of individuals, their habits, their laws, their amours, were founded on the invincible right of keeping the secret of themselves. Face to face, heart to heart, two lovers do not know one another. Everyone jealously retains his mystery and remains an enigma to others. The liberty of thinking for oneself alone was the true property of a human being; his sacred wealth, his supreme modesty, his ineradicable refuge.

And he was about to overturn that last rampart, to tear away that final veil? Was that not something impious and odious, a crime against humanity?

He was tempted to abdicate, to remain there, on his bench, between the sky and the water, in absolute solitude, until his redoubtable power vanished, until he had become a mere human being again, like all the rest...

What? Was he about to let the opportunity escape to know? There, a short walk away, in less than an hour, he could put the miracle to the proof. Was he going to abandon the task he had undertaken? The image of Lacaze standing in the dock, of Jeanne weeping, imposed itself on his memory. Compassion and curiosity prevailed. He rose to his feet.

Resolutely, he deplored the time lost in that sterile debate—for it was necessary for him to reconnoiter the terrain and map out his battle plan before being under the influence of the serum.

At a rapid pace, he went back to the quay, and headed for the lights of the casino, going through a deserted garden, brightly illuminated, florid with large red and white parasols. In the vestibule, he had to appear before a tribunal of solemn checkers and submit to vain formalities in order to obtain an entry ticket to the gaming rooms. He finally got in.

In a décor of banal sumptuousness, an ardent and silent crowd was already pressing around the gaming tables. Mirande perceived that the majority of men were wearing smoking-jackets. Unaware until than of the dress-code, he was dressed in a simple tourist costume. He could not help feeling the embarrassment one experiences in not being conventionally dressed. His timidity increased. Once again, the temptation traversed him to retrace his steps, so foreign did he feel to that milieu; but he got a grip on himself. In a few minutes, would be not be superior to all these people?

Suddenly, a hand clapped his shoulder and another was extended toward him.

"What the devil are you doing here?"

Mirande looked up. That tall stature, that energetic chin, that large black moustache, those dark eyes, that clear forehead! He recognized Captain Delacoste, who had commanded the battery in which he had served for two years as an artilleryman, and then as a quartermaster. He had met him again recently during a training exercise. The officer liked him. Rigid in service, benevolent outside, intelligent and worldly, he was reputed to enjoy his vocation and his pleasure equally. Mirande retained a pleasant memory of him.

"*Mon capitaine!*" he exclaimed.

"Commandant!" the offer corrected him, smiling. "Oh, don't apologize. That only dates back a week. Yes, I'm attached to the Ministry. Presently, I'm on leave, and I came to Dorville to watch the races. I'm fond of the sport. But you, a pillar of the laboratory, what are you doing in this place of perdition?

As best he could, Mirande improvised a story. He explained that he had come to spend a few days by the sea to recuperate from his labors. Alone and idle, he had allowed himself to be tempted by the casino.

"Are you a gambler?" the Commandant interrogated.

Mirande, congratulating himself on having found an experienced guide, refrained from denying it.

"A little game wouldn't frighten me."

On the way, he had meditated his chances of success. At games of pure chance, like roulette or little horses, his power of divination would be no help to him. At baccarat, his superiority over a normal punter would be scarcely perceptible. There remained games such as écarté and poker, which left a part to initiative, in which the fact of knowing the adversary's intentions would constitute a real and formidable advantage.

He admitted a secret preference for poker. He had spent entire evenings playing it in the ward-rooms where he spent time in the company of his comrades, hospital interns. But was it played at the casino? He had not yet had time to ascertain that. Perhaps he would have to fall back on écarté.

He confessed his predilection to the Commandant and asked him whether he would find competitors.

"They play a little of everything here," the officer replied. "Anyway, we'll make a tour of the rooms. You've never been here before?"

"Never."

"Then it's the moment to try your luck," the Commandant suggested. "Me, I play cards and bet gladly, but I've been in a black streak for I don't know how long. A real run of bad luck."

After a pause among the crowd amassed around the little horses and the baccarat, they reached a quiet room, illuminated solely by shaded lamps played over tables, the peace of which was only troubled by the rustle of cards and ritual pronunciations.

The Commandant raised his hand to salute four players grouped at the back of the room. Then taking Mirande aside, he asked: "Without indiscretion, do you have some money to risk?"

Mirande had brought a few thousand-franc bills borrowed on his inheritance. He was determined to multiply them. He answered in the affirmative.

"Well," Delacorte replied, "over there in the corner there's a table where you might try your luck. But they're good players, damn it! If you really have strength, it'll be a hard tussle, I warn you. I know three of the messieurs; the fourth is a newcomer."

"Who are they?"

"The handsome young man is Gomard, a Papa's boy—you know, Gomard, of the Gomard capsules. As for the offspring, he hasn't invented anything: a little popinjay, idle and snobbish, who makes the paternal millions waltz gracelessly."

"And then?"

"That noble trapezoid beard is Martigue, the notary, with one of the biggest operations in Paris. He boasts of being richer than his richest clients."

Mirande breathed out. He could, without overmuch scruple, vanquish such opponents. But a third person intrigued him: a true gentleman, proud and refined, soberly elegant, who was playing without departing from an attitude of great detachment, a lofty nonchalance. He pointed at him.

"Oh," said Delacorte, "that's the Marquis de Strezza. Genoese nobility, and a good player. It appears that he's just lost large sums in a very exclusive club in Dorville itself. Here, at the casino, chance seems rather to smile on him. He likes baccarat. He's the perfect banker, impassive and courteous. Indulgent even to small punters who hazard a modest stake, he goes so far as to calm the zeal of a croupier ready to take a hard line."

Mirande decided to spare that generous adversary. But the Commandant continued: "In that regard, I was witness last week to a rather amusing coup. It was a small game. He'd given face cards to two blockheads and two others to himself. Asked for cards he distributed an eight to the left and an eight to the right. Before serving himself he half turned to drink a lemonade for which he'd asked a few minutes before. Immediately, profiting from the banker's inattention, a good number of twenty-franc bets, not to mention a few chips, gently pushed, came slyly to increase the stakes. The marquis put down his glass, looked at his card again, took a card and drew…a nine. The gallery was most amused by the incident—except, of course, the pushers.

But Mirande was having difficulty listening. Feeble and scarce at first, strange thoughts were going through his mind. He was conscious of not having engendered them, but of registering them. The miracle of science was commencing...

Fortunately, Commandant Delacorte, attracted by a discreet conflict between two players, had drawn away slightly. Leaning on the mantelpiece, Mirande remained alone.

Doubtless the serum was not yet acting in its full force. Those thoughts were merely the advance guard of the ones that soon invaded him. They had to emanate from the nearest players, or the most energetic Then, very rapidly, they increased in number and strength, soon pullulating. There was a chaotic tumult of ideas in his head, a cerebral activity a hundred times more intense than that of the most exalting drunkenness.

He clasped his forehead with his hand, thinking that he was going mad.

He understood his master's striking image. Yes, one became similar to the wireless telegraph posts that vibrated with all the scattered waves. Innumerable messages, in fact, were flying from the four corners of the room and falling upon him, mingling, overlapping, in the disorder and extravagance of an unparalleled delirium. They were passing, passing…all the preoccupations of the games, chagrin, hope, the names of cards, calculations, alarms, triumph, anguish…and also the fortuitous reflections that go through the minds of players, trivial concerns, projects, desires, amorous obsessions…

But Brion's notes foresaw a kind of education of the new faculty, the possibility of extending his attention in a determined direction, of perceiving one thought more clearly than the others, as one hears the voice of a preferred interlocutor at table, in the midst of the hubbub of a general conversation.

In spite of his distress, Mirande attempted to train himself in that exercise. It seemed, after a few seconds, that he was obtaining some results. He succeeded in isolating himself relatively from the mental tumult, in choosing a subject, and reading better than any other the mind that he held most directly under this gaze.

But the Commandant summoned him with a sign. The unknown player had just quit his seat at the poker table. Delacoste offered to introduce the three of them to his young protégé. Mirande agreed, and on the officer's warm recommendation, was immediately accepted.

The game began. Determined to spare the Marquis de Strezza, Mirande engaged in conflict with the other two opponents, and tried to exercise his clairvoyance on them. Gomard was revealed to be prudent and Martigue audacious. Thanks to an extreme mental tension, directed his gaze alternately from one to the other, he succeeded in discovering their cards and their intentions. He folded when they had good hands and stayed in when they risked the adventure and attempted a bluff. He quickly reckoned with them; soon, a pile of gold and banknotes accumulated in front of him.

But luck had favored the Marquis de Strezza, who had obstinately refused to cross swords with him, and he understood that a final duel was imposed between the two winners. He experienced a genuine embarrassment that spoiled the joy of the triumph.

It was the turn of the Marquis to deal. Leaving Martigue and Gomard to one side, striving no longer to perceive the murmur of their thought, Mirande concentrated all his attention on the gentleman. Suddenly, he started; he did not see the gesture but he glimpsed his noble adversary's decision to substitute one deck of cards for another. The proud Genoese was nothing but a card sharp! That explained his indulgence for the push and the ingenious coup of the lemonade. Instantly, Mirande's scruples vanished. There was pleasure and profit in cheating a cheat!

Stimulated by that strange context, Mirande followed the subtle maneuvers whose plan he read in his adversary's thoughts. The Marquis served his opponents in such a way that at the draw Martigue and Gomard only needed one card. Mirande, with three of a kind, should have asked for two. That way, the fifth would go to the Marquis; it was the eight of hearts, which would have filled a flush and assured him of the winning hand.

But Mirande, when his turn came, only asked for one card instead of two, derailing the scheme.

The Marquis betrayed his surprise involuntarily. He raised his head sharply. "Only one card?"

"Yes, one card, please."

"I beg your pardon. I thought I'd misheard."

At the same time, Mirande kept watch on the aristocratic hands of his adversary, who, whether he liked it or not, had to give himself a club instead of the necessary heart. But he had more than one trick in his bag. As if by inadvertence, he dropped the card. It turned over.

"Excuse me—I'm so clumsy. Card seen, card burned, isn't it?"

He knew how to break the rules of the game pertinently. At that very moment, in the secrecy of his thought, he was evoking the names of the arbiters who condemned that practice. Mirande took a malicious pleasure in confounding him.

"Pardon me," he said, "but you must keep it. Schenck, Florence and Keller,[9] who are the authority in the matter, as you know, clearly declare that the dealer must conserve the overturned card.

The Marquis blushed slightly. He had just thought about those American authors. But he collected himself and conceded the point. "I only want to put myself at your disposal."

He kept his inconvenient club, but he had not given up yet. He would fall back on audacity. The flush had failed, but bluff remained. The other two folded. Mirande, who read his adversary's intention, was not about to be taken in by that reckless ploy. Pledging almost all the money he had in order to match his opponent's bet, he won the hand. The sweep was complete and the game ended.

---

[9] Robert C. Schenck and John William Keller published their definitive book *The Game of Draw Poker* in 1887, the former having determined the rules in 1872. William J. Florence published his *Gentleman's Handbook on Poker* in 1892.

Mirande stood up. It cost him not to unmask the noble Genoese, leaving him free to exploit dupes, but had he not himself—albeit in truly pressing circumstances and without a future—used an illicit weapon himself?

He did not have the leisure to linger over that debate of conscience. While he picked up his winnings—a small fortune—the Commandant caught him and congratulated him.

"My compliments. Damn it—I didn't know you were that good! And one of those strokes of luck, into the bargain."

Still stunned by his prodigious effort and his victory, he turned round and saw a curious crowd amassed behind him. He had, in fact, while concentrating all his attention on his adversary, perceived mute reflections, in which surprise and praise were mingled. The triumph of the debutant who had beaten those powerful players was an event among the regulars of the casino.

Delighted and glorious, Delacoste extolled his protégé.

"Look, here's Monsieur Favery, the director of the *Lumière*, who admired your clairvoyance greatly."

Mirande turned toward hm. What, Favery? Favery, whom he had tried in vain to approach in order to interest his powerful newspaper in the fate of Lacaze? He was a slender man, correct and polished, immaculately dressed, and who retained a juvenile appearance in the cut of his face and figure.

With all his power, Mirande strove to penetrate him. He discovered that Favery, at the moment of the introduction, ardently wished to surprise by his appearance of youth. He composed his features, tightening the line of his chin, giving his eyebrows an air of candor.

Mirande feigned surprise, and addressed the Commandant. "I would never have believed that Monsieur Favery, about whom people have been talking for such a long time, could still be such a young man."

Favery distilled a secret joy, but he pretended not to have heard the praise. "Believe an old player, Monsieur. You deployed there qualities of finesse combined with an audacity of the highest order."

A miraculous effect of the serum! The timid scientist heard his audacity praised! But he wanted to complete the conquest of the powerful director. Again he plunged into him. According to his custom, Favery was gauging the merits of his interlocutor, wondering how to make use of him some day. Then, by an association of ideas, he returned to the project that was haunting him, the mild but tenacious obsession that our greatest desire and our greatest affection pursue. It was a free newspaper, circulated in millions of copies, that would survive on advertising alone. Favery was hiding his plan jealously, ripening it, dreaming of only unveiling it at the moment of its execution.

Mirande replied to his compliment. "As for those qualities, Monsieur, you know them better than anyone, for you have often deployed them—and I'm certain that they will ensure the success of your next enterprise..."

Under Mirande's gaze, Favery raised his head. He had only confided his project to one person in the world, a mistress. He suspected her. Then, in a sharp tone, both anxious and haughtily, he said: "What do you mean?"

Mirande put on an ingenuous expression. "Don't you always have some affair in hand?"

Favery sketched a reassured smile, but he remained convinced that the young man had discovered his secret and held it at his discretion.

Mirande applauded himself. There was one man who certainly would no longer close his door when he came to knock on it. This singular struggle, with a new and invisible weapon, excited and intoxicated him. He looked forward to further battles, further conquests.

Just then, Delacoste, whose enthusiasm was still overflowing, appealed to another witness to the game, a man still young, rather short, with a clean-shaven face and luminous eyes. "What about you, Raucourt? Do you think the faculties of a good card-player would be useful in politics?"

Raucourt was one of those newly prominent députés in whom their colleagues are inclined to see a future leader. The rigor of his opinions, the purity of his life, and even a certain physical resemblance, had led to his being compared to Robespierre.

What? The Commandant also knew Raucourt? Miranda was astonished by that, but he reflected that his present situation of attaché to the cabinet must lead Delacoste to frequent journalists and parliamentarians. Raucourt might also serve to create a movement in favor of Lacaze. Turning toward him, he scrutinized him.

In order to respond to the officer's question, Raucourt retreated into himself. He would be a poor judge, for he did not play. He confessed, however, that in the evening, in the silence of his study, he played interminable games of patience, as much to relax his mind as to discover the dispositions of luck in his favor. He replied, gravely: "I believe that there's little correlation between the aptitudes of a card-player and a politician."

But Mirande, who had perceived the député's little confession, said: "You're doubtless correct, Monsieur. However, there might perhaps be me analogy between the unexpectedness of a public career and that of a card game. Hazard and initiative are similarly mingled therein. That's so true that great minds, at the summit of glory, retain in life a gambler's superstition. Famous men are cited—artists, scientists, legislators—who don't disdain to interrogate the cards, asking via indications of modest success for the disposition of fate in their regard."

Raucourt made a detached gesture. "It's possible."

As he drew away, however, Mirande acquired the certainty that the député retained a kind of fearful rancor against his perspicacity, at the same time as a gratitude for having assimilated him to illustrious colleagues in success."

The Commandant had drawn him into the baccarat room and suggested to him that he punt for a while: "While you're on a lucky steak..."

Mirande perceived that Delacoste, more of a gambler than he wanted to appear, desired to profit from that lucky streak by associating their chances, but he had excellent reasons for resisting. Then lassitude overtook him.

Amid that feverish crowd, so many desires, so many calculations, so many cries of avidity, satisfied or disappointed, so many ludicrous fetishism, had registered tumultuously in his brain that fatigue and nausea were prevailing over his curiosity.

Already he was preparing words to take his leave of the Commandant when a tall and statuesque young woman, haughty and cheerful, advanced toward them. He recognized her, having seen her on stage: Mademoiselle Lambrine, a star actress. She extended her hand to Delacoste. Mirande thought that this time, there was no connection with the Ministry.

"Well, Commandant," she said, "You're not playing this evening?"

"Not yet," he replied. "It's the fault of my young friend, who has just beaten Strezza, Martigue and Gomard magnificently, and who doesn't want to continue his luck at bac."

Mirande had bowed to the young woman. She scarcely interested him, but he was constrained to perceive her thought, and he understood that, offended by his modest dress, his subversive suit lost among the smoking jackets, that she did not want to be seen in his company.

More amused than insulted, he excused himself. "No, truly, it's too late. I came between two trains, as a tourist, and I perceive that I'm not correctly dressed..."

Convinced that he had surprised her glance, she was confused and annoyed, but he was already moving away. He went through the rooms at a rapid pace, impelled by his haste to escape the din of avidity that filed his head, finally to be on the beach, in the darkness, far away from people, alone—entirely alone—in the silence.

II

From the depths of the lodge, the hoarse voice of the concierge indicated: "Monsieur Nitaud, third on the left."

Confidently, Gabriel Mirande went along the corridor. His eyes, still impressed by the external light, could no longer distinguish anything in the old house in the Faubourg Montmartre. It was summer, and it could not be later that six o'clock, but the courtyard that illuminated the stairwell formed a veritable well itself, and the proprietor's parsimony only authorized the gas-lighting at night. Mirande had to feel his way, guiding himself by means of the handrail. His foot bumped into the steps. On one of the landings, a doubt assailed him.

It's not possible. I must have mistaken the floor.

An indicative plaque, however, glistened in the gloom. He struck a match and read: *Nitaud Detective Agency*.

He rang the bell, and was introduced into a small antechamber by a domestic who disappeared immediately. As his wait was prolonged, however, and as he could hear voices behind a door, he did not hesitate to open it, and he suddenly found himself in the policeman's study.

It was a large, banal room, clad in mahogany and moleskin. The walls were decked with numerous pigeon-holes labeled in white on green. Nitaud was sitting at a desk that collected all the glare of an electric lamp. His indoor jacket, the skull-cap on his head, his pen-holder behind his ear and the pipe between his teeth gave him the debonair appearance of a worthy tradesman satisfied with his business.

On the other hand, he was surrounded by people of unusual appearance who modified their attitude abruptly on seeing the door open to admit a stranger. There was a debilitated worker in a laborer's blouse; a priest, whose nose was plunged in a book of hours and who was muttering prayers; and finally, a kind of quakeress, with a shabby dressed and gloves with holes, who was hiding her face beneath the brim of her black hat.

Nitaud recognized Mirande and reassured his audience. "Have no fear, my children; it's a client." Then, dismissing them: "We'll resume the report later."

"All right, Boss," replied three masculine voices, in unison. And Mirande understood that the curé's robe, like that of the quakeress, and the workman's smock, disguised three agents of the organization.

"You're just in time—I was about to summon you," said Nitaud, examining his visitor curiously.

Endowed with a particularly faithful memory, the policeman recalled a Mirande of modest appearance, indifferent to fashion, like many scientists. He found, on the contrary, an elegant gentleman, whose silk-lined cloak partly dissimulated an evening suit. He could not retain a: "Sapristi! How handsome you are!"

"Yes, I'm going to the theater, and I ought not to go home," Mirande explained.

He sat down without being invited. Before Dorville, perhaps he would have waited until a seat was indicated to him, but money had inspired him with self-confidence. Furthermore, he had reflected on the necessity of giving an impression of fortune, or at least of ease, in order to ensure success with certain individuals, and he was constraining his natural reserve with that little comedy of ostentation.

He stretched his trousers, creased according to the fashion. Then taking a wad of banknotes from his side-pocket, he said: "Permit me first, Monsieur Nitaud, to complete my provision." He detached a thousand francs from the packet and passed the bill over the table.

"We've just sold our property in Chatigny," he explained, to reassure the policeman, whose astonishment he glimpsed. "I believe that we'll have need of all this money to succeed in our research, and I've resolved to spend it. I beg you not to spare any effort from now on."

With a delighted gesture, Nitaud approved the generous disposition. He slipped the bill into a drawer, replaced the key in his waistcoat, and waited to be questioned.

"What news is there?" asked Gabriel.

"Strictly speaking, Monsieur Mirande, not much," the policeman admitted. "I have, in accordance with your instructions, recommenced the Court's investigation. I've visited the houses of the Boulevard Suchet and the Avenue Raphael myself. I've interrogated the domestics of the Gagny house carefully. As for the journey that Lacaze accomplished by night in his airplane, I spent a week following it in an automobile, stopping at each village and asking questions left and right. I was hoping to unearth a peasant who had perceived your friend's signal-light that night. All that work brought me nothing."

"And the file?"

"The file, naturally, has been the principal object of my research. I've put my best sleuth on it, it must be said"—with a modest gesture he excused the word-play[10]—"the one you just saw in a blouse. I've sent him to live among his companions at Billancourt and Issy-les-Moulineaux. He's an active fellow, clear-headed, who soon found Lacaze's eight workmen and questioned them individually. Well, he obtained from each of them, minute by minute, checking their alibi, the employment of their time on the night of the crime. There's no point in continuing."

Mirande, dejected, concluded: "In a word, you've got nothing?"

"Nothing…except, perhaps for this, although it doesn't appear to me to be very interesting." Nitaud extended his arm toward a pigeon-hole and opened one of the box-files. It was the dossier of his mission. He took out a fragment of glass, soiled with a long stain. "This," he said," is something overlooked by the examining magistrate, which I discovered in the dust of the basement of the Gagny house, near the door opened by the murderer. It's a piece of the window he broke. The black stain is dried blood. It surely comes from the wound that was made in passing a hand through the breach. I didn't think the item could tell us anything, but I brought it along anyway, to acquit my conscience,"

Gabriel took the fragment of glass and examined it under the lap. The murderer's blood…what an irritating mystery! And what information, if the sanguine globule had presented a physiognomy unique to each individual, if the anthropological service had been capable of identifying an individual according to the appearance of his blood, as they could with the aid of his cranial measurements and fingerprints!

---

[10] *Lime* [file] and *limier* [bloodhound, or sleuth], lose their connective pun in translation.

In truth, biology had already inaugurated that system. Already, it could distinguish human blood from animal blood, but science did not go beyond that modest investigation, and the "sanguine imprint" was completely unknown.[11]

Mirande gazed avidly at that little debris, palpated it, turned it over, and invoked it, as if to obtain a supreme confidence therefrom.

"But this glass is yellow," he observed, suddenly.

"Indeed, the door had a window-pane of that color."

"Yellow...yellow!" repeated the young scientist, with a hallucinated insistence and a triumphant tone. Oh, the fortunate, the beneficent association of ideas. The liberating hope was suddenly illuminated. "Yellow...can you imagine that word? Yellow fever. Can you imagine that I haven't yet thought of it—me, a scientist, a pupil of Brion?"

He had risen to his feet—and, still incomprehensible for Nitaud, he cried, in a increasing excitement: "But that fever, he had it! If it's him who committed the murder, that fever is still there, dormant in the blood! If it's him, it's not possible that it won't be found. Oh, Brion, Brion the genius!"

This time, confronted by his apparent incoherence, Nitaud became seriously anxious. No doubt about it, the client had bats in his belfry. Probably, the Lacaze affair, descending upon a brain already overburdened by work,

_____

[11] In fact, the ABO system of blood typing had been discovered in 1901 by Karl Landsteiner, which permitted the first successful human blood transfusion to be performed in 1907. Couvreur could not have been unaware of that in 1911; perhaps the novel had been written earlier, although the frequent references to automobile taxis suggests otherwise.

had tipped it over the edge. Already, that unhealthy obstinacy in wanting to prove the innocence of the accused...this sudden metamorphosis in appearance, in dress...and all those thousand-franc bills that the citizen ruffled through with disdain, as if they were old newspaper clippings.

Oh, but no, beware! It wasn't the first time that a madman has come to sit down in that same armchair and pursue, in forms at first reasonable, a story whose meaning suddenly capsized. Dangerous to treat, affairs obtained in those conditions. The Prefecture would be only too glad to get something on a turncoat!

"I don't really see...," he objected, prudently.

Mirande saw the other's hand move toward his electric bell. He understood that the policeman was about to call for reinforcements. He calmed down suddenly.

"Have no fear, Monsieur Nitaud. I'm still in my right mind. But I understand your astonishment—because I've forgotten to cite an important fact in Lacaze's life."

And as Nitaud, half-reassured, cocked an ear curiously, he went on: "I've forgotten to tell you, in fact, that my friend, in the course of a recent aviation competition, contacted yellow fever..."

"Ah! I see! It's the color of that glass that recalled that memory?"

"Precisely."

"But I can't grasp the interest..."

"Capital, Monsieur Nitaud, capital. For my master, Professor Brion, who has just died..."

"Brion—yes, I know, a great scientist..."

"Well, Brion, among other biological endeavors, has studied the microbe of yellow fever."[12]

"And that microbe can still be found in the blood?"

"Science has denied it until recently. It believed that once the malady was over, the microbe disappeared with the organic debris, but Brion, among other prodigious discoveries, found the means to vivify—to resuscitate, so to speak—the bacillus, although it seemed to be annihilated."

"That's...amazing." The policeman thumped the table to signify his admiration. His eyes recovered all their intelligent mobility. He pushed his skullcap back over his head with a conquering gesture.

"So," Mirande concluded, "if I don't find the trace of yellow fever in this bloodstain, Lacaze can't be the murderer."

"Understood," said Nitaud.

For a long moment they contemplated the little piece of glass silently. Then Mirande added: "There's one point on which I'd still like to be informed. Does the law keep all the pieces of evidence for a time."

"Certainly."

"So it possesses other analogous debris, similarly bloodied..."

"You'll be able to repeat your experiments, which will then take on an official character."

---

[12] This is completely fictitious; yellow fever is now known to be caused by a virus, and even if it had been bacterial, the detection carried out by Mirande would have been impossible. The disease is, however, transmitted by mosquitoes, like malaria, and the malarial parasite—a protozoan rather than a bacillus—was detectable by microscopes in 1911, so the authors are presumably reasoning by analogy.

"That's sufficient for me," said Mirande. "I'll take away this piece of glass. And thank you again for having found it and picked it up."

Nitaud offered him a little cardboard box filled with cotton wool, in which Mirande carefully packed the precious splinter. Feverish and buoyant, he extended his hand cordially to the policeman, who shook it energetically before letting it go.

"Well then, eh? If you succeed, it'll be one in the eye for Dutoit. Oh la la!"

Outside, Gabriel headed for the boulevards. For her part, Jeanne had been invited to dine with friends, and he had promised himself an evening at the theater and music, a relaxation from his labors and cares. Nitaud's discovery added to his glad disposition. He gazed at the passers-by with an ingenuous affection. He was tempted to proclaim his confidence to them. He walked slowly, at random, in quest of a restaurant.

The display windows were lighting up. A mildness descended from the sky, and the murmur of the crowd seemed to acclaim the imminent success of his cause.

But a hand gripped his arm, and a cheerful voice behind him said: "Decidedly, then, it's a great life!"

"You, *mon Commandant*!"

He had just recognized Delacoste, whose overcoat revealed a white cravat. Undoubtedly, the Commandant had retained a benevolent memory of the evening in Dorville, for he immediately intimated to Mirande: "You're free, eh? You'll dine with me?" For the sake of discretion, Mirande risked a timid lie: "I was about to go home..."

"No, no—no protests! Passive obedience! I'm taking you to dine in the Bois, and then we'll go spend the evening at Lambrine's."

"Mademoiselle Lambrine? But I haven't been invited..."

"I'm inviting you. You've been introduced to her; that's sufficient. She's promised us ancient dances. It'll be curious, it seems. Then, I think a little bac will take us pleasantly through until dawn."

"Ah! Right,"

Mirande now understood the Commandant's insistence. His luck at cards had earned him this excessive good grace. A despicable prestige. He was about to make a further excuse, when Delacoste went on: "Come on, then. You'll meet interesting people. There are more Parisians in Paris that one might think, at present. You don't know, then, that Lambrine receives the cream of the magistracy, the arts, science and politics? That can always be useful."

This time, Mirande allowed himself to be tempted. Even so, he did not want to be introduced into Lambrine's home without his power of divination. The project was realizable—if he had time to leap into a cab, go to the laboratory in the Rue Méchain, inject himself and come back. He could then dine with the Commandant.

"I accept," he said. "You'll permit me, however, to go home..."

"I'll permit nothing at all!" protested the officer. "You're capable of not coming back. No, no. You're properly dressed. I have you, and I'm not letting you go."

And, indeed, a quarter of an hour later, he installed Mirande at a table set up in the open air, where, on the whiteness of the cloth, the delightful hues of flowers mingled with the pastel colors of the lampshade.

Authoritatively, Delacoste placed the order, like a man accustomed to those sorts of initiative. "Compote of ris de veau, roasted partridge, celery, camembert, flambéd peaches, extra-dry American Flag...and at the double!"

Slightly dazed, Mirande, who was penetrating that luxurious décor for the first time, contemplated the near-by hall, flamboyant with electricity, the diners in gala costume, and the garden, whose bright foliage seemed possessed of a tender freshness.

"So," asked Delacoste, "you've never been to Lambrine's? Oh, you'll see...a veritable little palace. And chic, tasteful."

Again he lauded the influence of the amiable woman. Without true talent, she hooked the premier roles. The press, aware of her prestige, did not spare its praise. In her home, nevertheless, Ministers could have held their council, there were so many of them. Even royal guests, passing through Paris, honored her with their visit.

"And clever! All those she's distinguished have remained her friends. She brings them together, so well that one barely recognizes the elect of the moment. For my part, I don't know who'll succeed Castillan..."

"Castillan? What Castillan?" Mirande almost shouted.

"But the only, the unique Castillan, the most worldly of physicians. What—you don't know that story?"

No, Mirande did not know it. But what upset him even more than that former liaison, was the thought of encountering Simone's husband.

Hazard had determined that during his student life he had never crossed the path of Dr. Castillan. He had heard mention of him as an audacious, brilliant, charming physician, but he had never seen him.

For a moment, he was tempted to renounce the soirée. But why? Was he not bound to encounter the man sooner or later? Already, in a pressing letter, Castillan had expressed the desire to thank him in person for the incredible resurrection. He could not avoid him indefinitely. On the contrary, the opportunity was tempting to meet him without the presence of Simone. And it was with a resolute tread that he approached the Lambrine house an hour later.

As soon as the porch, guarded by a valet of accomplished style, the high standing of the house was revealed. Valuable paintings were already hanging in the vestibule and along the stairway. An inestimable marble served as a lamp-stand. Oriental carpets extended over the steps. Two further valets, camped on the landings, indicated the way to the guests. But on the first floor, the three continuous drawing-rooms, under the abundant light of electric flowers, compelled his admiration.

Oh, how far away it was from the brutal luxury of the casino in Dorville, the halls of official fêtes, the gilt and finery of the exposition! Here, from the Aubussons at the entrance to the long mirror at the back, tempered by a Venetian veil, everything smiled with an intimate elegance and an aristocratic good taste. Wealth only revealed itself in the patina of the antique furniture, the rarity of the wood paneling, the harmony of the hangings, and the artful distribution of marbles, bronzes and choice trinkets in the display cabinets and on the sideboards. In the midst of that discreet splendor, an elite company of notorious men were striving by means of their prestige or wit, to dazzle and interest the beauty of women.

Delacoste grabbed Mirande's arm. "Look. You've never seen Castellan? That's him chatting to Lambrine over there, by the mantelpiece."

Mirande observed him avidly. At first, he could only make out a silhouette that was rather seductive, in spite of a somewhat rounded stomach, slightly emphasized by a whimsical waistcoat. Then he noticed the forty years inscribed in fine wrinkles in the corners of the dark eyes, the brushed hair, the pointed beard, brown and lustrous, and the warm coloration of the Oriental complexion. So that was Castellan! Simone's husband and master! That was the man he had detested, and cursed in secret, even though his heart was protected from hatred by so much indulgence and altruism...

Meanwhile Lambrine was approaching, followed by her companion,

Delacoste, having saluted her, said: "I've permitted myself to bring my young friend Gabriel Mirande, whom you've already met in Dorville."

She gauged him with a glance, doubtless deemed him better dressed than in the casino, and, while extending a hand heavy with rings to him in a regal gesture, she said to the Commandant: "You did very well."

On hearing Mirande's name pronounced, Castillan had not been able to retain a slight exclamation of surprise. He asked Lambrine to introduce him to the young man, and when that ritual was accomplished he immediately took him to one side.

"I'm delighted finally to meet you, Monsieur Mirande. Was it necessary that it should be elsewhere than my home? I have to thank you so much for your miraculous intervention. Don't think my letter sufficient to express my gratitude. My wife is waiting for you. Every day, she reproaches me for not having gone to see you. But you must suspect that the life of a Parisian physician is the most invaded, the most hectic…!"

The voice was musical, the tone discreetly important. Mirande was astonished to submit to the grace of the welcome, to sense his hostility flex.

"Has Madame Castellan made a complete recovery?" he asked.

"Not complete, but it's no longer anything but a matter of time and care. In any case, you can judge for yourself when you come to see us. We can talk about the miracle more at our leisure. Above all, don't fail. I have your promise?"

How could he refuse? Mirande consented. "Certainly, doctor."

But new arrivals were shaking Castillan's hand. He excused himself, leaving Mirande in a group where people were talking politics.

The scientist pretended to be listening, in order to put on a brave face, but he felt out of place and lost. Everything disorientated him: the scattered perfumes, the murmur of voices, the ease of the gestures, the profusion of light.

Oh, if only he had his serum! If only he had it in his veins, in order to find, if only momentarily, a little of his penetrating strength and superiority while facing these celebrated men and brilliant women! Being disarmed, he felt weak, confused and overwhelmed. He had the impression of being afflicted by a sort of infirmity, a mental deafness. On hearing all those people without being able to hear their thoughts he experienced the same embarrassment, the same malaise as if he could see them moving their lips without being able to hear their words.

Soon, his regret and his anxiety increased further. He had just recognized the glabrous face and inquisitive lorgnon of Monsieur Dutoit, the examining magistrate. Oh, that obstinate, vindictive face, how he had cursed it during the Lacaze affair! How he had trembled before it during the interrogation of the witnesses, before its irritation when he affirmed his friend's innocence.

Even now he retained a nightmarish memory of those interrogations, a persistent fear—and here was the enemy grinding out a polite smile and extending his hand.

"How are you, my dear Monsieur? Delighted to find you here. We met in circumstances so painful for you; I haven't forgotten your devotion to your unfortunate friend. Oh, you had no luck in that affair."

"Indeed, everything was in league against Lacaze," Mirande dared to reprove. In spite of himself, however, he retained his timorous reserve and his submissive tone.

The magistrate swelled with pride at sensing him once again in his power, as in the time when he had held him under question in his office, facing the raw daylight of the windowless curtain. Feline, he would have been able to continue playing with that prey, but the fact of wearing the same costume, of respiring the same joy diminished distances regardless and constrained him to an indulgence of goes company. Casually, he offered: "Shall we take a glass of champagne?"

For his part, Mirande could not savor it. His throat closed. He regretted more bitterly than ever the magic liquid that was asleep out there in Brion's cupboard. What absent strength! Twenty drops of the serum would have enlightened him so prodigiously! False compassion and apparent urbanity: how quickly he would have unmasked them in the magistrate. How quickly he would have opened a shutter in the skull of that little clean-shaven man and glimpsed the motives for his inclemency, his weaknesses and his flaws. How rapidly he would have dominated him in his turn. Oh, the splendid revenge...

At that moment, Castillan approached. Cheerfully, he said: "What—the two of you know one another?"

"We're even old acquaintances," said the magistrate indulgently, smiling.

"Oh, that's true—I forgot..." And he added, for Gabriel, in a sad tone: "Forgive me, my dear Monsieur."

Castillan's compassion, the sly irony of the magistrate...it was too much. Everything was colluding to make him sense his weakness, and he did not have his sovereign remedy at his disposal. What point was there in prolonging the ordeal? He resolved to flee.

But he had scarcely set foot on the staircase than Commandant Delacoste pounced on him. "What! You're leaving already?"

"Yes, I'm tired."

"But what about the bac?"

"That was true. He had forgotten. Alas, in the game no more than elsewhere, he would not have the talisman that gave victory. He smiled weakly.

"I sense that I won't win this evening."

III

Jeanne opened the glazed door to the fifth-floor balcony and leaned on the rail. She was watching for her brother. In the sunlight that had succeeded the recent rain the sidewalk was sparkling, the rails of the tramway shining like a nickel stream. The pedestrians who had taken refuge under the porches of houses were testing the sky by holding out their hands before resuming their route.

Jeanne amused herself with the movement of the street. Everything enchanted her this morning. She had recovered her interest in life since Gabriel, bringing her the fragment of glass, had explained to her the ingenious testimony that he hoped to obtain from it: how he counted on demonstrating the absence of the yellow fever microbe from the coagulated blood, and that it was possible, thanks to Brion's methods, to discover whether or not Lacaze had committed the crime.

Never had her brother's science enjoyed such prestige in her eyes. Culture media inspired a mysterious admiration in her; the objective lens of the microscope acquired a divine power for her.

Finally! The liberating proof, the blessed proof, Gabriel was about to bring at any moment, when he returned from the laboratory, for which he had set out that morning so confidently.

Why was he late in returning? Had he not promised to take an auto, in order to get home more rapidly? She imagined that he must have gone to the Palais de Justice first. And, with her eyes aimed into the distance, she grew impatient, reproaching every passer-by for disappointing her.

Certainly, he would bring her the proof of innocence. Her Henri, her dear Henri, she was sure of him, although everyone else turned away. Oh, how she loved him even more for having been thus afflicted and denied! For a moment, to relieve her impatience, she went back into the room and stopped in front of the portrait of Lacaze, placed in a prominent position. It was really him, it was his ardent visage, his intelligent and honest gaze, the proud bearing of his head, his customary fashion of folding his arms over his aviator's overalls. So the judges had been able to mistake him to that extent! They had not been touched, then, by that physiognomy, so righteous and sincere? Oh, the dear misunderstood, the great victim!

She was about to go back on to the balcony when the door opened behind her. Her brother came in.

"Well?" she questioned, feverishly. But she suddenly froze. Gabriel's constraint, his ravaged features confessed without words their common defeat.

"Speak!" she implored, in a terrified voice.

He did not reply. He went to collapse into a chair, and remained there prostrate. Then she shook him, almost brutally.

"Say something, then! I have a right to know! What have you found?"

"The proof."

"Of what? That he's guilty?"

"The blood I examined contains..."

"That's impossible!"

"It is, however." And, escaping his prostration, pressed to finish that confession, Gabriel continued: "My poor Jeanne, I would like to have been mistaken. Yes, I wanted to be...I consulted all my colleagues. I took them, one after another to my microscope and I asked them: 'What is that bacillus?' and they all replied: 'It's that of yellow fever.' Oh, it's the final straw. Now, there's nothing more for us to do than fall silent..."

But Jeanne, quivering, said: "I won't fall silent. On the contrary, I shall cry out more loudly than ever before this new error."

With a weary gesture, he criticized her, this time, for her obstinacy. To revolt against the judgment of men, so be it; but the testimony of science was irrefutable. However, on sensing her so fervent still, so passionately blind, he weakened. And he counseled her, in a soft voice:

"Believe me, I had every hope, like you...like you, I've fought...but I can't anymore; I can no longer struggle against the evidence. We have to concede, Jeanne. Tell yourself, if you like, that Henri went astray in a moment of madness. Tell yourself that he had good reason to hate Gagny, that he struck a wretched egotist unworthy to live. Even tell yourself that perhaps, unknown to him, it was his love that determined his action; that it was perhaps for you, to render you happy, that he wanted to bring forward the moment of succession, avoid bankruptcy. Yes, find attenuations, excuses, but don't veil your eyes any longer before the truth, my poor little Jeanne..."

At each of those phrases she had shaken her head obstinately. Her eyes dry, a rictus on her lips, she put her hands together. "It's you! It's you who talks like that! You, who have so valiantly supported me thus far! It's you who is drawing away from me."

"No."

"You're abandoning him, at any rate, and that's the same thing. For I'm his wife, eternally. So, I ask you to reflect, since, in dooming him you're dooming me. What do you want me to say to you? You're a coward before Destiny, as the jurors were. You're submissive to the same suggestions as them. Like them, you refuse to understand that an odious fatality can pursue a man..."

"Fatality, Jeanne?"

"Fatality, I repeat, I affirm. It exists, that fatality. I believe in it! I believe! Keep your conviction, but don't try to shake mine. Think, reflect! Ask yourself why Henri should be any more guilty today than he was yesterday. Is it because this testimony is more irrefutable than the others? It testifies to a new coincidence, to the obstinacy of hazard. What does it prove, in sum? That the murderer had had yellow fever, that's all. Is Henri the only man in Paris in that circumstance? There are mariners and colonials in the lower depths. Then why Henri? You see! You have no reply. Don't accuse, then! Stay with him! Stay with me!"

He shook his head. "I know that, I know that...but think...this new indication, added to so many others..."

Then, frightfully alone, her hands joined, she cried out her despair; "Oh, not to be able to share one's certainty!"

Suddenly, Mirande, illuminated, sat up straight. Why had he not thought of it sooner, since the examination of that drop of blood had rejected all doubt? Certainty...

But he could have it, absolute certainty, thanks to Brion's prodigious heritage. It was sufficient to see Lacaze, whose departure for the Île de Ré had been delayed by a slight illness, to read within him, to glimpse behind his forehead the confession of the crime or the

101

protestation of innocence. There was no hesitation. The serum would remove the final veil. The truth would appear. He did not even debate the arbitrariness of the means, the profanation of an amour, the espionage of a heart. No, no! First, to know...and to be finished with odious ignorance.

Impatient to act, but constrained to hide his decision from his sister, he took her hands and said to her: "Yes, it's you who are right, little Jeannot, I don't have the right to abandon you. So long as absolute proof doesn't intervene, I ought to remain faithful to my first conviction. And that proof, it's necessary for me to find. Do you believe me now? Do you forgive me?"

Her tears thanked him. But Mirande was already escaping. He hoped to obtain access to Lacaze—whom he had not seen since the assizes—by way of his friend Doisteau. He had scarcely an hour. He would find him at home.

In truth, he feared, by this new sounding, arriving at a definitive disappointment, but all the same, even if it were only a chance in a thousand, he ought to take it. Who could tell whether Lacaze might not really have succumbed to the obstinate blows of hazard?

While going along the Rue Monge, he recalled obstinately the gambler he had observed at the casino in Dorville before leaving the baccarat hall. He was one of those heroes in a smoking jacket, one of those parasites of beach resorts who, every evening, drag around their fear of the morrow and lie in wait for fortune like a bandit lying in ambush. His distressed features revealed, that evening, his somber misfortune. He had lost every bet. With what a tremulous hand, what a contraction of all his features, he had abandoned his last louis! Well, at that supreme attempt, his luck had turned. He won, and continued winning for a quarter of an hour, without a single defection of the cards, doubling, tripling and quintupling his stakes with equal good fortune. His resurrection at that moment! His exultant joy, at throwing handfuls of gold on to the baize! His bitter triumph when he saved himself, in time not to lose himself again, after having filled his hat with his sudden fortune And his grunting, like a hound thrown a morsel at the end of a hunt, or a wild beast over its prey, when, retired to a corner of the room, he had smoothed out the crumpled bills, lined up piles of gold coins and ivory chips!

Thus, fate, after having pursued Lacaze so relentlessly, might have reserved him a sudden revenge. In the chalice that one man empties for millions of others, in the obscure division of good and evil, Fortune might suddenly exchange the lees for a generous liquor.

Mirande arrived at the Place Maubert. With a backward glance, he made sure that he was not observed. Then, going along the buildings of the market, he joined an auto whose driver saluted him. It was a hired car that he retained permanently, which permitted him to save time in his steps. He had been obliged to hide it from Jeanne, because he could not reveal the origin of his small fortune to her. He gave Doisteau's address.

When he arrived, the surgeon was just getting out of a carriage. He was coming back from his service at the hospital, his expression both weary and joyful.

"Oh, my friend, what a morning! Three bellies, a breast, a shoulder and a knee! I'm worn out, exhausted, bowed down...but content, all the same."

"And why, great gods? Why this joy?"

Doisteau raised before his friend religiously, as if it were a pyx, a bottle full of liquid in which a piece of tissue was suspended

"I was offered this morning," he declared, "fifty centimeters of apache!"

"Apache?"

"Yes. There are amusing strokes of luck in our profession, and the macabre turns to vaudeville on occasion. Can you imagine that they brought me a little while ago a filthy scoundrel, one of those fortification rats who live on alcohol and 'thrusts of Père François,' who, after a battle with his peers—a matter of honor, it appears; where does honor go to build its nest?—had received a magnificent dagger-thrust in the abdomen. He was dying of it. No! He wasn't dying of it! I mean that he was dead of it. Exsanguinated face, absence of pulse, you can see it from here: a veritable corpse.

"Others had would have sent him to the Morgue, but you know my ideas. I think, personally, that people disinterest themselves too easily in subjects that present the appearance of death, when a rapid intervention might resuscitate them. The human body breaks down occasionally, just like an automobile. In brief, I had the pseudo-cadaver taken to the operating table, I opened up his belly, deployed his intestines, and encountered a lovely gash that had plowed the entire caecum. There are some, aren't there, who would have been content to stitch up the rent? And then, small chance. Well, me, I took out the lot, the entire perforated section. And here it is, that tube, in the alcohol. It ought to be well content. That one, I sutured, dried, drained, and my corpse..."

"Lives again?"

"Lives again! To the point that I was able to ask him: 'Is it true, my boy, that you burgle safes as easily as I've just burgled your belly?' And he understood, the animal; he laughed."

At that memory, he chuckled himself. But Mirande, absorbed by his project, remained anxious.

"I need your help," he said.

"Whatever you wish."

"Perhaps, in your capacity as a prison surgeon, you can get me into the Santé?"

Doisteau frowned. "That's strictly forbidden by the regulations," he objected. "What do you want to do in that hole?"

"I want to see Lacaze. You know that he's ill."

"Yes, I know. I've seen the poor devil several times." Perplexed, the surgeon tugged at his moustache. "I'd prefer it if you asked me for something else. But in the end, for a friend…a friend like you... listen, you're in luck. Just now, I'm replacing my colleague in medicine. If you promise not to get me into trouble, I could take you along as my assistant."

"Oh, thank you, Doisteau!"

"Yes, but above all, don't compromise me. They'd have my head!"

"Don't worry."

"Tomorrow morning, then, half past nine, at the gate."

"I'll be punctual. Thanks again!"

The following morning, Jeanne went out early. Mirande was glad of that. He would be able to proceed at his leisure to inject himself, in order to be fully under the influence of the serum when he arrived at the rendezvous, and he did not risk surprising the young woman's thoughts. He avoided the chance of an investigation that offended his scruples.

As soon as he heard the door close behind her, he consulted his watch. The incubation required an hour. He had time. At a quarter past eight he took out the medical kit that never left his person now. With the gravity of an officiant he passed the needle through an alcohol flame, broke off the tip of the ampoule, slowly aspired the substance and pushed it into his flesh. Then he tidied everything away, went to the chair at his desk and waited, his eyes on his watch.

At Dorville, on the beach that night, in the emotion of the first proof, he had not studied his physiological reaction to the serum. This time, he wanted to take advantage of the opportunity to monitor himself calmly minute by minute.

He was astonished not to feel any precursory symptom. Nothing. Not a wave within his skull. Had he mistaken the ampoule? No; error was inadmissible. In any case, Brion's notebook, consulted many times, did not indicate any preliminary disturbance. To while away the time, he tried to think about his old master, From then on, the time weighed upon him less. Once again, he saw the august face gained by the lividity of death. He heard the last words, broken by paralysis. There, still, a mystery remained. Had Brion hastened his end by the use, by the abuse, of the serum? Had the prodigious liquid had a toxic effect on his organism?

When the clock chimed nine o'clock, a tremor ran through him, the effect of an imperceptible vertigo. A slight transpiration moistened his brow. Then he felt an astonishing need for action, like an appetite for communication with others. A thousand energies animated him, brought him to his feet. In order to employ them, he arranged the papers on his desk, and then scattered them again. He made a feverish note of a chemical formula for which he had been searching for months, and which had just suddenly reappeared to him.

He watched the course of the clock's hands more feverishly, until the time he had fixed arrived.

"Quarter past nine—finally!"

He got up, but at that moment, he perceived a strange thought. At the same time, voices filled the neighboring antechamber. Furthermore, the cerebral language and the spoken language were so closely associated, expressing the same indignation, that he could not dissociate them.

He was preparing to intervene when Francette knocked and, as was her custom, irrupted into the room without waiting for a response.

"Would you believe it?" she exclaimed, immediately, her eyebrows menacing. "Would you believe that that animal won't leave his merchandise without being paid?"

"What animal, Francette?"

"The coal-merchant, of course. Mam'zelle went out without leaving me the money. And now he says he'll take his coke away of he isn't paid! Have we ever made him wait for a settlement? Sure, we aren't Rothschilds, but damn it, we're not paupers either!"

"Why didn't you advance him from your own money, as you've often done before?"

For a second, Francette was nonplussed, her mutinous head raised, her lips parted. But her thought, whose message Mirande received, confessed: *Oh, petit patron, if I only could! But I can't any more. I've used up all my savings, not a brass farthing left! Oh, my poor nest-egg! If I dared, I'd tell you that I poured it all into your household in the time when you were in the soup and Mam'zelle no longer looked at the book of expenses! Sure, it's for her that I'm cleaned out, and for her Lacaze too, but it's most of all for you,* patron, *because you're such a chic fellow, so decent, and I love you, oh, how I love you...*

But she had pulled herself together and, aloud, feigning confusion, she said: "Yes, that's true. I could have paid him. I didn't think of that..."

An admirable and touching lie! Mirande had received the windfall of naïve tenderness and generous devotion full in the heart. For two pins he would have gone to the worthy girl and planted two chaste kisses on her pink cheeks. *My poor little Francette...!* But how would he have explained such an impulse?

At least he wanted to compensate such discreet attachment with a facile generosity. He took out his wallet.

"Hold out your hand, my worthy Francette."

And into that poor little grubby hand he slipped a large blue bill. "Take it, Francette, Pay the coalman and keep the rest."

"For me?"

He's crazy. It's not possible. He's crazy, my petit patron, proclaimed the secret voice. At the same time, with a gesture, Francette refused the offering. He had to flee in order to leave it in her hands.

Still deeply moved by the naïve homage, he was going downstairs when the rustle of a dress attracted his attention. Someone was coming up. He leaned over the banister and recognized Jeanne.

So he was about to glimpse his sister's thoughts too? Oh, certainly, he admired her purity, her nobility, her moral beauty. But what if some shadow appeared on that whiteness, some trivial streak on the immaculate page? An impious suspicion. But the profanation would be even more impious. No, no, let the veil of illusion continue to envelop that fraternal tenderness.

And, out of fear as much as respect, he moved aside at the next landing and plunged into a dark corridor. Instinctively, he would have blocked his ears had he not been certain of remaining sensitive to the immaterial waves.

Alas, the corridor arrived quickly at a dead end. Scarcely two meters separated him from the young woman when she went past him without seeing him, and he could not escape her radiation.

But once again, he exalted in the discovery of a treasure. Dear Jeanne...she never ceased to love in her dolor. At that moment, as always, the thought of her fiancé filed her soul. She saw herself relegated with him to distant Guyana. She shared, and lightened, his harsh exile. She exhorted him to patience. She promised him a definitive triumph.

Oh, the divine canticle of pure and tutelary amour...the consoling apparition... Not all hearts, then, were rotten with egotism and turpitude. There were Jeannes, and there were Francettes...

Jeanne had passed by...

Mirande made haste, for time was pressing. He reached his auto, still parked in the Place Maubert, and gave the address of the Santé. On the way, he glimpsed the interior monologue of the driver, who was launching energetic abuse at his vehicle—and every time the vehicle passed close to a pedestrian, Mirande received the murmur of his thought on the wing, like the rapid rustle that one hears in an automobile as it passes the trees alongside the road.

Doisteau was waiting outside the prison gate.

"Am I late?"

"Slightly. It's nothing," the surgeon replied, politely. Internally, however, he expressed his annoyance at having been stuck on the sidewalk when urgent tasks awaited. Mirande excused him, effortlessly, for that slight divergence.

"Follow me," Doisteau ordered. And, in a whisper, his thought stirred an amusing apprehension:

You can follow me, my old Mirande, we can mock the regulations together. What do you have to say to Lacaze so urgently? Do you think he's innocent, for a start? Aren't you, rather, defending him with such energy to spare your own honor in the eyes of others? Yes, what do you want from him, our Lacaze? You haven't come, by chance, with the secret intention of helping him to escape? You aren't carrying in your jacket pocket, I hope, a false beard or a revolver? You know, my old Mirande, I like you a lot, but no tricks. Oh, no, no dirty tricks!

Meanwhile, they had gone through the heavy door where soldiers were yawning. They traversed a little courtyard crammed between severe walls and went into a maze of corridors and sonorous staircases.

Finally, they reached, at the heart of a vast intersection, a glazed office, elevated and isolated, a kind of enormous searchlight lantern, from which the view extended into the radiating corridors where the cells were aligned.

There, a warder greeted Doisteau with a familiar salute. The surgeon gave a signature and introduced Mirande as his assistant. All the reefs had been crossed.

Followed by his friend, Doisteau took one of the long brightly-lit, cold and bare avenues, bordered by narrow doors. To the warder who was guarding that span he said: "Monsieur is going to examine the prisoner Lacaze." Then, to Mirande: "I'll come and collect you after my visit. Be quick."

He drew away. And while the warder opened the cell door, with a great rattle of keys, Mirande battled with his supreme scruples. He was about to read the consciousness of his friend, delivered to him defenselessly, like an open book. That unequal struggle offended his sense of justice. Had he the right to surprise a confession that the condemned man had not wanted to be extracted from him? Was not that sly inquisition more odious than all the procedures of torture and interrogation?

But the warden, having opened the door, stood aside. And immediately, an infinite pity invaded him.

Henri Lacaze was lying on his bed. He was asleep. A heavy sleep had finally succeeded a feverish night. His bedcovers thrown off, he had only kept a single sheet. The cloth, which enveloped him like a shroud with rigid creases, emphasized the thinness of his body. And beneath the overly long beard, what a poor face, furrowed, reduced, ochreous, in which physical malady and moral torment were inscribed in dolorous lines. Oh, if that man was guilty, the suffering that he had already undergone had already paid more than sufficiently for his crime.

He was asleep, dreamlessly, for Mirande would have glimpsed the mysterious play. He was asleep, sunk in oblivion. Oh, to let him continue to forget! Impossible.

"Henri! Henri!"

At that appeal, the condemned man started and rubbed his eyes.

"You…! You…!" he stammered, stupefied.

At the same time, the brain awoke. Mirande perceived the commencement of the slow march of ideas. They expressed, first and foremost, a doubt as to the reality of the apparition.

111

"Yes, it's really me," he reassured him, immediately. "I've come to see you. I managed to get in here by means of a ruse. Doisteau helped me."

"Doisteau...indeed, I've seen him several times. He's not kind, Doisteau. He pretended not to recognize me, although I'd met him several times in your laboratory."

"Forgive him."

"There are too many people it would be necessary to forgive!" said Lacaze, grimly.

It was only a flash, a moment of drama. Already, the image of his fiancée had appeared in the mind of the invalid, with a beautiful intensity that expelled any other thought.

"And Jeanne?" he asked.

"Jeanne's anxious about you, naturally."

Lacaze misunderstood, thinking that it was uniquely a matter of his health.

"Poor dear...it's true, I'm not brilliant. Reassure her, though. Tell her that you found me well..."

"I can't tell her that, Henri, because I'm acting without her knowledge. It's even necessary that she doesn't know...don't tell her that I've come when you write."

"Why?"

Caught unawares, he invented: "To spare her the regret of not having been able to come with me."

Furthermore, his embarrassment was increasing. He searched for the word, or the phrase, that would unleash the association of ideas necessary to his investigation, which would provoke a confession of the crime or a cry of innocence.

A direct interrogation would have been brutal and wounding, especially at that moment, when Lacaze was allowing himself to be carried away by his memories. His thought evolved with an extraordinary precision, which Mirande had difficulty following. He relived enchanting moments in the little apartment in the Rue Monge, with his fiancée. Then, without any appreciable connection—perhaps the comparison of two intoxications, two purities—there was a flight into the blue sky, on the quivering wings of the helicoplane.

Oh, if he had been able to invoke that nocturnal excursion, in which the aviator claimed to have injured his hand on a taut wire. But no: no return to the drama. One might have thought that Lacaze feared that terrain, that he had forbidden his memory to slip into it. Aloud, he went on:

"I would have liked so much to see her, to thank her. Oh, her letters...her letters! They're so tender, so touching! That resolution to join me out there, in Guyana...but I don't want that. She'd suffer too much..."

This time, undoubtedly, he was about to return to the drama and thus yield his secret thought...but no. One might have thought that he did not know, or that he had definitively accepted the verdict of the law.

A doubt occurred to Mirande, however. If Lacaze, exhausted in any case by his illness, did not experience any need to protest his innocence, perhaps it was because he considered it to be evident in the eyes of his friends? For Gabriel, for his sister, it was an acquired fact. Their stubbornness in defending him during the trial was sufficient proof of that. What was the point?

And, in fact, Lacaze continued to avoid the past. He dwelt on his physical suffering, on the recurrences of his fever, on the minor incidents of his life in prison, with an absolute frankness that Mirande checked syllable by syllable. He was not hiding anything. He was expressing his thoughts faithfully—to such an extent that, incessant-ly recoiling from the brutality of a direct interrogation, Mirande drew away from his objective. He asked about the cellular regime, his relationship with the warders. Then, keeping quiet about the existence and intervention of the serum, he told him briefly about Brion's death, Simone's resurrection, and his recent encounter with Castillan at Lambrine's.

And suddenly, an inspiration illuminated him. "And guess who I met that evening? Dutoit!"

"Dutoit! Oh, the wretch! That ignoble individu-al…oh, if he fell into my hands…"

With an unsuspected energy, Lacaze had sat up on his bed. All his rage shone in his eyes. All his hatred rose to his face, inscribed on his fleshless cheeks in two fiery patches.

And within him, what a seething of revolt! What fulgurant indignation! What a dazzling oration! All that words could not express, his thought cried out, with an eloquence and an irresistible force.

And Mirande collected that generous protestation with so much avidity, remorse and joy that he could not contain himself. He seized the dolorous victim in his arms and hugged him furiously, covered the pitiful jaun-diced forehead with repentant kisses. And he stammered: "Oh, my poor old fellow, my poor good fellow. If you knew how I love you, how we love you, Jeanne and I. Come on, we'll get your revenge on Dutoit. We'll get you out of this…"

Such an effusion, succeeding the constraint and oldness of the beginning, disconcerted Lacaze, who thought, like Francette an hour before: *Ah! He's gone crazy…!*

But of madness like that, Mirande only asked that he could taste the delicious sweetness more often. And it was with an indulgent and light heart that he welcomed the secret confession of the good Doisteau, who reappeared at the door.

Let's see, good, all's well, He definitely hasn't brought a revolver, a gag or a false beard.

IV

"Innocent! Lacaze is innocent!"

His tread light and his heart joyful, Mirande was talking to himself in the solitude of the exterior boulevards. On leaving the prison he had immediately thrown himself into those vast spaces, to flee the buzz of strange thoughts while he remained under the influence of the serum.

So, all the judges on earth had run into that indecipherable enigma; they had never been able to know whether the accused who protested his innocence was sincere or lying. They had never been able to discover the truth that was agitating behind his forehead. But he, Mirande, possessed that supreme proof...

How glad Jeanne would have been to learn that her amorous instinct had not been deceived... Once again, he deplored his inability to reveal his secret to her. But he promised to reassure her without betraying it, and to penetrate her with his own certainty.

And what never strength he would be able to draw from that certainty, in order to extract Lacaze from prison, to prove his innocence! An entire plan was designed in his mind, in vigorous strokes. He would go to see Favery, the direct of the *Lumière*. This time, he would reach him. He would persuade him to share his conviction, without revealing its source. Oh, how warmly he would plead his cause henceforth! He would be able to demonstrate the advantage, for a newspaper, of opening a campaign whose success was certain, of being the first to denounce a judiciary error whose discovery was fatal.

Gradually, public consciousness would be awakened. People who had remained silent out of prudence might perhaps decide to speak. Generous minds, fond of equity, would become anxious, would want to study the affair. Even the law, if only to defend its work, would bring out its evidence, and thus betray its fragility.

Quickly, Mirande would be able to ameliorate the fate of the prisoner, loosen his chains, until the day of the definitive revenge, the overturning of his conviction.

Suddenly, however, he stopped. To obtain that revision, it would be necessary for him to produce a new fact, or identify the true guilt party. In his joy at knowing that Lacaze was innocent, he had forgotten the crime and its perpetrator. In spite of all his power, his divinatory faculty, how could he succeed in discovering and unmasking the true guilty party?

On returning home, he found a telegram form on his desk. He opened it and read the signature: Simone Castillan! He read it avidly. She was not yet fully recovered. However, she had invited a few friends to tea on the following day, to celebrate her convalescence. She absolutely insisted on the presence of her savior. Already, it had been painful for her to think that she had not yet had the opportunity to express her gratitude to him. Her husband had told her to insist on his behalf.

Mirande threw the note on to the table. His first impulse was to refuse, to keep his distance. But would not his avoidance of thanks end up by provoking suspicions? How would Simone explain it to her husband. That she had not seen her childhood friend since her marriage, Castillan would have had no reason to be surprised, but he would be astonished that Mirande refrained from reappearing after having snatched her from death. Alerted by that singular reserve, he might seek information, divine the disappointed amour...

No, the passion that the unhappy man wanted to stifle in himself, he had no right to allow the husband to divine.

Obscurely, he rejoiced in being pushed toward her by his very scruples. Certainly, it would cost him to see her at home, married. But at the moment when he was about to go fully into action, when the struggle in which he was engaged had entered a new phase, it seemed to him that the dear presence would have the bittersweetness of a cordial.

And abruptly, the temptation invaded him to know Simone's thought. A few days earlier, he would have rejected such a suggestion violently. He would have obeyed the concern for discretion and respect that, when Jeanne had passed by, had thrown him into the darkest and most remote corner of the stairway. But precisely because he had retained from that mental apparition of sorts such an impression of whiteness, of purity, of radiant splendor, he was confident, reassured, avid to plunge once again into those lustral waves.

Even the humble confession of the maidservant, the cry, involuntarily provoked, that had escaped poor Francette's heart, reassured him, inciting him to the tender proof. With a naïve egotism, he retained nothing of it but the certainty of being able to inspire love. His timidity, his suspicion of himself, had been attenuated by it.

Oh, he was not meditating either troubling Simone or deviating from the right path. Lies and treason were too repugnant to his own nature. No, he would find out what she thought of him, discover whether she retained the tender amity that she had shown him in the time of their adolescence. His curiosity was even more elevated, purified, free from all personal concern. With no hidden agenda, he wanted to interrogate Simone about herself, without her being aware of it, to make sure that she was happy, that she had no reason to complain about her life with her equivocal and charming husband.

So just and so strong were the reasons with which his desire to see Simone again was enveloped, that Mirande was intimidated to the point of anguish when he went into the Castillans' drawing-room.

He was not yet under the influence of the serum. He knew its effects with precision now. He had checked that they would only be manifest after an hour. He was, therefore, the master of the moment at which his power would commence. Thus, he only injected himself three-quarters of an hour before the visit, in order that its commencement would not be troubled by the buzz of nearby thoughts.

On the threshold, he congratulated himself for his caution. He thought he was going into an aviary. Four or five ladies, gathered around Simone, were all twittering at once. Already stunned by their chirping, he would have lost his mind if he had been obliged to listen to their interior voices as well.

Simone was curled up in an armchair near the fire-place. Her face lit up and she extended her hand to him. And she said, in a soft voice, when he bowed before her: "That's good."

Then the conversation was unleashed again, and he was soon able to contemplate the young woman at his leisure. She retained nothing from the terrible ordeal but a slight languor, in harmony with her natural grace, which added to her charm. He prolonged his ecstasy, simultaneously dolorous and delighted. She was alive...

119

The entire past of youth, poetry and amour, which he had thought buried forever, was resuscitated. She was alive, but for someone else. She no longer belonged to herself. The irony of destiny determined that she would always remain for him the inaccessible and distant idol.

Meanwhile, the conversation fluttered between the narrow limits that it is conventional to maintain in those sorts of receptions. There was talk of theaters and costumes. Then, Madame Castillan having deplored the departure of a chambermaid who had revealed expert skills, all the visitors erupted in condolences. One could no longer keep a good domestic, and the worst of them were acquiring such pretentions that it would soon no longer be possible to obtain service.

Mirande was hardly listening. In a few minutes, the serum would take effect, and he feared being unable to use its power usefully on Simone in the midst of all that frivolous chatter. Already, in his meeting with Lacaze, he had felt all the difficulty of orientating someone's thought in a specific direction, and then leading them to formulate the thought in perceptible terms. How could he lead Simone to descend into herself, to reveal her sentiment regarding him, regarding her own happiness, in the midst of that cackling?

He became worried about the time. For the first time, he inspected the vast drawing-room, where the soft light of electric bulbs clad in silk caressed the furniture, the hangings and the trinkets, revealing an ensemble with the sober sumptuousness of a museum.

Finally, he discovered a Louis XV clock hanging on the wall near the chimney-breast. Past six o'clock; the truce was complete. And the twitter of the aviary did not stop. Resigned, he waited, his eyes on the floor. And gradually, the light babble was doubled for him by another concert, almost as frivolous and almost as tumultuous: thoughts if praise and envy for the furniture and the arrangement of the drawing-room; lacunae discovered in the menu of taste; shrill criticisms of the dress and mannerisms of the neighbor; concern to appear elegant and pretty oneself, more so than the others.

In passing, Mirande collected a few impressions regarding him. One mocked his mutism; one disapproved of his cravat; one admired his abundant hair, his svelte shoes. But one note dominated, by its force and its abundance: the desire to get it over with, the urge to leave. Some were harassed by the need to stack visits upon visits, other by the hour of an appointment with a milliner, a couturier, or someone else, and others by the simple desire to finish the chore, to be outside: a unique refrain of all those songs, which gave the disparate chorus a kind of harmony. And Mirande, irritated by that interior verbiage, thought in his turn: *Since they're in such a hurry to leave, why don't they go?*

He knew that by looking directly at Simone he could grasp her thought more especially. What was the point? At that moment, constrained by rigid social law, she must be agitated, like her companions, by futile concerns. And then, he would have had to look at her insistently. He did not dare. And, hanging his head, he waited, dumbfounded.

Fortunately, the doorbell was heard through the drapes. At that signal, one lady got up swiftly. Two others, incapable of resisting her example, imitated her almost immediately. They took their leave, with effusions, regrets and anguish in their voices, while singing internally the joy of taking flight.

They crossed the path of a visitor that Mirande recognized immediately: Quatrefin, a wealthy man who was involved in major industrial deals and was interested in aviation. Svelte and solid, his beard fine and his gaze frank, he was reputed to be honest in financial milieux, where his boldness and skill were admired.

Convinced of Lacaze's innocence, he had testified in favor of the accused. He had affirmed that at the moment of the aviator's arrest, he was about to make him a large loan. Mirande retained a gratitude for that attitude, which he had expressed several times in the course of the trial.

Completely at ease, Quatrefin brushed Simone's hand with a kiss and congratulated her on how well she looked.

"I permitted myself," he added, "to order a few flowers in passing, for your convalescence."

And suddenly, Mirande perceived that the man's thoughts surpassed his words. He experienced more pleasure than he had marked in finding Simone reestablished, in celebrating her return to health. He was more attached to her that he allowed to appear. She pleased him.

Mirande felt his heart pinched by jealousy. Immediately, he tried to reassure himself. A woman like her, of a grace so touching, of such gentle beauty, could not go through life without inspiring fervor and admiration. But what about her? Could she be insensible to such homages?

Forgetting his prudence and restraint, he fixed his gaze upon her ardently. He breathed out. She remained placid, indifferent, simply recalling that Quatrefin was a friend of Castellan's, she asked him: "Have you seen my husband?"

He replied, secretly annoyed by her calmness: "We arrived together. He'll catch up with me."

Already, he was shaking Mirande's hand with an energetic grip.

"Glad to see you again," he said.

He was thinking that—but at the same time, he was wondering why he had never encountered Mirande at the Castillans' before, and was astonished to find him so different from his appearance at the trial, so confident and well-dressed.

Castillan appeared. The last female visitor took advantage of that to get up. He said to her in a heart-broken tone, although she was utterly indifferent to him: "What? You're running away as soon as I arrive?"

"No, no," she replied, "but I'm dining in town." She did not add that she had to call in at her hairdresser' first, because her temples were beginning to lost their gilt since the last lotion.

At that moment, Quatrefin asked Mirande, in his warm, brusque voice: "Well, what about poor Lacaze? He's definitely going to the prison colony? You haven't discovered any new indication?"

Mirande was obliged to keep silent about his research. "Nothing," he said. But once again, he protested his friend's innocence. The necessity of masking the origin of his certainty excited his zeal further. He wanted to compensate for the absence of proof by persuasion. Eager to convince, he proclaimed his faith in the ultimate success, the discovery of the real guilty party.

In the gazes and behind the foreheads, he watched for sentiment. And suddenly a thought as strident and clear as a burst of laughter mocked: "Go on, my lad. You'll do well to find him, your guilty party..."

Castillan? Only Castillan could jeer like that. Did he know something?

His gaze taut, Mirande concentrated, pouncing upon him mentally. He wanted to concentrate his thought on the crime.

"What about you, Doctor? You haven't found the slightest indication? It's known that you were associated with the victim..."

Castillan replied, casually: "Oh, as for me, I respect the judges' decision. Since the verdict, I haven't given the matter any further thought."

And slyly, he added internally: *And besides, it would be futile. In truth, at the present moment, I'm incapable myself of finding the poor devil who struck the blow...*

He knew! He knew the murderer. Was that possible?

Oh, the rage of not being able to leap his throat, not being able to howl in his face: "I divine you. I can hear you. Speak. Say who killed him. Quickly. Immediately."

But no. Brion was right. He would be taken for a madman. He would be locked up. He must even be careful not to give himself away. Alerted by a sign, a presentiment, Castillan might turn his mind away from his memories. With a new effort, he brought him back to the drama.

A poor devil, Castillan had thought. Mirande therefore affirmed: "Personally, I can't get away from the idea that the crime was committed by a professional."

"Do you think so?" said Castillan, skeptically.

And silently: *What tells you that, honest Mirande? And what a professional! I can still see him, when they brought him to me at the hospital, that great body emaciated by liver disease, a distant repercussion of an old bout of yellow fever. I can hear his hoarse voice, his slum accent. Oh, a fine cure! But where the devil did gratitude take him? That cowardly wild beast, that river poacher, that pirate of the Seine, didn't he want with all his might to thank me for my care by getting rid of an inconvenience for me? A skin! He offered me a skin as one offers one's physician a copper coin. How many times did I find him outside the hospital door, waiting for me to leave, harassing me, tempting me with ingenuity. In truth, the opportunity was too good. Like a good hound, he almost divined the trail on which I wanted to launch him. He only needed the double indication: the blow to strike and the name of the man who had to be accused. Damn! Time was pressing, it was necessary to clear the way to the inheritance!*

Abruptly, however, the train of thought changed course, at a word from Quatrefin. The financier attributed the murder of old Gagny to a vengeance.

Then, cordial and affectionate, Castillan took him by the shoulders and shook him familiarly. "Quatrefin, Quatrefin, my friend, let's leave that affair tranquil. In France, we have the malady of judiciary error."

Mirande had received the confession like a bullet to the head. It had penetrated him rapidly, with a murderous violence. His hand clenched on the back of a chair, he stiffened in order not to fall.

So, Castillan had guided the murderer's hand, deflected suspicion on to Lacaze! Castillan, Simone's husband! Oh, the necessity of remaining impassive under the frightful revelation, of being as calm as if one still did not know…!

But the name, the name of the guilty man? He needed it, in order to bring the truth to light, for he could not admit how it had been discovered. He needed, at all costs, to extract that name from Castillan, to make it light up in his memory.

He strove to recover his composure and his voice. "However, Doctor, what if the police were to discover a guilty party who confessed?"

"In that case," Castillan declared, gravely, "I would concede."

And he continued, within himself: *And it wouldn't cost me anything. The man would never betray me. These brutes have their special honor. Wounded in a brawl, his peers remain obstinately silent about the man who struck them. That savage, at the same time as he offered to rid me of an inconvenience, promised never to give me away. He'll keep his word. Furthermore, it's in his interest. Once taken, he'll still be doomed, with or without an accomplice. Free, unsuspected, I can save him from the guillotine; sitting beside him, I can no longer be of use to him. But what's the point of these chimeras? The man has sunk back into the lower depths. He'll never be found there. I wouldn't be able to find him myself if my life depended on it. At the hospital, he refused to reveal his identity. I don't even know his name. He's unknown to the anthropometric service. He's a number over a bed, something vague, non-existent, evaporated. So, what can happen?*

Mirande suppressed a gesture of despair. He would get nothing more out of that wretch. Thus, he was certain of Lacaze's innocence, and certain of Castillan's culpability, but he could do nothing to prove it! For he had to keep the secret of his certainties—and the murderer himself was out of reach.

Nevertheless, by combining the indications scattered in Castellan's reminiscences, perhaps he could succeed in discovering his accomplice. Dominated by the instinct of the pursuit and the desire to triumph, distressed by his discovery, he wanted to think clearly himself, to escape the buzz of thoughts that were henceforth importunate, breathe the air outside.

As he took his leave of Simone, she said to him, afflicted: "Already? It's given me pleasure to see you."

Instinctively, he sketched a gesture of doubt. Then she insisted; "Yes, yes…and you must come back, you hear?"

Short phrases, but Mirande was moved to tears by them, for the words were the faithful echo of her thoughts. Better than that, they were wedded to them, like the tune and words of the same song: an accord that gave the sound frankness, a hymn of the heart, a delicious harmony that a human being was savoring for the first time…a music so sweet and so pure that it removed him from the world, that he forgot therein, momentarily the lying voices, the frightful discovery, the bloody cloaca that a forehead could conceal.

PART THREE

I

So, that monstrous thing was possible, certain! Castillan had ordered the death. That worldly doctor, flourishing and sought-after, was nothing but a murderer. And what a murderer! The most cowardly, the most vile. He had not even had the audacity to strike the blow. He had exploited, to make use of it, the gratitude of a brute.

Oh, that one of those pariahs, an item of the debris of the social organism, might lie in wait for his prey and fall upon it, was certainly abominable. But at least that one had suffered; he had been hungry; he had envied the felicity of the other bitterly; no interior voice had turned him away from evil; in his narrow mind he estimated the right to pleasure, to enjoyment. Crime is less unjust for the man crushed by injustice.

But Castillan...

Castillan, heaped with success, power, money! Castillan the murderer, Castillan unpunished, was that not the most revolting challenge hurled in society's face?

In the street, after having left the Castillan house, Mirande abandoned himself to his indignant rage. So destiny, which had already given him that man as a rival, now designated him to his just condemnation. The same hand that had led Simone to the altar, had shown the path to the murderer, designated Lacaze to the tribunal...

His execration was exasperated. His hatred over-flowed. He felt ready to be drawn to immediate imprudence. His scorn and his disgust spread out over humanity entire. He drew away from passers-by, in order not to glimpse some new abomination at every encounter.

However, the keen and chilly air outside gradually calmed him down. He strove to classify the facts he had acquired methodically.

So, Castillan, in order to assure the community of the entire Gagny inheritance, had killed the old man in such a Machiavellian fashion that the suspicions of the law had been sure to fall on the co-inheritor, Lacaze. And the man he had employed for that task was a grateful apache, a pirate of the Seine, whom he had treated during his service at the hospital for accidents indirectly consequent to yellow fever. A bandit, alas, whose name Castillan did not know, of whom he had lost track.

He had prescribed the act, as a great lord, to the hired killer whom gratitude had delivered to him. How had the murderer studied the house in the Avenue Raphael? How had he procured the file marked with Lacaze's initial? How had he taken advantage of a day when the old man and his young cousin had quarreled violently? How and where had he hidden from all research? All that, Castillan did not know. And that was frightening for Mirande. He was advancing, plunging deeply, into the enigma, but it still remained just as obscure.

Would that grateful patient, well-founded in the power of the crime, never appear again to his master, to his savior? Castillan had faith in his discretion, in his special honor. Who could tell whether he might not surge forth in an hour of poverty and hunger, breathing threats and blackmail?

But how could he find out about that possible return of the pirate? How could he keep watch on Castillan closely enough to be immediately informed on the event? Ought Mirande to renew his visits, slipping into the intimacy of the household? He only envisaged the project to reject it. No, no. He would have suffered too much. Such a role was beyond his strength.

However, he admitted the utility of an active surveillance. Would it not be appropriate, in order to protect Simone, to penetrate her husband's true attitude toward her? The bandit had shown his measure; he was capable of any cruelty. Eventually, on the day when, alerted by his subtle intelligence, he sensed that he was suspected, would he not seek to escape punishment, to take to the sea with his fortune made?

But who could he employ for that delicate work? For a moment, Mirande thought of Nitaud. Of his own accord, during their first meeting, the policeman had wanted to orientate his research in the direction of Castillan. But how could he explain and expose suspicions whose origin had to remain secret? Finally, Mirande admitted it to himself; it was repugnant to him to place near Simone, to install in her house, one of the shady associates he had glimpsed in Nitaud's office.

He hesitated again when he went into the little apartment in the Rue Monge. Francette, who was agitating in the kitchen, was in loud conversation with Jeanne, who was occupied in her bedroom.

"Mademoiselle," shouted Francette, "in your place, do you know what I'd do?"

"No, what?"

"I'd wouldn't bother any more with the law, because it has nickeled feet, the law."

"So?"

"So, me, I say that it wouldn't be a bad idea to go save a man from prison. Do you know Latude? I've seen Latude at the Théâtre des Gobelins. He was a rude fellow of olden times. So, why shouldn't one see it again?"

The sound of the door closing cut the conversation short.

But that naïve ardor enlightened Mirande. Why seek elsewhere the intelligence, the bravery and the malice necessary for the investigation? They were there, at the service of devotion? And had Simone not said that she was looking for a chambermaid? By polishing Francette, dictating her role to her, she was perfectly capable of getting the lace...

Immediately, his decision was made. He would employ Francette. But it was necessary to prepare Jeanne for that new tactic. Already, he had let her know—and with what eagerness she had accepted his confession!— that he shared her faith, that in spite of the disquieting analysis of the bloodstain, he was fully convinced of Lacaze's innocence. There was nothing surprising in his pursuing his investigation. He therefore invented a long conversation with Nitaud. The policeman—she would recall—wanted to look in Castillan's direction. They had deflected him away from it, but he came back to it with insistence. He was not far from thinking that the physician knew the murderer. He therefore wanted an incessant surveillance around Castillan. Who could exercise it better than Francette, enrolled as a chambermaid?

In spite of her amazement, Jeanne was too pressed, too avid to succeed, to liberate her fiancé, to reject such a grave suspicion, or to question the means of clarifying it. Francette was, therefore, summoned

"You know, Francette, that we love you here?"

"And me the same."

"Well, it's necessary for you to render us a great—a very great—service."

"At your disposal..."

"It's a matter of the affair of our friend Lacaze. You can help us directly."

Oh, the excitement, the joy of that singular girl, when she learned that she was to count for something in that story, which had been holding her under the grill for months! Finally! She was going to join the dance! Finally, they had thought of her! Yes, truly, she was intoxicated by the heady breath of battle, quivering with the heroism of a conscript about to risk his skin for his fatherland.

Gabriel Mirande, Jeanne Mirande and Henri Lacaze: her entire fatherland!

Never had the living contrast of her entire person been so striking. The furious bar of the brows, the fulgurant copper of the hair, and the long legs, boldly planted, expressed a vengeful ardor, and the pert tip of the nose, the teeth of a little puppy, the cunning gaze declared the malicious joy of succeeding where the law had failed.

"Understand me well, Francette..."

"Yes, yes, go on...I'm not a blockhead."

And Mirande ventured to expose his plan.

Castillan had been suspected for some time. They were astonished by his bizarre appearances, certain shady relations, seeing him spend money beyond his means, to such a point that they wondered whether he might not have an interest in the crime that brought him a new inheritance. But they needed someone in the house to observe him, to keep watch on him, to protect Madame Castellan if necessary, for anything was to be feared on his part, if he were capable of such a calculation. A place as a chambermaid had just become vacant. The opportunity was there to fill the role, to unmask a possible conspiracy....

"Well, Francette, what do you say?"

Her attitude had changed while Mirande spoke. Her nose was tilted, her lips had closed, her gaze was extinct.

"Oh, me…it bores me, that chore."

Well, no, it didn't "bore" her. It pained her; it frightened her. Oh, what did he think he was asking of her, the *petit patron*? To serve Simone Castellan, that woman who had hurt him—him, who had never had the courage to ask for her in marriage! And then, the more direct chagrin of leaving her masters, that little nest that had become her own, this furniture, that parquet, those saucepans, everything that she polished, everything that she loved...

"It bores me…it bores me…," she repeated.

Poor Francette. Even though his clairvoyant power was extinct, Mirande divined her. A tender pity invaded him. Without his sister's anxious gaze, he would have renounced the idea. But Jeanne persuaded him.

"Francette…I'm asking you as a personal favor."

Oh, in that case, since it was a personal favor for the *petit patron*, to please him, in that case, Francette no longer had any hesitation. She drove back into her inner depths all her repugnance, as she would have stowed clothes beyond use at the bottom of her trunk, and buckled the lid. Finished, the romance. She would attack! And, as quickly as they had darkened, her features resumed their radiance. Her nose lifted, her teeth shone.

"It bores me!" she said, this time joyfully. "But so what? Necessary to march? Well then, at the double! I march."

Combatively, she abandoned the doorpost on which she had learned to receive the blow. She strode back and forth across the drawing-room, her head held high, like a Bellona. Her eyebrows were already devastating the enemy.

"Wait," said Gabriel. "That isn't all. It's not just a matter of getting into the house. It's necessary to stay there."

"What! Why shouldn't I stay there, in that boutique?"

"Precisely because the house isn't a boutique, as you put it. It is, on the contrary, a very imposing town house, with a very stylish personnel. Now…this isn't to make you any reproach…but your vivacity of language, your character, might be surprising in an another environment, where people don't know you…"

"Understood," she said. "Here, I don't have to pose, do I? But do you want to know how I hold myself in society?"

Surprised, Gabriel and Jeanne saw her retire to a corner of the room, and then come back toward them, with a measured step, her eyes lowered, her little face suddenly masked by a serious modesty. Without awkwardness or affectation, she bowed to an imaginary individual: "Bonjour, Monsieur le docteur. Are you well, Monsieur le docteur? Yes, yes, Madame is well too, she has slept like a log. You should do the same, Monsieur le docteur, you work too hard. Patients? Yes, there's a full waiting room. Necessary to make them wait, Monsieur le docteur."

She bowed again, so comical in her grave gentility that the brother and sister burst into benevolent laughter.

"Well, Francette, that's a talent we didn't know you had! One or two more rehearsals and you'll no longer have anything to learn."

In a single evening, Jeanne completed that apprenticeship. She informed Francette of the virtue of mutism and initiated her into the mysteries of the third person."

And the following morning, equipped with a certificate of complaisance extracted from the worthy Doisteau—for she could not be coming from the Mirande residence—Francine presented herself at the Castillan house. After an hour, she returned triumphant. She had been hired on the spot.

The moment came or the final advice Above all, at the slightest suspect visit, the slightest hint of anything shady, sound the alert as soon as possible. There, a fortunate circumstance served Mirande, permitting him to remain in close communication with Francette. Always animated by a desire to act quickly, he had been thinking for some time about installing a telephone in his domicile. Again, he had experienced some embarrassment at confessing his plan to Jeanne, for he could not reveal his secret resources, his winnings at Dorville. He attributed it to the benefits he was obtaining from his new position at the Brion Institute, and the resultant necessity of remaining in constant communication with the laboratory.

"So, notify me immediately by telephone, Francette. The apparatus will be here in two days, and I already have the number, 1900-05. As for the laboratory, that's 1326-21.

Francine became alarmed. "I'll never remember that!" Then, traversed by a sudden inspiration: "Wait!" And she wrote the two numbers on the inside of her cuffs. "Now I'm a telephone directory," she remarked, incorrigibly.

But when the time came for adieux, she wept.

Mirande and his sister leaned over the balcony to follow her with their gaze. At the door of the fiacre that was transporting her, her little trunk beside the coach-man, she waved a large handkerchief.

When the cab had disappeared, Mirande said: "The brave girl! As long as nothing happens to her!"

"What do you expect to happen to her?"

"I don't know. Perhaps it's a presenti-ment…perhaps remorse."

Francette went three days without sending any news. She reappeared on the fourth, like a gust of wind, thanks to an errand that had brought her to the neighbor-hood. It was the first time she had been out. Immediate-ly, although out of breath after five flights of stairs, she explained her silence. To tell the truth, nothing extraor-dinary had happened. She had been well received. She had not made any gaffes. Madame was better. She was very nice. But she must be hiding a chagrin. What? Francette will find out, for a chambermaid becomes the confidante, more or less of a mistress the employer ne-glects. Oh, as for the neglect, Monsieur doesn't spare her. At the most, he says bonjour at breakfast—but he's never there to say bonsoir, of course. At six o'clock, when he finishes work, Monsieur has himself pawed by the masseur, primped by the wig-maker, puts on his coat and goes out, not to reappear again in the apartments until morning. In the servants' parlor, they don't talk much in front of her yet, but it will come. But what a society, those good-for-nothings! All that one can imag-ine of the worst rabble. Not to mention the chauffeur, always between two glasses of rotgut, and a kitchen-maid, a slut who doesn't do a stroke of work; there's one couple, valet de chambre and cook, one wouldn't have to

137

search for in a chamber-pot. Doesn't the wife boast of getting two sous of scratch from a simple box of carrots? And doesn't the husband confide that, in order to get his own back for an observation of Monsieur's, he spits in the dishes while bringing them to the table? So, Francine doesn't dare eat. She lives on hard-boiled eggs and chocolate. And that's all she knows for the moment.

Another four days passed before she gave any sign of life. Disorientated, Mirande did not know what to do. He deplored the flight of time. More than a week without acting, without getting any further forward...

Again he thought about confiding a parallel investigation to Nitaud. Only the flair of a sleuth seemed capable of discovering Castellan's complicity.

Then, one morning, Francette arrived early. To begin with, he had difficulty recognizing her. She was transformed, certainly dressed in one of her mistress's old dresses. A thin mauve veil dissimilated the pallor of her complexion and attenuated the brightness of her coppery hair.

Before interrogating her about her metamorphosis, however, he uttered a brief: "Well, what's new?"

Glad to be finally able to risk a little argot, she clocked her fingernail on the enamel of her teeth and declared: "*Peau de balle!*"[13]

"You haven't discovered anything, then?"

"No, nothing, It's always the same routine. It isn't that I have my peepers in my pockets. Report that the valet de chambre is ill, that it's me who introduced the doc. No. Toffs come, but no apaches. I stick my ears to

---

[13] Literally "ball-skin" (as in scrotum), loosely signifying a worthless wrapping.

doors. When an envelope's badly sealed I even read the letter before Monsieur. Well, *peau de b*alle."

So, decidedly, he would go to see Nitaud—but he wanted to hide his disappointment from the poor girl.

"Sapristi, Francette, how beautiful you are! Are you on leave, then?"

She blossomed. "As you say, Monsieur. I'm a god-mother today, of a kid in my family..." At the same time she displayed a cargo of beribboned packages at arm's length.

Mirande remembered vaguely that Francette had once confided to him her gratitude to worthy people who had taken pity on her, had collected her almost from the cradle and brought her up until the time came for her to go into service. Not rich, the foster-parents, and yet they had just offered themselves the luxury of a sixth child, her step-brother. So she was profiting from it to render them a kindness, Oh, she had spared no effort. The *petit patron*'s famous bill had gone into it to the last sou. She had paid for the layette, a crib with a green lining, an ivory rattle and money. Follies, in sum.

She listed her generosities with a face warm with pleasure. The lovely soul, full of released tenderness, of a treasure of latent maternity!

Suddenly, Mirande pricked up her ears.

"For sure," said Francette, "when you've towed all your life like them, you're entitled to a tow one day.

Hastily, he asked: "Towed, you say? What do these worthy folk do?"

"They're bargees."

"Where?"

"On the Seine."

"On the Seine! And they live...?"

"Everywhere, as you do. In their barge. But their home port is at Charenton."

"You've lived there too? You know that whole society of boatmen?"

"What a question!"

"Tell me, among those people, is there also bad seed? Are there pillagers of wrecks?"

Offended, Francette stiffened. "Not in my family, Monsieur!"

"Oh, Francette," said Mirande, "don't take any offence at what I'm asking you. You don't suspect the importance of my question. No, I'm not casting aspersions on your parents. I'm talking about the wretches that one sees everywhere that there's poverty, apaches of the river, water poachers, pirates…yes, the pirates of the Seine, I stress that word…pirates of whom you've heard talk."

"For sure there are, and I've known some of them."

"Oh, Francette!"

In his enthusiasm, Gabriel had seized her hands: a simple gesture of hope, but it touched the worthy girl so profoundly that a catastrophe followed. The whole fragile edifice of gifts and boxes of candy collapsed.

"My bonbons!" she moaned.

"It's nothing! Wait!"

He helped her to repair the disaster, and without delay, taking advantage of Jeanne's absence, he unmasked himself. Well, yes, he suspected the veritable murderer: one of those very pirates. He told her all he knew: the old malady, Castillan's treatment, the cut on the wrist. By returning out there, living among the boatmen again, perhaps she might succeed in discovering him…

"His name?"

"I don't know."

"His mug?"

"I don't know."

"How old?"

"I don't know."

"Oh, right, right…that's quite a job."

She was very perplexed, in truth. Her packages, balanced on her fingertips, threatened another fall.

"So, it's necessary to change again? Necessary to go back to the barge, become a hauler? Quit the Castillans?"

He had not envisaged the alternative. However, the surveillance of Castillan, the protection of Simone, remained urgent.

"Well…if it's necessary…"

She saw his hesitation.

"I see what you need. Continue service with Madame and then, in the evening, do as the kitchen-maid does: decamp and go on the spree in Charenton. That's it, eh?"

Confused, he stammered: "You'd do that, Francette?"

She did not reply immediately. The night…all the menace of the black banks and smoky hovels, the reek of burnt-fat, bare-headed girls, the breath of drunken cutthroats, the songs the cries, the battles, the whistle-blasts, the flash of blades, the pools of blood: the whole vision, the whole concert of horror danced noisily before her.

But she looked at Mirande at that moment. His eyes were imploring. Then she stood up straight and vibrant: "All right!"

And the decision was made. She exalted in her new sacrifice. An old ancestral leaven of challenge, adventure and heroism was seething within her. The peril, momentarily redoubtable, now enthused her. After all, her skin wasn't sable.

But the key scraped in the lock. Jeanne came in. Mirande put a finger over his lips.

Understood, signaled Francette, with a wink. She was definitely delighted. She had a secret with her *petit patron*...

II

It was the evening of the dress rehearsal at the Théâtre de l'Athénée. Everyone knows that those previously-unseen spectacles are sought-after, at least by those whose métier does not constrain them to watch them. One rubs shoulders there with people whose names are whispered and whose faces are recognized. One can be seen there. One can talk about the play the following day, before the newspapers, and show that one was among the elect.

Thus, it is very rare that a spectator leaves his seat for the apparent pleasure of pacing up and down outside the theater. That was, however, was Mirande was doing. Striding back and forth in the impasse that the Square Boudeau forms at that spot, he was waiting for the end of the second act. But several reasons justified his retreat. In the power of divination, he feared the mental tumult of the auditorium. He wanted to keep his lucidity fresh, because he would soon have need of it. But above all, if he had deserted his place before the curtain rose, it was because at that moment, Simone and Castillan had just sat down in a front-of-stage box.

The sight of them had been a dagger-thrust: he strutting, cynically displaying his importance, his beard lustrous, his waistcoat loud; she opposing her blonde charm, her delicate grace, to her husband's audacious tranquility. By virtue of her effaced, almost constrained, attitude she even contrasted with the sumptuousness of her dress, the sheath of lace that enveloped her entirely, the rare pearl necklace whose pallor glistened over her low neckline.

143

He admitted it: another man, bolder and more adventurous, would not have hesitated to approach the couple. For more than a month he had not seen either of them. The opportunity was propitious. He owed it to Lacaze to reach once again into Castillan's somber soul. He owed it to his love to read more of the secret book of Simone's life.

But if he did not fear the physician, his scruples and hesitations with regard to the young woman revealed themselves more sharply than ever. Certainly, she had married Castillan in order to obey the rules of society. Utterly ignorant of his crimes, she did not love him. But he possessed such gifts of charm and seduction! Who could tell whether, unconsciously spurred by the return of that savior, that distant companion of childhood, he had not employed them to please her? Could the heart of a spouse, which had only been brushed by a pale memory of an idyll, resist a pressing husband?

Those questions, Mirande no longer dared resolve. And that, above all, was why he had deserted his seat.

He paused momentarily in front of the posters stuck on the façade of the theater. As the star, Lambrine's name was displayed there in large letters, overwhelming those of the other performers. What was that woman's exact influence on Castillan? Was their liaison still continuing? Or had she broken with him, as Delacoste claimed? Was it for her that the physician had so ferociously pursued old Gagny's inheritance? That was what Mirande wanted to know. If the revelatory serum was coursing through his veins his evening, it was in order to extract the secret from Lambrine. In advance, he had had a spray of flowers sent to her dressing-room, and soon, he would go to congratulate her.

A few spectators appeared on the threshold of the theater. The act had just finished. Mirande was already climbing the steps that led to the entrance when, from the top of the stairway someone said: "Monsieur Mirande! I regret that you're arriving just as I'm leaving!"

He recognized, emerging from a thick fur coat, the Robespierre mask of Raucourt, the young politician who had just been appointed as Garde des Sceaux in the new cabinet. After his fortunate introduction to him in the salons of Dorville-sure-Mer, Gabriel had seen the former député again several times. He had not failed, on each of those encounters, to espouse the views of the man who was justly nicknamed the Incorruptible of the Third Republic. Again, the opportunity was offered to flatter him.

"Oh, Monsieur le Ministre, I'm glad to congratulate you—and also to congratulate the country. It's a great fortune for it to have a man like you in power. I'm sure that your reformist spirit will finally be given free rein..."

He was all the more sure of that because, at that very moment, in his brand new zeal and enthusiasm, the young minister was dreaming of audacious initiatives.

Raucourt allowed it to be seen that he relished the compliment. Before his benevolence, Mirande almost evoked the Lacaze affair. He admitted, however, that it was neither the time nor the place to importune a man in haste to get away and intoxicated by recent glory. He marked for the future the new progress he had just made in the minster's esteem.

Already, Raucourt was extending his hand. "Excuse me, Monsieur; we're so overloaded with work..."

Ah! No, this time the Incorruptible was translating his thought falsely. His day was finished; he had only one great desire: that of soon putting himself between the sheets, not without having laid out a few preliminary games of patience.

But Mirande excused that innocent weakness.

The act had scarcely finished, and the majority of the spectators had not yet invaded the corridors. Mirande took advantage of that relative emptiness to reach the stage rapidly. He had twenty meters at the most to travel, but the thoughts that it was necessary for him to pick up through the partitions!

A few burst forth quite clearly:

And I thought he'd never recover from his typhoid.

It's quite an art, to appear to be applauding without making any noise.

Further on, from a colleague: *Well, well—not bad the idea at the end of the act; I must make use of that in my next play.*

Elsewhere, someone was congratulating himself sincerely—but that was a money-lender: *This will make money. My deals are good.*

An entire ingenuous racket of envy, baseness, in which were mingled the profound meditations of women on Lambrine's dresses and jewels.

Mirande would have liked to get away, to suspend his divinations. He could not. However, he respired a fresh bouquet of tributes.

The author's children: *All the same, it's our Papa who did that. How proud we are of him! All those people who are here for him! How they applauded!*

But that was only a fugitive perfume. Immediately, he was obliged to plunge back into pestilence.

He passed by as quickly as possible. He finally drew level with the director's box, where he collected on the wing a: *How mistaken one can be...me, who dreaded a terrible flop...* And he reached the little door that separated the auditorium from the stage.

It opened to give passage to Favery, the director of the newspaper *La Lumière*. Mirande, who had not seen him since Dorville, gave him an emphatic salute. He was counting on having recourse to him as soon as he had unmasked Castillan's accomplice. He perceived an effort of memory on the part of the young "paper king": *Who's that? Oh yes...at Dorville...a chemist at the Institut Brion. Nice fellow.* Then an ardent wish: *Has he noticed that I've been decorated?*

Mirande took care not to neglect that alert. He congratulated Favery on the red ribbon that a recent exposition had earned him. To which the director replied, with a detached air: "Oh, that's ancient history..."

He drew away. Mirande climbed a few steps and found himself in the wings. There, the reflections eased. One might have thought that the penumbra was tempering them. A fireman was ruminating his incomprehension of the play. Stage-hands attentive to the next change of scene were only thinking about their work. One of them, however was secretly cursing importunate spectators. Another, with hollow cheeks and a burning gaze, was meditating the explosive effect of the abrupt declaration of a strike, at the moment.

But Lambrine appeared. She emerged from the stage, after four curtain calls, as if intoxicated by her art—but Mirande perceived that in the midst of the ovations she had not ceased to admire Simone Castillan's necklace, for which she retained a bitter covetousness.

"Why, it's you!" she said, extending her hand to him. "You're spoiling me. Those lovely flowers! Come and see them in my dressing-room." And on the way: "How do you like the play?"

"A great success!"

"Isn't it? I'm so glad...so glad to interpret something truly beautiful!"

Something beautiful, oh, I believe you! the actress corrected herself, internally. *What a bore it promises to be! Repeating the same words and gestures for an entire season, two hundred times in succession, every evening...*

Hitching up her dress and followed by Mirande, she went up the administration stairway and traversed a corridor. He reached the dressing-room, a flowery candystore, a luminous boudoir. On the threshold, however, he recoiled in disgust. Castillan, sprawled on a divan, was waiting for the actress to return. At the sight of Mirande an anxiety and an irritation invaded him. He did not let it show.

"My dear friend," exclaimed the physician. "Isn't Lambrine superb?"

"Superb," Mirande repeated, mastering himself.

Castillan had placed an expensive jewel-case on the Louis XVI dressing-table, and the was waiting for the moment when Lambrine would perceive it, perhaps utter a cry of joy, of gratitude...thus, undoubtedly, their liaison was continuing.

The physician's secret impatience was testified by a so much humble fervor and imploring frenzy the Mirande was able to measure at a stroke the enormous empire that the actress had acquired over him.

And her? Lambrine, sitting at a table, was retouching her make-up. He could see her charming painted features in the mirror. He concentrated his attention on her.

Oh, how easily he would have been able to avenge himself on the physician! How he could have annihilated him by revealing the secret thoughts of the avid and lovely woman! At that very moment, she was speculating on the amour of a rich and noble Milanese who, during a recent excursion, had made enquiries about her and wanted to marry her. She was dreaming of becoming a Comtesse and a chatelaine, under the skies of Italy, as soon as she had extracted the last louis of the Gagny inheritance...

Finally, she deigned to notice the jewel-case. Concealing her satisfied cupidity beneath an impassive mask, she took out the admirable string of pearls, weighed it, made an expert appraisal of the luster and ended up attaching it around her neck. The necklace was worth ten times as much as Simone's.

"Very nice, very nice!" she murmured.

Castillan stammered, in an ill-assured voice: "Really? You like it?"

Negligently, she replied: "Yes, of course."

Embarrassed by Mirande's presence, he dared not insist further. He contented himself with enveloping her with a submissive and burning gaze. But how much it said, that gaze!

Oh, the mute, frightful confession that Mirande surprised, that deeper plunge into unsuspected depths, into the horror of that monstrous soul...

That's all, then? That's all that you can find? Not a word, not an impulse, not a tender gesture? Never, then? I'll never retain you, never enchain you, even by gratitude, even by interest? But if you knew what I've done for you, to satisfy you, to keep you...

Oh, if I could speak! How many times have I been tempted? Perhaps the crimes themselves would touch you more than the money I've extracted from them: the old man that I had killed, the innocent I've sent to the prison colony, all that was for you, to have more money, always, to our out for you. But that wasn't enough. That money, I had to have to myself, alone, without division, in order to be able to give it to you entirely, without control. And when that unfortunate Simone was struck by catalepsy, it was you, yes, still you, that tempted me. So if I used my authority, my prestige, to keep the official medical examiners away from her coffin. If I signed her death certificate myself, it was for you, it was still for you. For I wasn't sure...no, I wasn't sure that she was dead...

III

The Ceinture train only deposited one passenger that evening, a woman, on the platform of the Point-du-jour station. One would scarcely have recognized Francette under the great mantle that enveloped her from head to toe, behind the thick dark veil drawn around her face. As soon as she had quit her compartment, she tucked a parcel of old clothes wrapped up in a sheet under her arm, hitched up her skirt and set off deliberately toward the exit. She pushed her ticket to the employee, disapproved of his slowness with a grunt, went down the stairway leading to the foot of the viaduct and found herself outside, on the sidewalk of the Boulevard Exelmans.

There, a lighted kiosk indicated a cab-stand. She headed for it hastily, consulted the clock, which marked ten o'clock, and dived into the first automobile taxi.

"Billancourt, Rue de Meudon; I'll tell you where to stop." Then, putting her head out of the window, she said: "Go via the quay."

When the barrière was crossed, about five minutes remained before reaching the end of her journey. That was more than she needed to transform herself. She unpacked her old clothes, replaced her mantle with a red woolen shawl, took off her hat and veil, which she placed on the seat. She tousled her hair, brought it down over her forehead and covered it with a common mantilla.

"There's me decorated," she murmured. Through the mist-covered windows she tried to peer at the landscape. It was drowned in darkness, which the December mists rendered even more sinister. A recent downpour had filed the gas conduits with water; the street-lights were out. To the right, one divined walls, the foliage framework of a cheap restaurant, the mass of some dormant factory, whereas on the left, there was dense mystery, an entire boulevard of darkness opened by the river, scarcely contained in its bed, where vague reflections played, broken up by the current.

One might think it was black coffee with eyes on top...

That poor comparison restored her courage. Coffee led her to think about cheap brandy, and she had faith in brandy coffee. Recently, too, she had consulted a gypsy fortune-teller who, interpreting the pattern of the little black grains at the bottom of a cup, had predicted the success of her enterprise. And that confidence had sustained her for a month during which, to obey her *petit patron*, she had gone almost every evening, at least one night in two, when fatigue hadn't overwhelmed her, to run around the riverside dives attempting to unearth the famous pirate.

Oh, the adventure wasn't comfortable. First of all, in order to leave the Castillan house in the evening she had had to bribe the concierge, allowing suspicions to weigh upon her virtue that sickened her when she thought of it. Then it required courage to risk herself on the banks of the Seine, to go into drinking-dens, creating abominable frequentations there.

She had beaten the entire upper reach of the Seine from Bercy to Port-à-l'Anglais. She had retained frightful visions thereof, the impression of having brushed peril at every plunge, especially in the beginning, when she had made contact with a band as an intruder, and sensed that she was suspected of being a police spy. Terrible eyes had interrogated her; muzzles had sniffed; one

152

would not have experienced more terror in a lair of wild beasts.

At those times, a maladroit gesture would have condemned her. Knives would have fallen upon her pitilessly. But she knew that by making use of her laughter she could tame the most ferocious individuals.

So, her strategy was invariable. She went into the dive, looked the crowd up and down, sat down at the counter, ordered a drink and dipped her lips in it with evident relish. Then she waited, in the great silence provoked by her entrance. Gradually, whispers rose up; her identity was being discussed. One of the ladies came to sit down beside her, engage her in conversation. Francette didn't put on any airs, oh no! She immediately told her story, a lamentable barrière odyssey, deploring the arbitrariness of the police, the departure of a friend sent to the Bat d'Af.[14] Magic words! They classified Francette, and her confidante immediately introduced her into the circle.

There was a fine rabble there: boatmen, out-of-work stevedores, and their companions. They drank various kinds of rotgut, corrosive mixtures, devastating absinthes that the neophyte had to accept—unless, as was more frequent, she offered them. But she avoided their deadly effect by washing the parquet with the liquor when the fire of speech permitted her to slip her glass under the table without attracting attention. They even ended up finding her resistance astonishing, and that reputation as a solid drinker would have amused her as much as her

---

[14] The shorthand term for the Bataillons d'Infanterie Légère d'Afrique: penal battalions based in Tatouine in Tunisia, made up of ex-prisoners who were still required to do their military service or unruly soldiers.

subterfuge if her instinct as an economical petty house-keeper had not revolted at spending the *petit patron*'s viaticum on such largesse.

She ended up, however, no longer regretting her liberality when, after an hour, she found herself taken in hand by the rabble, being *tu*ed and *toi*ed along with the celebrities of the bank. Quickly initiated into base pleas-antries, even seeming to understand those that she had never encountered, she responded tit for tat. And the ob-scurity of her repartee passed in the eyes of the brutes for a boldness more emphatic than their own.

Then there were bursts of gross laughter, warm ap-proval and thunderous admiration when she wiggled the tip of her nose and twitched the rebarbative arch of her eyebrows. They writhed, they thought it hilarious. They could have carried her in triumph. And she clapped those messieurs on the shoulder and arranged the greasy chi-gnons of the ladies. No mistake: for the filthy gallery, Francine was one of the gang, and they no longer hesi-tated to tell her about their misdeeds, to display the gory of their evil escapades.

She listened then, avidly. She concentrated her intu-ition on their boasts, encouraging them, and leading them, as if by chance, to converse about the murder in the Avenue Raphael.

Alas, so far it had been without result. The men knew the affair well, which was famous. Blowing out the smoke of their cigarettes, they expressed their opin-ion, always disdainful—for Lacaze, whom they believed to be the murderer, was not one of theirs. They were not interested in him.

One of them however, might be able to resist the communal boasting, to hide his game. Then, Francette abandoned the collective strategy. Under the menacing gaze of their companions, she interrogated them individually, drew them apart. Had they traveled? Where had they done their time? In order to engage them to confession, she repeated the fable of her friend sent to the Bat d'Af. She enquired as to their health. She talked about the colonies, the evil climate that produced fevers. And she only abandoned her investigation when she had recognized its uselessness.

But things became complicated at closing time, at about two o'clock in the morning, when it was necessary to get away and repel the affection of a gallant who offered to see her home. To refuse that base protector she had only found one means to begin with: flight, a solitary hectic race through the darkness. She seized the moment of a song or a brawl to reach the door and disappear.

But those escapes could, at length, have become suspicious. Then she preferred to attach herself to a *cavalier servante*. One evening, she chose one, as feeble and as unfavored by nature as possible. His name was Popol, nicknamed Asticot[15]—an appellation justified by his degenerate face, his pear-shaped skull blurred by stringy hair, his extravasated and melancholy blue eyes and his moist mouth, which hung down at one side. As for the silhouette: a skeletal chicken with short legs. Francette had no fear of him; she could have flattened him with one punch. He only had to his credit, moreover, a few petty thefts, during which he had stupidly got himself caught and condemned to minimal punishments.

Throughout one evening, Asticot had adored her in silence; and she had left him some hope, on condition of quitting her at the threshold of the tavern, never follow-

---

[15] i.e. Maggot.

ing her and never enquiring as to her domicile. He obeyed. Thanks to that inoffensive companion, she was able to continue her investigation all the way to Alfortville. When she had finished, without result, she arranged one last rendezvous with Asticot and did not go.

Now, it was downstream of Paris that Francette was operating. She had set her sights on Billancourt first, nearer and more infested than any other shore. But there, people were on their guard. In the three nights that she had been directing her exploration, she had only been accredited with one gang, and she had not discovered anything useful therein. She was rendering one last visit this evening, before passing on to another.

Suddenly, Francette tapped the glass. The driver had gone past the Rue de Meudon.

"Where are you going? You've missed it, old man. Necessary to go back."

Cursing, the man stopped his auto, battled with the gears, turned round and finally resumed the right route.

"Turn left now. Go as far as the square." And after a short trajectory: "Stop!"

Vague streets led away from a crossroads, scarcely illuminated by an anemic light, dormant causeways trailing through the mud. The fog, denser in that spot, limited vision to twenty paces. A tram went past, devoid of passengers, and continued its noisy progress without even stopping at the station.

"Wait for me here," Francine said to the driver.

The other looked at her in surprise. Who was this new client? The transformation did not suggest anything good. He feared not being paid.

"Hey, little lady," he said, "you think you're going to leave me like this, without provision?"

Francette understood. She took a hundred sous out of her pocket and gave them to him. "You're afraid of a fare-dodger, eh?"

"It's not often that a client gets into my cab like a lady and gets out again like a serving wench."

"You worry too much, my lad. I'll be back shortly."

She left him with that. She went around the center of the square, planted with trees surrounded by railings, and went straight ahead. Under the sheet of fog, the place was grim and deserted. She recognized the frontage of the drinking den at a distance, however, three paces from the first street-light. She hastened her steps. Before going in, however, she darted a glance inside through the misty window. It seemed abandoned, as usual, devoid of clients. The proprietor Monsieur Achille, a plump man with his sleeves rolled up over arms with prominent sinews, was indolently plunging his glasses into the sink behind the shiny counter, and then wiping them with the same dirty rag that he had just used to mop his ruddy face.

But that was only a décor for passers-by, the mask of a second room into which only the initiated penetrated. From that discreet lair such a concert of songs and drunken exclamations was presently escaping that Francette almost obeyed an intimate voice that deterred her from risking herself there that evening. However, she shook off her fear, bravely pushed the door, greeted Monsieur Achille's smile with a grimace and went into the den. The songs ceased at the sight of her.

"Why, it's Casque de Lune!"[16] a crapulous voice baptized her.

---

[16] Loosely, "Moon Hair."

"For sure, and it's a red moon too!" applauded another.

"It's true she's a shapely one!" enthused a third.

Then Francine joined in the chorus and cried, showing all her teeth: "Hey, you, I've got cash. I'll buy a round for all the mates."

She was acclaimed. They moved aside to make way for her, to permit her to reach the back of the infamous hole. By the ruddy light of an oil lamp, one divined that it was borrowed from a small courtyard between two blocks of houses. The walls were scarcely roughcast, covered with coarse inscriptions that betrayed both the sentimentality of hearts and hatred of the police. *Death to the Cops!* sat side-by-side with hearts pieces with arrows and daggers suspended over ingenuous protestations of eternal love. A glazed roof formed the ceiling. The breach of a broken window let out the tobacco-smoke, the reek of alcohol and the heavy emanations of a cast-iron stove consuming coal-dust in a corner.

Two greasy wooden tables constituted the whole of the furniture. They were surrounded by twenty equivocal clients: boatmen, stevedores, mechanics, the majority out of work, only adopting a social label to cover their shady exploits. In the three times that Francette had approached them, she had already got to know almost all of them.

She saluted with a tap on his skull, bald before thirty, Nemeses, alias l'Anguille,[17] a tall fellow with a skeletal fame who had no equal for catching a lit cigarette in his mouth when it was tossed into the air. Then there was Jules Crevard, an indolent colossus, whom she greeted with a punch: Crevard, le Rempart de Sèvres, an

_____

[17] i.e, the Eel.

occasional bargee, but who preferred wrestling at fairs, playing the amateur in the crowd who accepts the trunks and pins down a professional, or is pinned by him, at the discretion of the huckster.

Francette then imitated, with her used lips, the sound of an engine for Julot le Rossignol,[18] a premature-ly-aged young man with a pockmarked face and lips perpetually drawn back in a smile over his blunt teeth. He remained faithful to elephant's-feet trousers, a canine coiffure, and did odd jobs as a mechanics, hired from time to time by an automobile factory but was soon sacked for inveterate laziness. But an invincible success with the ladies was achieved by his voice, a poor falsetto tenor, pierced like his face with numerous holes, in which he warbled with conviction, striking at the heart.

And others, with whom Francette forced herself to ludicrous familiarities.

She expended no less effort on the ladies. She sensed, however, that they were venomous, irritated by the empire she had achieved over their companions. The tall Paulette, known as Gloire de Dijon—no one knew why she shared the name of a rose; she scarcely had the bloom, with her faded complexion, consumed, one might have thought, by the furnace of her eyes—assassinated her with a rictus, while Emilie Rouquet, a vast sphere whose three chins dangled over an adipose bosom, spat an insult as she went past, and Marie Lalèque, also known as Bille d'Ivoire[19] because of her anemia, had no hesitation about extending her feet to trip their common rival. But Francette was not caught; she avoided the trap, leaping over the legs, and sat down next to an individual

---

[18] i.e., the Nightingale.
[19] i.e., Billiard Ball.

she did not know yet, the mere sight of whom made her tremble.

"It's Le Crabe that has the honor!" yapped Emilie Rouquet.

Forteau, alias Le Crabe, was a man of about thirty-five, stoutly built, with a stupid and bestial face, pierced by enormous gray eyes flush with their orbits, whose lids were afflicted by a chronic conjunctivitis. His tawny moustache escaped from an earthen skin, revelatory of a compromised health. The most impressive thing, however, was his bone-structure, especially his hands. Succeeding wrists as hard as flint, they looked more like the appendices of a crustacean. Enormous and hairy, they developed like formidable pincers. He liked to show them off; they were his ornament, his pride. He owed advantageous triumphs to them, when he displayed them on the counter before a stranger, wagering a pastis that he could bend a ten-sou coin as easily as he could drink that absinthe; and if they took the bet, he twisted the one in order to drink the other. Those exploits had earned him his nickname.

He did not move aside when Francette slipped in between Julot le Rossignol and him. He expressed his contentment by turning his bloodshot eyes slowly toward her. As she looked at him without apparent fear, he leaned toward his neighbor and observed, in a hoarse voice: "Goes without saying that she's quite pretty, the kid."

"Not too ugly either!" riposted Francette.

That exchange of courtesies immediately led to intimacy. Le Crabe displayed his pincers and commenced measuring them against a silver coin. Vexed at passing unperceived, Julot le Rossignol also wanted to show off, and prepared his voice by coughing. The eternal instinctive rivalry resurfaced in them.

"Look, there's no fakery," Le Crabe emphasized.

But Monsieur Achille appeared, bearing liters. He had heard Francette's offer when she came in, and was not a man to neglect it. He caused his abdomen to pivot through the customers, distributing the blue liquor. Nénesse, alias l'Anguille, grabbed a bottle and juggled with it perilously. Then he uncorked it for the vast Emilie Rouquet, who approved of the nectar with a click of the tongue. Seeing that, Jules Crevard, le Rempart de Sèvres, did not take long to empty his glass. He lifted a liter level with his nose, opened his mouth, and without direct contact with the bottle, swallowed the wine, making a noise like a gurgling tap in his throat. La Gloire de Dijon and Bille d'Ivoire applauded noisily, guffawing.

"And you? You're not drinking?" Francette asked Le Crabe, who extended his pincer over his glass as a sign of refusal. The brute shook his head sadly. "Because of my fevers," he explained.

"You fevers?" Francette repeated, pricking up her ears.

"Yes," the doctor's condemned me to the white stuff. "Will you pay for a milk, Casque de Lune?"

"A milk for my pal!" Francette shouted to the tavern-keeper.

An inexpressible emotion oppressed her. "Was she on the track? Had those same fingers that could bend silver plunged the file into old Gagny's heart? She didn't want to believe it, at first. It had happened to her so many times before in the course of her expeditions that she's latched on to a deceptive clue.

She overcame an impulse of repulsion, however, and put her trembling hand on the brute's shoulder.

"What fever have you had, mate?"

"The yellow."

"Where was that?"

"Not in Paris, for sure. In the colonies."

She thought she was about to faint. The road was mapped out and illuminated. She had only to march along it, throwing in a few capital questions as she passed. Did Le Crabe know Castillan? Was he a Seine poacher? Had he worked in the Lacaze factory, or, at least got close enough to the workshops to have procured the murder weapon? Finally, had Le Crabe studied the house in the Avenue Raphael, to discover its disposition, to notice the basement door and the manner in which it was locked?

Immediately, the last thought obsessed her. She fixed her gaze on the monster's right wrist, looking for a scar. But a trace of it could have existed without her being able to see it under the thick hair. Better to act by other means, to use facile perfidy, extract the revelations one by one, by means of oblique suggestions.

Already she was imprinting a pitying tenderness on her face when she perceived that Julot, his ears pricked, was listening to them jealously.

She turned toward him and encouraged him with a grimace. "Well then, my handsome Rossignol, you're not giving us one today?"

And as the other, flattered, arched a smile over his blunt teeth, Francette stood up. "Shut up!" she cried to the assembly. "Open your lugs! The Rossignol is going to sing!"

Indeed, Julot announced: "*Dans les étoiles!*"

Then, while the singer, his hand on his heart, gargled his ballad, with languors and ecstasies that made Gloire de Dijon's eyes shine, dilated Emilie Rouquet's throat even more and put an incandescence into Bille d'Ivoire's waxed cheeks, Francette embarked on a duel with her grim neighbor.

Oh, how sorry she was for him for having a bad liver. Was it raging? When one had all that was needed to succeed with the in-life, and with the ladies! How had Le Crabe got stuck with it? It was in the colonies, was it? During his service, undoubtedly. One more injustice, to send folk to die abroad. But necessary not to despair. There were good hearts in France, friends who would help you. While slaving away from time to time—because of the police, who poked their noses in everywhere—one could, on Sundays in summer, idle along the river, catching fish, and if the sun shone too much, taking one's cup of juice.

"Slaving...slaving," grunted Le Crabe. "Necessary, for that, not to be bone idle...for, truth be told, I'm bone idle."

"What do you do, then?"

"What I can. Depends on the occasion. At times I tout on the Seine. At times I help the birds at Issy-les-Moulineaux."

Francine went pale. She had understood that the birds in question were airplanes. She did not want to press the point, for the moment. But the criminal was delivering himself by the minute. She filled the glass of milk and handed it to Le Crabe.

"You'd rather have a *mêlé-cass* [20], eh?"

"You bet!"

---

[20] Short for mêlé-cassis, a mixture of cassis with brandy or absinthe.

"It's your doctor who put you on milk then? Necessary not to believe them, doctors. They're all liars. Work to make you lick sawdust."

"Not this one!" swore Le Crabe.

"Oh? Who's that?"

Did he sniff espionage? Or was it a generous scruple? He contented himself with replying: "He's one of the best." But the voice was suspicious, the intention evasive. Francette understood that she could spoil everything in an instant. She changed tactics, set the stage, watching every muscle in her adversary's face.

"Possible for that one," she said. "There are good ones, evidently. I once knew a good one myself, who cured me, at the Hôpital Boucicaut..."

And as Forteau manifested an increasing interest, she dropped the remark: "You don't know Castillan?"

Le Crabe could have confessed his crime and Francette would not have been more convinced when she glimpsed the violent and instinctive contraction of the pincers at that moment. At the same time, a flash escaped from the man's bloodshot gaze and penetrated her. No doubt: it was him. But he contained himself, kept quiet.

"Don't know," he declared.

The interrogation was becoming dangerous. Francette was afraid of having ventured too far already. A terrible threat had passed through the brute's eyes. Anyway, what point was there in continuing? She would not have learned any more without danger. She only had one goal now: to run to the nearest telephone, to tell Mirande that she had the pirate, to indicate the hovel, and then get back into the dive to keep watch on the rogue until the *petit patron* arrived with the police.

She turned back to Julot le Rossignol. He had just finished his ballad with a highly effective swoon. She complimented him, while bravos rang out around. But for having crooned, he must lack saliva, poor friend! He'd accept something nice for the beak, then?

Francette seized the pretext. "Hang on, mates. I don't have any more cash, but I'll go see if there isn't a means of making an arrangement with Monsieur Achille."

She stood up, saluted by cries. Le Rempart de Sèvres offered her his hand, Nénesse, alias l'Anguille, recommenced juggling in her honor. Even the demoiselles showed themselves sensible to her generosity. La Gloire de Dijon smiled, Emilie Touquet swelled a fourth chin and Bille d'Ivoire helped her over the bench. As soon as she had left the room, though, Le Crabe stood up, his pincers clenched.

"Go see if she's really talking to the boss."

"No more than to the Pope!" proclaimed l'Anguille, his eye stuck to the gap in the door. "She's off, the bitch."

Then Forteau declared: "No mistake, mates, as true as I'm Le Crabe, Casque de Lune is with the cops, Necessary to get out of here, double quick!"

There was a panic. However, before leaving, the bandits held a brief conference. Then Forteau left first and soon caught up with Francette, whom he followed, galloping through the night.

For Francette was running. She was running at top speed toward a telephone. The office was closed at this hour. She was counting on addressing herself to a waterside restaurant, where she had noticed a sign advertising a telephone. Oh, my God, as long as the flood-water hadn't cut it off. As long as they weren't suspicious of her, that they wouldn't make difficulties for her in the place. No. She would explain. She would pay. She would say that someone was sick and dying. She would even affirm, if necessary, that she was employed by the police,

And she ran, through the night thick with mist, feeling her route more than seeing it, bumping into sidewalks, trees, walls, and heaps of paving-stones. She reached the Rue de Meudon, and turned on to the quay, still running. In broad daylight, at that sped, the trajectory would have required two minutes. She took ten.

Fortunately, things worked out. The restaurant, that evening, had been abandoned by its masters; Francette only had to address herself to the domestic, who let her into a redoubt forming a cabin. Feverishly, she appealed: "Hello! Mademoiselle, give me...

Ah! The numbers! She had forgotten the number! Quickly, she consulted her cuff, which she always wore, in accordance with the recommendation of the petit patrons, but when she wanted to resume the communication, the telephonist had gone. She had to wait for five minutes. She stamped her feet. Weren't the others, out there, going to be suspicious of her absence? Wasn't Le Crabe already alert? He had given her such a look just now...

She thought momentarily about leaving the capture until the following day, about making a rendezvous with the pirate somewhere else. But the telephonist responded to the appeal.

"Finally! It's you. You were having a snooze? Give me 1900-05, and at the trot, eh?"

A further wait. Then confused, distant voices. She demanded, impatiently: "Monsieur Mirande? Is that Monsieur Mirande?"

When she finally heard the voice of the *petit patron*, she poured out, without even waiting for the response: "Ah, Boss, I have him. Come quickly. He's in Billancourt right now, in a dive in the Rue Nationale... Yes, it's the only one open, a hundred meters from the square... Yes, I'll try to keep him there. But what if I can't?... If not, I'll bring him to the Rue de Meudon, and then along the Seine, on the left. For sure he'll follow me, like a dog. Bring agents... Why not agents?... Nitaud?... You've alerted him?... He's with you? Good. Listen, Boss: take the quay as far as the Rue de Meudon. That way, you're certain... See you soon, Boss." Then she added, replying to another voice: "Yes, that's right, as many men as you can... See you soon, Monsieur Nitaud."

Oof! They would arrive. They'd arrest him. And vive Lacaze. Vive Mademoiselle! Vive the entire world of worthy folk!

She hung up the receiver. At that moment, she heard a noise in the next room, as if someone were moving away, knocking over chairs in the darkness. She didn't pay any more attention to it. Perhaps it was a dog. She was in haste to rejoin the bandits and serve them up a story in her fashion to explain her long absence. She gave twenty sous to the maid and left the restaurant, sniffed the fog, turned right along the quay and moved into the roadway in order to run more freely. She had not gone ten meters when she heard footsteps behind her. Surprised, she made a detour, but the sound followed her, drawing closer. Then she stopped, fearfully.

"Go on your way," she said to a shadow that was now almost touching her.

"Is that you, Casque de Lune?"

Then she recognized the voice. "Le Crabe...,"

"Yes, my chick, it's me who's Le Crabe." And he sniggered. "Ah, you're not afraid of wanting to deliver my meat to the Widow!"

She understood. Frightened, she tried to get away, but the monster's pincer had already closed on her throat. A violent blow in the middle of her chest stretched her on the ground.

She wanted to scream, to cry for help—in vain, for the air was lacking. At the same time, it seemed to her that a hard point was withdrawn from her left side, which caused her to suffer atrociously for a second. But the pain was dulled. She realized that her aggressor was running away, that she was alone on the road, in the fog, incapable of movement, that autos were going to run over her as they passed. Oh, the brandy coffee had deceived her this time...

Then she felt cold. All sensation died away in her, in the infinite despair of never seeing the *petit patron* again. And there was a gentle slide into oblivion.

A long quarter of an hour weighed upon the crime. The nearby river was already thickening its shroud of mist over her. The large round eye of an auto headlight cleaved through the fog, however. Ten meters from the body, the brakes screeched on the wheels.

"What is it?" asked a voice.

"A woman lying in the road."

"Should we take a look, Monsieur Nitaud?"

Two men got out. Aided by the policeman, Mirande unhooked the headlight and projected the light on to the victim.

"Francette! It's my poor Francette!" he croaked, his throat tight.

"She's had it," Nitaud estimated, having leaned over Francette.

"Is she dead?"

"I fear so. She's no longer breathing, and her heart isn't beating."

Gabriel suspected the genesis of the drama. He did not pause to debate it any more than he persisted in the idea, impracticable in any case, of pursuing the pirate. He owed it to that admirable associate to occupy himself exclusively with her.

Suddenly, under the insistence of pity and gratitude, Doisteau's opinion regarding the frequency of apparent deaths came to mind. What if Francette were not doomed? If she were only in that transitory state when the flame was flickering before going out? What if that state could be prolonged until the intervention of the surgeon? Oh, let her be saved! Let her be brought back from the gulf!

"I'll carry her," he said to the policeman.

"Where?"

"To a clinic, to confide her to the care of a surgeon, one of my friends."

Nitaud shrugged his shoulders. What was the point in persisting? If the unfortunate woman were still alive, she wouldn't resist transportation. Better not to torture her final minutes…

Then he changed his mind. "After all," he said, "perhaps you're right. At any rate, we can't leave her on the road like this. It would be necessary to tell the police. More stories, complications. Necessary to expect anything on the part of those fellows. So if you have a clinic, the best thing is to take her there…without me, for I need to wait for my men, who will be arriving shortly.

Aided by the driver, they transported Francette gently to the vehicle. Mirande took his place there after giving the address of a clinic in the Rue du Sergent-Hoff, in the Ternes quarter, where Doisteau generally carried out his operations.

Oh, that return through the darkness! That funeral proximity, with the head tilting at the slightest shock, the arms dangling along the body, sometimes seeming to be animated by the jolts of the vehicle! And that sensation of cold dampness, that blood in the darkness, which Gabriel collected when he placed his hand on the young woman's breast in order to monitor the inert heart.

So many other concerns were clawing at Mirande's sincere despair. If it was all over for Francette, if her mouth remained closed for ever, what a new disaster for the cause! The thread scarcely glimpsed had broken abruptly. The whole web required to be rewoven, and in far more difficult conditions!

It would be necessary to attack a criminal who was now alerted, who might perhaps put Castillan on guard in his turn, and whose name Mirande still did not know...

They were about to arrive at the customs post. Mirande feared delays, the miserable formalities of inspection. He shouted to the driver through the lowered glass: "Don't stop! Go on! I'll answer for everything!" And the auto went through like a whirlwind, then to go even more rapidly along deserted streets, without even slowing down at the intersections. What if there were a collision at that frightful speed? Not important. Every spin of the wheel added to the chance of Francette's salvation.

Finally, the auto turned into the Rue Demours, swerved, and slowed down. They had arrived.

"Go collect Doisteau from his home," Mirande ordered the chauffeur. "I'll alert him by telephone."

It was necessary to wake up the house, bring to the threshold the director, still dazed by sleep, and shake up all those energies in repose. Mirande gave the full measure of his methodical organization. His fever and anguish found a brief distraction therein. Francette was transported again to the operating theater. She was warmed up by radiators, and the instruments were prepared.

Ten minutes later, Doisteau appeared.

Francette was lying on the operating table, ready for an attempt by the surgeon, if he judged it useful. The light of two hundred electric bulbs, powerfully focused by reflectors, illuminated her chastely uncovered breast, the milky tint of her skin contrasting violently with the warm patch of her coppery hair and the blood coagulated around her wound. She was resplendent, on her altar of white linen, like one of the expiatory victims of legend that a sacrificial blade had immolated.

The surgeon examined his patient with minute attention. He lifted her eyelids, consulted her pupils. He stuck his ear to the cardiac region, after having taken care to interpose a sheet. Then he straightened up. A moue expressed his opinion.

"Well?" interrogated Gabriel, avidly.

"Little hope," he confessed. "The blow has struck full in the heart; the pupil's no longer active. I doubt…and yet…"

"And yet?"

"And yet, I thought I perceived a heartbeat…but so weak, so weak…"

"Oh, attempt the impossible!" the young man begged.

"I believe you've said the word: impossible."

And while he put on a long white blouse, and proceeded, in front of a series of taps, with the scrubbing of his arms and hands, Doisteau explained: "My friend, one can't suture a wound in the heart like any other. One can scarcely ever reanimate an organ so delicate, so compromised!" He shook his head. "Anyway, let's try!"

He tried.

Oh, the valiant attempt, the incomparable audacity!

Gabriel watched, confounded by a horrible admiration, while the surgeon, seizing his scalpel, began his struggle against death with a long incision. Retreating into a corner, wanting to escape the spectacle but brought back to subject himself to it regardless by the force of his anguish, he saw the terrible mutilation unfold.

He saw, under the action of the fulgurant instruments, bones that were broken, blood swept away by means of compresses immediately thrown to the floor.

He saw fingers that plunged into the red hole, lacerating, tearing, twisting, accomplishing as much work as the implements.

But he saw above all—and with what respect, what fervor, which could have made him fall to his knees!—was that profound, ardent flame, that reflection of interior force, of will, of energy, which magnified the surgeon's eyes while he deployed his liberating gestures.

From time to time, a brief order escaped his lips: "Separators... Forceps... Scissors... Wipe..."—orders immediately obeyed by the perfect discipline of his assistants.

Four ribs had been broken, with a noise of snapping twigs, when he announced: "The pericardium!"

It was the sheath of the viscera, the scabbard in which the organ was set. Doisteau cleaved through it, expelling a bloody mass—after which all his faculties were focused in the minute examination of the heart that he held in his hand with a religious precaution.

He lifted it, and ran a proud glance around his entourage.

"My friends, I have the wound, and the organ is still functioning! Who knows?"

He bent over his work again. The most delicate moment: to suture the perforated organ, make it palpitate again, render the momentum to the pendulum that was beating its last oscillations.

"Catgut!" he cried. "Prepare the induction apparatus and the serum!"

And plunging the needle, the stopper of genius, he applied himself.

From then on, the rest of the operation no longer offered, for Gabriel, the same horrible interest. The surgeon's "Who knows?" expanded within him a softness compounded of hope and stupor. His nerves gave way; he had to sit down.

He witnessed, in retreat, the last peripeties of the duel, the practices of the electrification of the heart, the propulsion of the physiological serum into Francette's side.

And when, finally, the dressing was finished, the body, still similar to a cadaver, was taken away, his soul capsized. He venerated, with warm tears, everything that was carried off tenderness, virtue of bravery in that poor little livid muzzle, pointing its mutinous nose above the covers and retaining even in the grip of death the contrast of her absurdity and her heroism.

PART FOUR

I

Majestic and essential, two men were enthroned before a little table dressed in green baize, in the middle of the large vestibule with colonnades, where a few paintings, darkened by time, relieved the whiteness of the walls.

Mirande, sitting on a bench, whiled away the time by observing the two men who had, a little while before, received him with the arrogance inherent in their function. He had brandished the letter granting him an audience with the new Garde des Sceaux, Raucourt, but the austere guardians had not appeared to be dazzled by it. Faces shaven, chins high, gazes distant, doubtless lost in vast thoughts, they were reminiscent of two sphinxes on the threshold of a Temple guarding the enigma of Justice.

The attempted murder of Francette—still suspended, after two days, between life and death—had decided him on this step. Until then, only the secret thoughts of Castellan had revealed the existence of the pirate to him. He could not offer evidence to anyone. But the man had committed a new murder, Henceforth, therefore, Mirande could move out of cover, pursue his research in broad daylight, launch the police of the trail of the wretch, excite the zeal of sleuths. Poor little Francette, who, even on her death-bed, was still serving him!

He took out his watch. Four o'clock. He had wanted to be in possession of his power of divination before Raucourt, in order to contest with him at an advantage, to know his state of mind at every moment, to know whether he was gaining his cause. Not knowing how long he would have to wait, he had therefore injected himself an hour before entering the Ministry, in order to be ready for any eventuality.

He was astonished not to feel the first effects of the serum yet, the mental rumor that ordinarily rose up gradually within him. He ought to be able to glimpse the thoughts of those two stolen sphinxes...

Had the talisman lost its power, due to some unforeseen circumstance? Had the liquid deteriorated? Or had he become insensible to it?

Already, he was anxious. Without his prodigious clairvoyance, he would be nothing more, before the Minister, than a paltry solicitor. It would be a futile step, perhaps even a backward step, for he would lose the scant prestige that he flattered himself on having acquired in Raucourt's eyes. And if, henceforth, he was no longer sure of his weapon, if he could no longer make use of it, he would fall back into impotence sand discouragement. He would not be able to finish the task that he had undertaken...

At that moment, a door opened with a dry click, and a short young man, with a false collar and shoes with built-up heels, swiftly traversed the room, darting a superior glance at the banquette.

Then Mirande received the impact of his thought: *Another cretin who must be waiting for the Boss. Let's flatten him.*

He was not offended by that stupid reflection. On the contrary; he applauded it, for it proved that he really was under the influence of the serum. But the stupid young man disappeared and mental silence fell again.

He was not alone, however. The two sphinxes were still enthroned before their little green table. And suddenly, light dawned in his mind. The Ministry's ushers *were not thinking*...

Shortly afterwards, a bell rang, and Mirande was introduced into a room that was solemn in style and dimensions, where Raucourt, in a casual jacket, seemed very small behind his desk.

While the Minister shook his hand, and indicated a chair with a gesture, he perceived behind his forehead the naïve and new satisfaction of appearing in his power.

Mirande had meditated his request carefully. He explained the Lacaze affair briefly, and the attempted murder of his maidservant. Then he concluded: "I have reason to believe that the two crimes have been committed by the same murderer. That is to tell you the importance I attach to his arrest.

Raucourt had listened to Mirande with a somewhat distracted attention. Ignorant of the objective of his approach, he had initially imagined that the young scientist had come to request his influence in favor of a red ribbon. He was relieved to learn that it as a matter of a judiciary error.

For a moment, he was amused by the ironic comparison. The task of extracting a man from a prison camp seemed less onerous to him than getting someone decorated!

Nevertheless, the prospect of a press campaign, a resounding revision, sobered him. *Complications already, stories...to hear them, in truth, one would think that there wasn't a single guilty person in prison.*

His faith in the law was firm, since he presided over its destiny. In sum, he rejected the hypothesis of a connection between the two crimes. Mirande, who had surprise his incredulity, could not help exclaiming: "You don't believe me, Monsieur le Ministre!"

Raucourt was astonished to be divined. He flattered himself on cleverly concealing his opinions. It was a political habit.

"I don't say that!" he protested. "I still need to study the dossiers..."

Mirande did not want a false and preconceived idea to take root in Raucourt's mind. He went on, with more emphasis: "But you're already rejecting my conviction, Monsieur le Ministre, and I want, on the contrary, to penetrate you with it. Remember that, since Lacaze's arrest, I have dedicated my life to seeking the truth. I can't go into the detail of my enquiries and my means of investigation, but believe me, believe me—my friend is innocent and the guilty party has just committed another crime."

Shaken, Raucourt thought: *It's possible, after all.*

Immediately, he searched the wind: where did his interest lie? Ought he to get involved? In what direction?

To mask his calculation, he said, gravely: "You're not unaware that the process of revision must follow precise regulations. No one can change the course..."

Mirande, reading the hesitations of the ambitious politician, sure of touching the sensible fiber, exclaimed: "But one can hasten or slow them down. Now, once again, believe me, Monsieur le Ministre, that revision will happen. If you are hostile to it, the event will do you harm. You'll regret too late not having believed me, for neither your friends nor your adversaries will forgive you for an error. If you show yourself favorable to it,

178

you'll receive the benefits of having seen clearly, of having preceded the law on the right path, and you'll come out of it even stronger..."

Raucourt interrupted him with a modest gesture. "Let's leave personal considerations out of it. It's sufficient for a cause to be just for me to take an interest in it."

And he thought: *Yes, but that's it: is it just? Oh, of course, if I were sure, I'd start moving immediately.*

That was the opportunity for Mirande to deliver a final thrust, to touch his precise objective.

"It's necessary to search and have the man arrested, Monsieur le Ministre, and he will give you the proof you lack himself. With nothing left to lose, he'll talk. Except that he's being pursued for a rather banal murder: a working-class girl stabbed by a marauder. That's scarcely enough to excite the zeal of an examining magistrate or his agents. But you can simulate their zeal, you can make sure that they treat that humble news item as a resounding drama, so that they bring more attention to it and more ardor. Do that, Monsieur le Ministre, do that, I implore you. At a stroke, you'll make your clairvoyance shone, and you'll be enlightened yourself."

Raucourt made a few rapid notes. The he rose to his feet: "So be it. I promise to do everything, in that direction, that is within my power."

He was sincere. His words were in accord with his thought.

As he quit the Minister, Mirande savored once again an impression that no human being had known before him: he was exactly edified as to the nature and the value of promises that were made to him.

Under the porch, he almost bumped into Dutoit, the examining magistrate. When he had encountered him for

179

the first time, on the evening at Lambrine's house, he had felt disarmed, for want of the serum. His rancor re-awakened against the man who had worked to doom Lacaze, but the fortunate outcome of his interview with Raucourt, and the certainty of finally reading the magistrate's thought, incited him to clemency. He saluted him without stiffness.

The other conserved the unctuous bonhomie that he only set aside in order to harass accused individuals and witnesses. Internally, however, he was anxious. What the devil was Mirande cooking up with the Justice? Was it a matter of that accursed Lacaze affair again? To engage him to confessions and dazzle him with his own importance, he said: "I have a meeting with the Minister..."

"I've just left him," Mirande admitted, candidly.

Without allowing anything to appear, Dutoit was alarmed. Oh, but…but this was becoming serious. He enquired, graciously: "Do you know him well?"

Decidedly in a good mood, and delighted to torment the torturer, Mirande played with words: "He has no secrets for me…"

Suddenly, the magistrate took fright. The young man before him had a grudge against him for having condemned his friend, for perhaps having mistreated him somewhat as a witness. Was he about to become an adversary, to take his revenge, to weigh upon the Minister? Was that nomination as a counselor, so keenly coveted, about to retreat again?

So Dutoit was preparing to solicit a promotion...

Mirande congratulated himself on learning that. By virtue of that, he might have a hold on him, for the magistrate might be dangerous. If he mentioned the Lacaze affair incidentally to the Minister, Dutoit would want to defend his decision. He might shake Raucourt's fresh conviction.

"Some good advice," said Mirande, in a peremptory tone. "Avoid as much as possible mentioning the Lacaze affair to Raucourt. You won't be of his opinion. You'll risk annoying him. You know as well as I do what these interviews are like. It's a matter of explaining one's desire clearly and leaving the Minister with a good impression. So, you have nothing to gain by it, and you might lose by it. Adieu."

He left Dutoit resolved to a prudent silence.

He would be under the influence of the serum for a few hours yet. Buoyed up by the result of his interview with the Minister, he had himself taken rapidly to the offices of *La Lumière*, in order to attempt an analogous step with Favery. A shift of opinion would stimulate Raucourt's zeal. For a Minister, the press is often a second conscience.

On the first floor of *La Lumière*, he found employees almost as solemn as the sphinxes of the Justice, but he did not have the leisure to spy on their thoughts because, in that late afternoon, visitors were crowding the newspaper's antechamber, from the debutant who was bring his first article or launching his first novel, and the complainant who had come to demand a rectification, to the petty actress who would exchange a smile for three lines of publicity.

They were all ruminating the speeches that would seduce, convince or conquer the director—except that the fear of not being received by him that evening traversed their meditation. Ardent prayers and disparate invocations were launched toward the omnipotent Favery, a canticle that buzzed in Mirande's brain, sometimes troubled, like the bell of a choir-boy in the meditation of a mass, by a strident alert: *What if he won't see me!*

But the employee who had announced Mirande showed him into a waiting room, doubtless reserved for select visitors. There, two mature men, decorated, sitting on a settee, were conversing in low voices. One of them, dressed casually, with a cigar in his lips, seemed at home: some administrator of the house. He was mainly listening. The other, gloved, fastidious and comfortable, was speaking abundantly.

Suddenly, Mirande perceived the name of Quatrefin. What did the man want? Habituated now to disentangling the double thread of speech and reflection, he followed both.

Aloud, the loquacious individual was criticizing the financier with moderation: "An intelligence of the first order. Very enterprising. Very audacious. But he wants to have everything. So, he's launched this affair of electrical wires and cables, which, well directed, would have the finest future, thanks to the development of distant transport and the increasing employment of hydroelectric power. He ought to devote himself to it entirely and be content with it. Well, yes. Today he covets the furnishing of military airplanes. He wants to found a company of which all the small constructors of airplanes will be tributaries, and to centralize those considerable orders in his hands: all the inconveniences of a monopoly without the advantages. It's too much, too much. The fellow will end up breaking his back. In the interests of the army, it's important to warn him of the danger."

And silently: *Inasmuch as I want to appropriate that enormous supply myself, Quatrefin is a hindrance to me. He has to disappear. He's supported by his wires and cables. That base has to crumble. Classic proce-*

dure. I'll buy all the shares in that company surrepti-
tiously, and once I control the market, I'll provoke a fall
by spreading nasty rumors, until there's a panic and a
debacle. My man is down and I have an open field...

Mirande was beginning not to be indignant any longer about the murderous thoughts that so often rolled around behind foreheads. So someone was meditating Quatrefin's ruin...what should he do? Warn the financier? Let him sink?

But a door opened and, neat, polished and astonishingly young, Favery was framed in the bay.

The two men continued talking in low voices on the settee. Mirande went into the director's office. For a second time, he exposed himself to the double drama, strive to impose his conviction, lauded the benefit and the advantage of a campaign assured of ultimate success.

Like Raucourt, Favery appeared attentive and as sometimes distracted. While nodding his head gravely as a sign of acquiescence, he noted that Mirande must have shaved himself, for little islets of hair persisted in the folds of the neck. He judged the form of the collar becoming and promised himself to adopt it. Unlike the Minister, however, he allowed himself to be won over without resistance. His adhesion was rapid and complete.

"Understood," he said, standing up. "I'll put you in contact with one of my reporters, who'll occupy himself with these questions. He's a man we've just released from prison by means of a vigorous campaign. Although his innocence was recognized, he's had difficulty finding employment. I took him on at the paper. You'll see that he knows about judiciary errors!

Indeed, he knew them very well. Of the Lacaze affair he assimilated rapidly everything that Mirande could unveil without revealing the secret of his power. He promised to follow the plan traced by his employer, to pique the curiosity of the public by semi-revelations, to stimulate the zeal of the people in place. At the back of his mind, however—where Mirande penetrated—he was resistant. He was more difficult to convince than Favery, or even Raucourt. By a singular irony, the man unjustly condemned did not believe in the innocence of others!

Outside, the memory of Quatrefin imposed itself on Mirande. He was not, for him, some marionette whose fall or rise one regards with an indifferent eye. No, he was the man who was courting Madame Castillan discreetly, the man who had spoiled, by a surge of jealousy, the pleasure of seeing Simone again. But he was also the man who had had the rare courage to testify in favor of Lacaze, the man who was ready to aid him with his fortune.

Certainly, Mirande only had to disinterest himself in the struggle, of a kind so frequent between rich men. Quatrefin would sink for a while, cease to cause him umbrage and at least deliver him from one anxiety. But ought he to let one of those who had dared to extend a hand to the accused Lacaze go to his ruin without a gesture, without a warning, purely out of personal interest?

Generosity prevailed. Ten minutes after leaving the offices of *La Lumière*, he entered Quatrefin's, and rediscovered his warm handshake, his rude voice and his direct gaze.

As soon as the words of welcome had been exchanged, the financier asked: "Have you seen our friend recently?"

And Mirande, who still had his power, perceived all the pleasure that Quatrefin had in evoking Simone: a brief and sharp torture that he was able to master and which did not deflect him from his project.

Unable to confess how he had learned the truth, he explained that he had overheard a conversation in one of the waiting rooms of the *Lumière*, and revealed to Quatrefin his adversary's plan.

"Of course!" Quatrefin exclaimed. "It's that animal Chardin. I knew he wanted the cake." Then he offered thanks that Mirande recognized as sincere: "My dear Monsieur, you've done me a great service. In our world, a man warned is worth a hundred. Alerted in time, I can ward off the blow. On the other hand, unaware that Chardin was buying my shares surreptitiously, I wouldn't have been able to avoid the storm on the day it burst forth."

"What are you going to do?" Mirande asked. "I'm entirely ignorant of matters of the Bourse."

"It's quite simple. My shares are at five hundred francs or thereabouts. I'll let Chardin maneuver. I'll let them fall to two hundred. But then I'll set myself against the lowering. I'll buy them back and keep buying them back at constantly higher prices. By that means, I'll force the value up, and ward off the danger. Except that I'll need a lot of capital. I'll find it, because the business is good, but it's thanks to you that I'll have the time to assemble it. Once again, I truly don't know how to thank you." He struck his forehead. "But I've thought of one…it's necessary that you profit from your information. Now you know the double movement that the share price will follow, speculate at the low point, at two hundred, and then sell at the high. It's child's play. You'll only need a small cover. If you want, I'll facilitate the operation for you…"

Mirande felt himself blushing. Did Quatrefin suspect him of a calculation? He sounded the financier's thought. No. Quatrefin really want to prove his gratitude in his fashion, as a fighter preparing to enter the lists and who wants someone to bet on the combat himself.

Before that sincere impulse he hesitated momentarily, tempted. But he was still far from having spent all his winnings at Dorville, and he hoped to complete his task before having exhausted his reserves.

"No, thank you," he said. "Truly, that would spoil my gesture for me."

He went back to the Rue Monge rapidly, on foot, through the fête of the street, where the denser crowds and the brighter shop-fronts were celebrating the approach of the new year. The action of the serum, the dose of which he had moderated, wore off. He savored the serenity of sorts that succeeded the fever, the vertigo and the alerts of the divination.

He reviewed the few hours spent under its influence. Oh, how much another, more ambitious and more avid than him could have accomplished with such a talisman! How he could have extended himself, increased his power...building a fortune in an instant by playing the stock market...glimpsing the hidden flaws in all human life and holding at his mercy all those whose secret shame he had discovered!

And what if, in spite of his master's will, he allowed his power to be gradually divined? The man who could read the depths of hearts...

Oh, how people would tremble, how they would kneel before him. How broadly he would be conscious of his domination...but he was not born for those strong intoxications. And were they, fundamentally, worth as much as the obscure joy of obtaining a little justice?

II

Warmly wrapped up in his fur coat, Dr. Castillan came down the perron of the hospital, traversed the courtyard and passed through the gate. His chauffeur, having perceived him, had already started the engine.

Just as he was about to get into the limousine, however, a hoarse voice breathed behind him: "Pardon, M'sieur. Apologies. A few words."

He turned round with a start, and recognized, with as much anxiety as chagrin, old Gagny's murderer.

Since the day when he had launched him on that trail, he had not seen him again. He thought himself definitively liberated. And now the man had risen up from the lower depths, emerged beside him...

Careful not to embolden his accomplice by too much benevolence, and not to irritate him with too much abruptness, he asked: "What do you want?"

"Well, this is it, my prince. It's in regard to the affair that you know. I believe someone's looking for me. Even women are mixed up in it. Two days ago, I was forced to take care of one who was certainly with the police. A little more and I'd have been pinched. She was already hanging on the telephone in a bistro on the quay. Fortunately, I'd followed her. Without that, I'd have been swept up. She was asking all the time for a Monsieur Maran...Moran..."

"Mirande!" exclaimed Castillan, involuntarily.

"Yes, that's it, Mirande. He's surely someone at the Prefecture. Do you know him?"

Swiftly, Castillan replied: "No, no, I don't know him. So?"

"So, well, it was necessary to settle her business. Oh, you can be tranquil. That one won't talk anymore."

In a muffled voice, Castillan asked: "Dead?"

"Rather. Anyway, one's being tracked, no? Necessary that you be up to date. Above all, don't get upset. You see, Monsieur Castillan, I have it. Time comes when you read about my arrest in the papers, don't worry. Even if I'm done, nothing to fear for you. I don't know anything. I won't talk. That's sworn. I'm all honor and gratitude, me."

Castillan inclined his head gravely. He was embarrassed by the presence of his chauffeur, by the comings and goings of the hospital personnel. But so what? Humble patients often came to see, even in the street, the physician who had saved them.

"That's good," he said.

He was already climbing into his auto, but he changed his mind.

"Oh, how can I find you, if necessary?"

The man moved closer. "I've moved—because Billancourt, you see, smelled bad for me. My name's Forteau, known as Le Crabe. Necessary to write to me at the Deux Goujons, a bistro in Charenton."

This time, Castillan took his leave with a glance. To his driver he said: "To the house."

He lay back on the cushions and closed his eyes. In spite of the brute's oath, a frightful anguish oppressed him. Mirande? Mirande was on the track of the pirate, then? Did he suspect the plot woven against his friend Lacaze? Get away! So many chimeras for such a simple alert. Alone in the world, he and his accomplice knew the truth, and neither one of them had talked.

But that woman—who as she? How did she know Mirande? Oh, in that direction, he would make enquiries. He would discover the identity of the victim that had been found two days earlier on the suburban quay.

The auto stopped. He resumed his mask of smiling indifference.

As he went into his study, Simone said to him: "You know that Francette hasn't returned. Don't you think it's time to notify the police?"

Suddenly, a suspicion crossed his mind. That girl has disappeared two days ago. Perhaps she had been placed in his house in order to spy on him? Perhaps she had been executed by the pirate?

Initially, he had not attached any great importance to her disappearance. That Francette had seemed odd. He had thought it some caprice, some amorous flight. He had expected her return at any moment. But now, all kinds of small indications presented themselves to his memory: papers disturbed, drawers open. He had only seen it as the traces of a venial curiosity, frequent among domestics. Perhaps, however, they were the signs of a serious espionage.

His resolution was quickly made.

"You're right," he said to Simone. "I'll go today to notify the commissariat of the girl's absence. But before then, I'll go look in her room to see whether she's left any indication useful to the police."

Refusing any aid, he armed himself with a hammer and chisel, climbed the service stairs and immediately went to the trunk: the poor trunk with the furry lid, made of plywood, which simultaneously served as a wardrobe, writing-desk and strong-box. Three blows broke the fragile lock.

Feverishly, the scattered the carefully-folded garments and thin piles of underwear around the room. Nothing in particular. Already, he had reached the bottom and was despairing of his search when he fell upon a clipping from a newspaper: Mirande's portrait!

It was a half-tone photograph, a good likeness, doubtless published at the time of Brion's death, which a pious hand must have cut out with scissors.

Castillan sniggered. So, he had not been mistaken. The girl knew Mirande well. And she even retained a tender enough memory of him to keep his image hidden away like a treasure.

But perhaps he was still in error. It was necessary not to take a false track. The girl might have served in his house years ago and, flattered, simply clipped the portrait of her former master out of the paper. Had she remained in contact with him? That was what it was important to know.

He finished emptying the trunk, scattering its contents on the parquet. He did not discover any other clue. So be it. In the meantime, the portrait sufficed to affirm his conviction. Mirande and Francette were acquainted.

He was inspecting the room with one last glance when he noticed, standing on the dressing table, two worn cuffs that Francette must have taken off at the moment of her departure. There appeared to be characters inscribed in pencil on the fabric.

He drew closer and read, indeed: 1326-21…1900-05.

1326-21. But that was the telephone number of the Institut Brion. It was requested often enough at the hospital, in order to obtain serums. As for the other, he did not know it—but perhaps Mirande had a telephone in his private domicile, since he had, in a sense, replaced his former master at the institute. The fellow was singularly spruced up since Brion's death.

He noted down the number, went downstairs and consulted directories. A recent supplement confirmed his anticipation. Francette wanted to have the two telephone numbers incessantly to hand that permitted her to communicate with Mirande, either at his laboratory or at home...

For a moment, he was subject to the disturbing impression of being besieged, of being watched from the shadows. But he was not a man to give in without a fight. After all, of what was he afraid? Who could establish the proof of his complicity? The pirate would never talk, even with his head under the blade.

And then, exactly what did Mirande know, for what was he searching? Immediately, Castillan made his decision. He would confront the enemy. He would take the offensive. That was always the secret of victory.

Under the cover of demanding that petty scientist to account for his espionage, he would discover his intentions, his goal, his information and his suspicions. It was the only means of paralyzing his action in future.

The following morning, he presented himself at the Institut Brion.

Mirande read Castillan's name on the card that the porter brought him with an anxious amazement. What did he want? He regretted not sensing himself armed with the power, all of whose advantage he had felt the previous day in his meetings with Raucourt and Favery. Oh, if only the serum had acted instantly, how quickly he would have had recourse to the divine injection. Immediately, he would have unmasked and undermined the monstrous bandit's plan.

He received him in Brion's old laboratory. Perfectly at ease, Castillan sat on the divan where the dying master had revealed the incredible discovery to his pupil, his arms posed on the cushions, his legs crossed, the tip of his boot swinging.

"My dear Monsieur," he said. "I have some information to ask of you. A…domestic matter. Can you imagine that my wife recently took into her service a girl named Francette. She hasn't reappeared in three days. Yesterday, before notifying the commissariat of her disappearance, I wanted to carry out a summary investigation myself, and I discovered, among her clothing, your portrait…"

"My portrait!"

Poor little Francette, that was just like her, to take the image of the "*petit patron*" even into Castillan's house. Mirande's embarrassment and confusion was extreme. How could he explain…?

"Yes," said Castillan, "Your portrait. Oh, a simple newspaper cutting. I immediately imagined that the girl had been in your service and that, justly proud of her former master, she had taken that souvenir from some newspaper. Am I mistaken?"

Was he mocking? Was he sincere? Mirande dug his fingernails into his palms. Oh, not to know his adversary's true thoughts…! And there, two paces away, was the little cupboard in which the talisman reposed. What should he do? He could not hesitate any longer. What if he hid the truth? But Castillan might be keeping evidence in reserve to confound him. He made his decision.

"Indeed. My sister and I had a maidservant of that name."

"And she left you recently?" Castillan enquired. "I beg your pardon for these questions, which are taking on the appearance of a small interrogation, but you'll understand the interest, from the viewpoint of the poor girl herself. Perhaps you know her family, her associates?

192

Perhaps she continues to see Mademoiselle your sister? Perhaps, even, you have not broken off all communication with her yourself?"

Mirande was under torture. This time, the necessity of a lie was imposed. "No, no…we haven't seen one another…since her departure."

Castillan stood up. His face hardened. "Why, then, have I found your telephone number and that of the Institut inscribed on cuffs that she had just taken off? Was that also a pious memory? A testimony of amour, like the portrait? Come on, Monsieur Mirande, masks off. It was you who placed that girl with me. You're spying on me. I have the right to know why. Speak."

Mirande had stood up in his turn. *Why?* Castillan asked. Oh, the temptation, the keen desire to hurl all his crimes in his face! But no, no. He could not, before having laid hands on his accomplice. Incapable, however, of hiding his indignant scorn completely, he said to him, in a profound and contained voice: "And it's you who's asking me why…?"

"Yes, of course I'm asking you," Castillan retorted. "And I insist. I won't tolerate, do you hear, anyone interfering in my affairs. And I took you for a good young fellow! In truth, it's very easy to make one's maidservant one's mistress, and having thus softened her up, to send her to spy on one's friends to find out what's happening there!"

So much cynicism…to sully thus little Francette, of whom Doisteau still seemed to despair of saving…must the bandit think himself unsuspected, to venture thus on the attack, to push audacity so far?

Mirande succeeded in containing himself, however. He disdained to interrupt Castillan, who continued: "For you are one of our friends, Monsieur Mirande. I haven't

193

forgotten that I owe you the salvation of Madame Castillan. I retain for you, believe me, the keenest gratitude. Although, on thinking about it, I have difficulty understanding why, in the middle of the night, you were leaning over close enough to her tomb to hear her plaints. An umbrageous husband might be anxious about such a sharp grief on the part of a childhood friend. And you'd be quite capable, after having seduced the soubrette, of employing yourself in other gallant projects..."

To dare to touch Simone! No—anything except that. Mirande threatened him with a gesture.

"Shut up! Shut up! Don't push me too far. You can see that I'm trying to contain myself. But you also sense that I hate you, that I despise you, that you horrify me...in sum, that I know you. Do you understand? I know you..."

But Castillan, ironically, provoked him with his gaze. "Bah! That's jealousy, and the most base. The rage of an ousted lover who sees his beauty in another's arms. But you shan't have her. I know how to keep her..."

That was too much. Mirande burst out: "By burying her alive, no doubt!"

Castillan, impassively, immediately demanded: "What are you saying?"

"I'm saying that you wanted to kill her, as you had Gagny killed, out of cupidity, for that Lambrine..."

Mirande shut up, afraid of having betrayed himself. At least he hoped to have overwhelmed his adversary—but no. Very calmly, almost smiling, Castillan nodded his head.

"Is that all? Have I not committed other crimes too? Well! Is it the atmosphere of this laboratory? Has that old madman Brion bequeathed you his insanity? For between us, at the end of his life, he was losing his mind.

The pessimism and the misanthropy that one finds in his last papers testify to a senile dementia. But you, at least, aren't waiting for old age. Come, come, young man, it's necessary to pay attention, damn it! One doesn't throw such accusations at people's feet without proof."

Mirande did not reply, So much impudence disconcerted him. He had begun to doubt Brion, the serum, having discovered the bandit's secret.

Castillan had picked up his hat from the table and brushed it carefully with the back of his hand.

"Take note that I'm not annoyed. I'm anxious for you. Do you know that this game risks putting you in a straitjacket?"

But Mirande did not reply to the insult. He had said too much. Fortunately, he had kept the secret of his power. And the concern of not allowing that to be drawn from him sealed his lips. He merely grated, swiftly: "Go away…get out…"

"That's the first sane thing you've said," Castillan sniggered. "I believe, in fact, that my presence can only excite you further." And he added, in a severe tone, his finger menacing: "But remember my advice. If you don't want to be locked up, never repeat those absurd accusations unless you can justify them. And that, I defy you to do."

He adjusted his hat on his head with a cavalier gesture. And as he went out he repeated: "I defy you to do it."

III

Leaning over the balustrade of the main staircase in the Ministry of Foreign Affairs, Mirande watched the guests come in. A diplomatic soirée in all its banal splendor: black suits, uniforms, bright dresses unfurling their polychromatic ribbon along the steps. An usher posted in the embrasure of the large salon collected the names and titles with an urgent ear and proclaimed them in a stentorian voice, mangling them. Further away, the Minister and his wife bowed, briefly or deeply, shaking hands with a fixed smile and an inexhaustible good grace.

Mirande was watching for Raucourt. He had seized this opportunity to see him without importuning him with a request for an audience. Here, on an equal footing, he could stimulate the minister's zeal. Castillan's arrogance and cynicism, his recent provocation, had pushed his impatience to unmask the monstrous individual to paroxysm. But the incorruptible did not appear. Was he disdaining his colleague's soirée? In the meantime, Mirande collected the thoughts of the crowd, for he had put himself under the influence of the serum.

The booty was meager. The desire to appear, a somber ennui, occupied numerous minds. Puerile concerns held the others. A petty Balkan attaché, wedged into a gilt-laden costume, was deploring not having received his emoluments. An austere ambassador was composing the seduction of a love-letter. His beard fanned out and his saber rattling against his boots, a Russian warrior coveted the savor of the champagne at the buffet. A Japanese was regretting the smooth water of his gardens, where lotus leaves lay dormant. A power-ful American despised the anemic races of the old continent, from the height of his firm corsage.

"His Excellency the Ambassador of Italy!" announced the usher.

Gabriel followed that short, bald man with his gaze, pale even in his moustache. His presence at the soirée was particularly significant, at a moment when French and Italian influences were disputing preponderance in Cyrenaica under the equally interested eye of Turkey. Relations between the two nations, after being extremely tense, had finally eased. His Excellency bore in his short person all the amenity and good grace of a conciliator. The Minister shook his hand for a long time. He introduced him into the room reserved for diplomats, near the entrance, where their manifest sympathy was celebrated.

But the iridescent ribbon on the steps of stairway became even more compact. A few pretty women were secretly in quest of the homage due to their beauty. A polychromatic group went past; Mirande was ingenuously astonished that their thought was strangely mathematical. Here and there, mothers were guiding their daughters, slender in their pastel dresses. The same concern occupied them all: would they find a husband? He recognized a few faces at a distance: Favery, Delacoste, and then Dutoit, whose inquisitive lorgnon appeared over the shoulders of his neighbors: Dutoit, avid for prestige, who was secretly regretting that the counselors of the Court—he had finally been appointed—were not allowed to show the splendor of their robe at official soirées.

In the distant hall, an orchestra of violins struck up a waltz. Gabriel listened, sadly, seeking in the voice of the strings a diversion from all the human voices. Was the contrast between the décor of the fête and his life of drama and alarms, in which checks succeeded victories, a new effect of the serum, or an abrupt reaction? Under the almost dolorous influence of a keen sensibility, however, the harmony stretched his nerves, running like a frisson along his vertebrae.

He abandoned the balustrade and wandered through the salons at random. People were dancing almost everywhere. Interrupted in his passage by bounding couples, Mirande advanced with difficulty.

And he received, along with the jostling, involuntary confidences: concern to keep in time with the waltz, anguish over finding a topic of conversation, tender desires, gallant thoughts, confessions that lips retained, an entire round of petty romances that twirled and leapt under the eyes of mothers who were dreaming about the benefits of sleep.

But the kaleidoscope was turning too quickly. He wearied of it, and darted another glance toward the entrance. Raucourt had not arrived...

Perhaps he was in the diplomatic room, entrance to which was forbidden to the profane.

He stopped modestly on the threshold. No Raucourt—but the Excellencies were still congratulating one another.

What were they hiding behind their grave foreheads? He extended his clairvoyance toward the ornamentations. To his amazement, he perceived nothing but a strange cacophony, in which only a few comprehensible thoughts were mingled. What was happening? Was his prodigious faculty troubled? Was it functioning abnormally? He sharpened his attention, but the waves remained untranslatable.

Suddenly, an inspiration enlightened him. *Of course—that's it. These people are thinking in their own languages. It's the Tower of Babel!*

But just now, at the entrance, he had penetrated the petty gilded attaché, the booted Russian and the expansive American. But they had become Parisian! The son of the Balkans had completed his studies in Paris, the American spent eight months of the year there, and the Russian his entire career—and their reflections had crystallized in their adopted language...

Mirande deplored his ignorance. It was serving him poorly this evening, diminishing his power. Apart from Italian, which he had practiced at length in a study voyage in company with his master Brion, he was ignorant of all foreign languages. For absolute power, the trigger of the serum had to operate on a polyglot.

His interest therefore concentrated on the Italian ambassador. Closer to him, he was also more comprehensible. Prostrate at that moment before a dowager in a white wig, he was confirming the conciliatory role that he had just played in the Cyrenaica affair. In all respects, he admitted, the conflict would have been disastrous for the two nations. Were they not sisters? Did not the same Latin soul vibrate within them? Would not war have condemned it forever? Was not the great harmony of peoples, entrusting their disputes to international arbitration, along with the common efforts of pity and justice, the sole aspiration of sovereigns worthy to rule? But one could be reassured now. The misunderstanding had been so completely dissipated that the king was thinking of traveling, of going on a cruise...

And the dowager, satisfied, approved with an oscillation of her wig.

Alas, what a terrible shock for Mirande! What emotion for humanity! The man was lying, lying with an ironic satisfaction, a secret voluptuousness. He had learned that very evening, by special courier, of the imminent demonstration of his king, who intended, during his cruise, to land in Tripoli, to mark the old African soil with a dominating heel, and to establish, by means of a surprise coup, his preponderance over that disputed region.

A manifestation concentrated, moreover, ripened in advance, inspired by avid financiers, ambitious potentates, supported by all the ready-aimed cannons of the Triplice,[21] and capable of igniting a formidable conflagration, if France did not capitulate!

Mirande stood there, overwhelmed. All his horror of war vibrated, exciting him. Quickly, quickly! Avert the frightful explosion, avoid the gunfire, deliver that secret capital, shake up energies, avoid the fatal gesture, prevent the bloodshed, the weeping mothers and wives!

It was his imperious duty. But who should he warn? Raucourt. That was his first impulse. He was the only man in power that he knew. Furthermore, he was active, ambitious in the generous sense of the word, and would avidly seize an opportunity to save his country from a war or a humiliation. And what gratitude he would have to the man who brought him that providential role!

Miranda ran away, jostling people. Outside, it was freezing, The cold gripped him. Renouncing finding his car, taken away by the servants on duty, he leapt into a prowling taxi.

---

[21] The shorthand term for the Triple Alliance forged between Germany, Italy and Austro-Hungary in 1882, which endured until the Great War.

"To the Ministry of Justice, Place Vendôme!"

"Monsieur will keep me?"

"Go, go!"

The streets filed past. There were only a few passers-by, warmly wrapped up. Rare automobiles, flying over the frozen ground, revealed in passing a vision of luxury, a somnolent couple returning from a dinner, a woman huddled in furs.

The Place Vendôme was deserted. On the threshold of the Ministry, two agents were stamping their feet to keep warm. Mirande looked at his watch. It was not yet eleven o'clock. Raucourt should still be up and about. Some light filtered through the shuttered windows of the façade. He went under the porch. Only then did he realize the extravagance of what he was doing, the difficulties that awaited him.

"Where are you going?" a uniformed concierge shouted at him, bounding out of his lodge.

"I want to see the Minister."

"At this hour? Is he expecting you?"

"No, but it's necessary for me to speak to him. I have very serious things to communicate to him, and I'd like..."

He stopped. He glimpsed the man's anxiety: *Another madman! It's been raining them for some time...*

Exhorting himself to calm, he resumed in a complaisant tone: "Yes, you must find my arrival unusual, at this hour...but have my card given to the Minister, with a few words. I know him."

He took out his notebook and prepared to write.

"It's futile, Monsieur," the Cerberus interrupted. "One doesn't get into the Ministry without a letter of audience. He won't receive you. Write tomorrow..."

"His *chef de cabinet*, then. I'll explain my reasons to him, and hen..."

"Monsieur le Chef de Cabinet isn't here at this hour."

"And no one in the offices?"

"No one."

Gabriel had an inspiration. "Listen, my friend, here's a louis...five louis...ten louis, if you can get me in to see the Minister immediately."

He understood that he had not convinced him. The money tempted the concierge, but professional dread retained him. He would not risk his job for so little.

"It's impossible."

Mirande became more pressing. "Listen. I swear to you that it's an exceedingly seriously matter. You won't forgive yourself for having sent me away. You won't forgive yourself, for your sake, that of your family, your country...

That's it! He's a madman! thought the concierge, who got ready to throw the visitor into the street violently.

Mirande became exasperated. After all, a Minister ought to be accessible to all, when superior interests were at stake, when the fate of the fatherland depended on news received that very evening. He must be allowed to get in! No one must prevent him from getting in!

"It's pointless, my poor Monsieur! Go to bed, that would be better!"

At the paroxysm of his wrath, Gabriel cried: "I tell you that I shall get in! I'll strangle you rather than not get in!"

Oh, it couldn't go on. The man lowered his head, fell upon the importunate individual, seized him like a parcel round the body, and, gripping him hard enough to choke him, carried him outside.

Mirande struggled vainly. The grip of the two policeman, come to help, paralyzed his resistance. And there was the painful spectacle of an unkempt individual in evening dress, bare-headed, struggling and howling as two servants of public order transported him to the nearest police station.

On the way, in spite of his fury, he perceived the pity or criticism of the passers-by. *He's a madman!* estimated some. *He's a drunkard!* granted the others.

"I'm neither drunk nor mad! Let me go!" he implored, suffocating, garbling his words.

But the agents shook their heads, and continued on their way.

At the station he was thrown, fearfully, on to a bench. The influence of the serum wore off. In the vicinity of the agents he could hear nothing but faint murmurs. Calmer, he took better stock of the situation. It did not seem desperate. He could not be reproached for any crime. He had simply struggled. The wrong was on the side of the public force. As soon as he explained himself to the Commissaire de Police, he would be released. He would still have time to act.

The magistrate soon arrived. He was a stern administrator, zealous and fearful of stories. He bowed to the military salute of the guardians and went into his office. First he listened to the concierge's report, and that of the agents who had carried out the arrest. Then he had the prisoner brought in.

"Sit down there on that chair."

By the severity of that greeting, Gabriel understood that the Commissaire was expecting to give the incident a serious complexion. The presence of two guardians by his side confirmed his fears. He felt weak before the authority. His timidity, driven back under the influence of the serum, invaded him again.

"Monsieur le Commissaire," he said, "I'd like to speak to you alone."

"That's not customary, Monsieur."

"I have, however, something to confide to you..."

"Wait until I interrogate you."

He questioned methodically. He demanded papers that Gabriel could not furnish. He asked his name, his address, his place of birth, his profession. He transcribed that information in a register. He enquired about previous involvements with the law, and, on Mirande's protestations, rang for the duty secretary and asked him to request urgently, by telephone, a judiciary file or an anthropometric record. All those services were to be awakened, the entire administrative machinery set in motion. It was a matter of a Minister.

Those preliminaries accomplished, penetrating his interlocutor with a keen gaze, he placed is head in his hands and gave his authorization.: "Go on. Speak."

Oh, that accused timidity! That irrational embarrassment! That retreat of personality! The necessity of lying, of concealing the existence of the serum... With every sentence, Gabriel became more incoherent. Stammering, searching for words, he nevertheless narrated his adventure as best he could: that he had discovered a diplomatic secret and had thought himself obliged to report it immediately to the Minister, whom he knew.

"You were in the diplomatic salon, then, Monsieur?"

"No, Monsieur, I was standing at the door."

"Ah! And what persons were exchanging this confidence?"

Gabriel hesitated, and then: "The ambassador of a foreign county and an aged lady."

"French?"

"I don't know."

"Was the conversation in French?"

"I think so..."

"You think so?" The Commissaire reflected momentarily. Then, letting nothing show of his impressions: "And what was this confidence?"

"It's of capital importance for the security of our country. I will say more, Monsieur; it involves the peace of Europe. That's why I desire to transmit it to Monsieur Raucourt. I beg you to excuse me if I don't surrender it to you."

"As you please, Monsieur. But I will point out immediately the implausibility of your story."

"Implausible? In what way?"

"In that you don't even know in what language this capital secret, revealed according to you by an ambassador to an old lady, was confided."

Gabriel attempted to backtrack. "It was in Italian, naturally. I misunderstood your question..." Floored by that logic, he understood that he had betrayed himself.

The Commissaire seemed, however, to consent to that explanation. He went on: "Let's admit that. But one thing astonishes me even more in what you're saying. That is that you were able to overhear, from the door where you were standing, a conversation that must have been exchanged in low voices, by reason of its character of gravity. And all that, naturally, in the midst of the rumor of a numerous assembly. Is that possible?"

"Certainly, since I heard it."

The Commissaire mocked, sarcastically: "He was shouting, then, your ambassador? The lady was deaf?"

"No. It is, in any case, evident that they wouldn't have compromised themselves in that fashion..."

"Then I can't understand how their words reached you."

Mirande became irritated. "What do you want, Monsieur le Commissaire? Admit, if you wish, that I have particularly keen hearing. Admit anything you wish."

At that response the magistrate turned to his secretary. They exchanged a knowing glance.

"But what does it matter how I overheard it?" Mirande went on. "The secret was nevertheless acquired, and I repeat to you that it is laden with threats, that one day's delay in its divulgation might lead to frightful consequences! I beg you, therefore, in the name of your patriotism, in your interest, to release me, and even to help me to see Monsieur Raucourt...."

The Commissaire raised his arms. "Release you! How you go on! Remember, Monsieur, that your conduct is utterly extraordinary. What? You seek to introduce yourself by night, without authorization, into a Minister's abode. The concierge stops you; you want to go on regardless. He takes hold of you, which is his duty, and you strike him!"

"The concierge is not telling the truth."

"At any rate, you struggled. It's the same thing. The agents arrive to lend a hand, and you strike them too!"

"That's false!"

"One of them has a face labored by scratches. I've seen them! And you're asking me to release you? I'd still need a serious explanation to explain your anger. Oh, if serious interests were really at stake, I wouldn't refuse, but you serve me this ludicrous fable about an

206

ambassador and an old woman, and that's all! Give me a valid reason, and then I'll see what I can do for you."

"Listen Monsieur."

Suddenly, Mirande made a decision. He would confide the secret itself to the magistrate. Thus, he would justify his conduct. And if the Commissaire did not agree to release him right away, at least he could avert the peril by making a prompt report.

He stood up and took a step toward him. But the agents held him back.

"Let him go. He isn't dangerous," the Commissioner reassured them

Gabriel started. "Dangerous? What do you mean by that? Do you think I'm mad?"

"No, since I'm listening to you."

Leaning over the desk, face to face, he whispered his secret: the quarrel between the two countries reanimated, the manifestation planed by the Triplice. The Commissaire appeared to listen with gravity, even with anguish.

"That is, indeed, very serious," he murmured.

Gabriel was exultant. "If our diplomacy doesn't prevent that sovereign's gesture, it's war, Monsieur. It's war, with its ruination and disasters. It's our unfortunate country crushed by the coalition. Now you understand my haste my imprudence, my anger. For the negotiations require time. It's necessary for orders to leave Paris tonight, tomorrow at the latest. One day's delay might cost billions of dollars and millions of lives. Do you believe me now, Monsieur le Commissaire?"

"Certainly."

"And you're going to help me?"

"Certainly."

"Finally!"

The Commissaire scribbled a few words in haste and confided them to the secretary, who left, without further explanation. Then he said, very benevolently: "Well, we'll sort all this out. I'll have you taken to your Minister. Be patient for a moment. Someone's gone to fetch a vehicle."

"For such a short journey…," Gabriel protested.

"Monsieur Raucourt has kept his private domicile. He doesn't sleep at the Ministry," the magistrate explained. Then he left in his turn, leaving the prisoner with the two agents. The wait, a quarter of an hour long, was cruel to Gabriel's impatience. Finally, the purr of an automobile told him that he had not been forgotten. The secretary arrived at the same time, and handed him a battered hat that he had found in the street.

"I'll accompany you to the Minister," he said.

"You're too kind, Monsieur."

They left the office and went through the station, where the drowsy policemen did not even look up. Oh, the worthy fellows! They scarcely suspected that their recent victim was about to save them from an atrocious calamity, an unspeakable scourge. But Gabriel forgave them their violence. He felt that he had the heart of an apostle.

Outside, the pure air soothed him after the emanations of the station. Moonlight caressed the roofs of the houses. He consulted the luminous clock of a nearby kiosk. Scarcely one o'clock in the morning. He still had time.

However, when the moment came to get into the taxi he was astonished. He was shoved very rudely into the back of the vehicle. That the secretary got in too was legitimate, but why that escort? Why were the two agents piling into the second banquette with a rattle of sabers? Why was a third getting in next to the driver? He was also disquieted by the fact that the vehicle pulled away without the address being given to the driver. Were they playing with him?

On the way, he tried to follow the itinerary. Where were they going? Where did Raucourt live? For pride's sake, he did not want to interrogate the policemen. He grasped too late the odiousness of the situation.

The vehicle stopped. The faint light of a street-lamp illuminated a bleak frontispiece. An agent took him by the arm, drew him through a low door. A brief conversation, a clink of keys, corridors, a sort of cell: he finally understood. The Commissaire had judged him to be mad. He had sent him to the special infirmary at the remand center.

Mad...he thought he would go mad. Thus, on the whim of a stupid Commissaire, everything was collapsing. Lacaze's cause was lost, Castillan was triumphant, and the fate of the country was compromised.

He wept, in the sheets that seemed still damp with other tears. Oh, the broken, fitful sleep, in which the vision of dear   people, an impious war, filled his dreams and his insomnia!

And yet, in the depths of his distress, one hope still gleamed, No, he did not have the right to allow himself to be defeated by human stupidity, when he possessed a superhuman power. If he was obliged, at the price of a sacrilege, to reveal his power, he would not succumb...

In the opaque darkness of his cell, he thought he could still see, like a tutelary gleam, the fluorescent ampoule...

IV

In the morning, when Mirande was summoned before the little man in the black frock-coat, with a rosette in his buttonhole, a denuded forehead and a gray beard, he suspected immediately that it was the official medical examiner.

Finally, he was hoping to be able to explain himself. He was sure of convincing him, of quickly dissipating the misunderstanding. His plan was entirely traced. He had meditated it for a long time during his hours of insomnia. He had resolved not to abandon himself to violence again. And he would certainly be able to avoid the traps that were set for him.

He observed his judge. Profound wrinkles furrowed his cheeks, going astray in the undergrowth of his beard. The gaze was sharp, disillusioned, but the ensemble was honest, almost sympathetic.

Certainly, Mirande knew his name, his reputation. He searched his memory, evoked portraits published by the newspapers. And suddenly, a memory surged forth: Brimmel, the alienist. His story had caused a brief scandal in medical milieux. It was claimed that his rosette had been bought by his complaisance. In a medico-legal report, he had concluded the madness of a troublesome Minister. Later, events had justified his diagnosis, but the opposition press had made a great fuss at the time.

Mirande judged it prudent not to recognize him. And, following that strategy, he lent himself tranquilly to the examination. He willingly placed himself facing the light, as was demanded of him. He responded calmly to the first questions. He smiled internally at Brimmel's ruse, representing himself as an envoy of the Court rather than a physician. He hid his irritation at seeing that the scientist began the conversation with the preconceived idea of madness.

In fact, Brimmel deployed the benevolence and amenity that one uses with an interlocutor whom it is unwise to contradict and whose confidence one wants to capture. He declared that he knew of Mirande's fine work beside the lamented Brion, and the preponderant place that he had taken at the laboratory since his master's death.

Then, arriving at the adventure of the previous evening, he seemed to accept its plausibility. It was, in sum, the convenient procedure that the Commissaire de Police had used: flatter the lunatic, pretend to believe him.—with the variant that Brimmel was preparing his traps, noting in passing the points of the narrative that would later appear extravagant.

But at the first attempt of that sort, Gabriel cut him off: "Come on, Doctor, don't use trickery with me."

"Doctor? Who told you that?" said the physician, astonished.

"That you're an alienist charged with examining me? But it stands to reason—the reason of a rational mind, at least. I ask you, would a magistrate have placed me facing the light to observe the equality of my pupils? Would he have interrogated me like a madman, flattering my supposed mania? Would he have praised my laboratory and my work so eloquently, to see whether I gave evidence of an unhealthy pride? No, no, the Court doesn't take so many precautions! They reveal a specialist, a manipulator of madmen."

He applauded himself for that engagement. Then, very calmly, he went on: "Well, so be it, Doctor. You need to make observations for your report. I will, if you'll permit me, furnish you with the elements. Let's begin with the reflexes."

Methodically, he crossed his legs. He gave himself a sharp tap under the knee, on the tendon that links the tibia to the patella. At that stimulus, his leg gave a brief jerk, which testified to a normal nervous system.

"You can see that my reflexes are intact?" he said, smiling, and added: "You've doubtless also remarked that my voice isn't affected by any tremor, which denotes the integrity of my rachidian bulb; that my march is assured and my movements are precise, which affirms the good state of my spinal fluid. I have not, thus far, manifested any ambitious delirium, in spite of your excessive praise. In a word, I don't present any of the symptoms of the cerebro-spinal inflammation for which you've looking for ten minutes. Do you want me to lend myself to further experiments now, to come, to go, to debate?"

"You've studied medicine, then, Monsieur?" asked Brimmel, nonplussed.

"I have at least frequented the wards of hospitals, including those of Bicêtre and the Salpêtrière, where the sick are treated…very different from me, believe me. I can swear to you, Doctor, that I'm not afflicted by any flaw similar to those I've studied."

The physician sketched a vague gesture. Gabriel interpreted it immediately.

"Yes, I see. You're telling yourself that many of the insane escape the physical observations…that it often happens that the organism doesn't denote them…that the entire drama is played out far from science, in the mysterious centers of thought…and that it's necessary to put the demented on the path of their delirium to be persuaded of their condition. Well, so be it. Let's get on to my obsession, let's talk about my life, Let's see whether my faculties are troubled from this moment on."

For the first time, Brimmel found himself confronted by a subject who was discussing his own case, posing in advance the questions that he was going to ask. He was disorientated by that. But madness reveals itself under so many unexpected aspects, and sometimes so much logic, that he was still suspicious.

"Yes, let's go into my mania," Gabriel went on. "How have I manifested it, this mania? By claiming to have discovered a state secret in the midst of a diplomatic soirée, and by having difficulty explaining to the Commissaire how I came to possess it. That's it, isn't it? There isn't anything else? For what happened thereafter, my attempt to reach the Garde des Sceaux, my exasperation when I was opposed by force, can all be explained by my impatience to communicate my discovery to him right away. And you would have acted as I did, Doctor. You would have revolted as I did, wouldn't you?"

The physician nodded. He still had no comment to make.

"All the charges against my mentality, therefore," Mirande continued, "can be summarized as follows: I gave an explanation of the origin of that secret that seemed suspect to the policemen. But suppose, for example, that I had that confidence from a person that I can't name…or that I surprised it thanks to a method I can't divulge. Isn't it logical that I would improvise a story…maladroitly, in truth, since it brought me before you…but which was imposed by necessity? That's the whole of it! Am I exposed to you as a madman?"

"Absolutely not."

Gabriel had a flash of victory. His strategy was succeeding. He was triumphing without having to embark on the redoubtable struggle regarding the existence of the serum. All his assurance returned to him. He glimpsed imminent liberty.

"Furthermore," he added, "one doesn't deliberately lock up a man—even a maniac—who doesn't pose any danger to public safety. I'm not dangerous. And a decision you make against me would be severely interpreted by the press...the press that easily accuses a physician arbitrarily, that willingly charges him with partiality...sometimes of interest...."

No allusion could have been more sensible to the medical examiner. Since his adventure with regard to the rosette, the fear of scandal had dominated him.

"In fact, the press isn't always convenient," said the alienist, reaching for the inkwell. Undoubtedly, he was about to write a favorable report, concluding with Mirande's release.

At that moment, however, a warder came in, and pronounced a few words in Brimmel's ear; the latter got up immediately.

"Wait for me, and have confidence," he said, as he went out.

Unfortunate Mirande! Would he have retained the joy in his eyes if he had been able to suspect that Castillan was on the other side of the door, asking for Brimmel?

A brief item published at the last minute by the morning newspapers had alerted Castillan to Mirande's misadventure. What an admirable opportunity! For him, the young chemist represented a constant danger, a living threat. For he knew. How? That, Simone's husband could not understand. At any rate, he knew. And Castel-

Ian had already been thinking of ways to harm him when that news item fell under his gaze. One again, destiny was offering itself to him, tempting him.

Knowing the time of the medico-legal examination, he had arrived just in time.

He approached Brimmel cordially. He had known him for a long time, encountering him frequently at dinners of a body of which he was the president. Serious questions were rigorously banished therefrom. Sympathies were sealed there by the warmth of good wine, and Castillan excelled at spreading charm and enthusiasm at those feasts.

He said immediately that, passing the remand center, he had seized the opportunity to notify his dear colleague of a change in the date of the next banquet.

"The January promotion has offered our society three new decorations," he said, in a satisfied tone. "It's appropriate to give a certain splendor to the monthly feast. That's why I've put it back for a week in order to bring together more people. That's all right? You'll come?"

"I'll come."

They were about to separate when Castillan, indicating the office door, said "You're on duty?"

"Yes, I'm examining Mirande…you know Mirande, Brion's pupil…"

"What! Mirande's been arrested?" said Castillan, feigning surprise. He seemed to reflect momentarily. Then, slyly, he filtered between his teeth; "Of course, it was to be expected."

"Why is that?"

"But he's mad!"

"Well, he doesn't seem so to me…I wasn't about to conclude that."

"Be careful, my dear, be careful!" His voice and his physiognomy expressed such conviction that Brimmel became anxious.

"Do you know something?"

"Me...not at all," said Castillan. At the same time he extended his hand, to bid farewell. He was manifestly removing himself for the sake of discretion—so Brimmel restrained him by one of the buttons of his impeccable jacket.

"But yes—you know something, I can see by your expression. Come on, admit it."

"Professional secrecy, my dear, what can you do?"

"Between us?"

Castillan hesitated; then, generously: "No, it wouldn't be charitable." And he attempted to withdraw again.

Then Brimmel pressed him to speak, alleging their good relationship, the services that colleagues owe one another, his fear of further troubles with the satanic newspapers.

"Well, yes," Castillan consented, vanquished by that pressure. "Yes, I've known the poor fellow for a long time, and I pinned him down with a solid diagnosis long ago. He has the most dangerous persecution mania...can you imagine that I've even been the victim of it?"

"You?"

"Me, my dear."

"In what circumstances?"

"Quite recently, in fact. It's necessary that you understand that I know him slightly through my wife. Quite recently, he presented himself at my home, and in what a state, great gods! What agitation! And there, without

216

warning, he accused me of several crimes...several, you hear? All as frightful as one another."

"Tell me..."

Castellan shrugged his shoulders. "So ludicrous that it's not worth the trouble of taking about them."

Brimmel insisted: "But yes, yes..."

"Well, he claims that I had a cousin of my wife's murdered, from whom we inherited. He added that in order to profit alone from that inheritance, I had my wife buried alive after plunging her into a hypnotic sleep...and other inanities even more ridiculous, such as can germinate in the mind of the persecuted. Oh, he won't go away and remain quiet. And note that he presented these enormities to me with such an appearance of reason that if he'd accused another person in the same terms, in truth, I would immediately have gone to the public prosecutor."

"Sapristi! You've done well to warn me. I was about to sign his release!"

"At least keep him under observation for a few days," advised Castellan. Then, before going away, he politely offered to wait for his colleague, to drop him at home when he had finished with Mirande. As the alienist hesitated, fearing that he might be too long delayed, Castillan protested: "No, no! We so rarely have the opportunity to chat."

"All right—we'll go back together," Brimmel agreed.

When Mirande saw him come back in, he understood that his dispositions had changed. Something had turned his judge against him. But he was careful not to let his suspicion show, in which, Brimmel, forewarned, might have been able to discover persecution mania.

He therefore waited for a new interrogation. Questions did, indeed, fall upon him, striking the same point with irritating insistence. How had he discovered the diplomatic secret?

"I've allowed you to divine it, Doctor: from a third person."

"What third person? That's very vague information you're giving me there. I could consider it an evasion. It's necessary that I know, do you understand? That I can check..."

"I've also told you that the check was impossible."

"However, what if I gave you my word of honor to verify your affirmation personally? What if I promised to go alone to find your confidant, to ask him for his evidence and to forget it immediately?"

"That can't be done, Doctor."

The struggle continued, stubborn on both sides. And suddenly, war weary, Brimmel reached out toward his penholder again.

"In that case, what do you expect? I'm obliged to keep you!"

Mirande collapsed, desperate. He had glimpsed a chink of the sky through the breach. It was being walled up again. Oh, how could he put an end to it? How could he recover the necessary liberty?

Certainly, one means existed: to reveal Brion's discovery to the Doctor. But had not the old master demanded secrecy? Would he not be dishonoring his memory, breaking his word?

He debated the matter internally, very rapidly. Evidently, in ordering silence, Brion had not foreseen such complications. His indulgent and generous heart would have yielded to the force of circumstance. And it seemed to Mirande that an encouragement from beyond the tomb came to him from the Great Seeker, a generous, tutelary: "Go on, I permit it."

Then, recklessly, turning an anguished face toward the alienist, he said: "Forgive me, Doctor. Well, yes, I haven't told you the whole truth. You're pushing me to a confession that costs me dear, but I owe it to you. Know this: I have no confidant in this affair. I alone discovered the diplomatic secret…and this is by what mysterious power…"

Oh, the emotion, the dolor, the solemnity of Mirande when he dared to make the august revelation. One might have thought that he was drawing it from the depths of an abyss. He veiled his face as if before a sacrilege. He trembled throughout his being.

Alas, to end with what! With a smile of compassion! Brimmel did not believe him. Brimmel inclined his head with pitying skepticism.

Then the unfortunate embarked on a theoretical explanation of the serum. To convince a scientist, science would perhaps serve? Not at all! The alienist was no longer even listening. He had picked up a pencil and was tracing vague figures on a piece of paper. Then he abandoned his drawing and looked for his portfolio.

That gesture inspired Mirande. For half an hour he had been exhausting himself trying to convince him; why had he not thought of the decisive testimony? But he was carrying it on him, the proof! It was there in his pocket!

"I can see that you don't believe me, Doctor."

"But yes, my friend, but yes."

"No, you don't believe me. But I'll oblige you to believe me, because I'll inject myself in front of you. Only consent to summon me in an hour, the time for the serum to act, for me to be fully impregnated by it, and none of our thoughts will escape me. I'll repeat them to you—all of them! And I'll finally have reckoned with those who want to doom me."

The alienist raised his head, interested. "In truth, I'd be curious to see that!"

Buoyed up by hope, Gabriel took out his medical kit, which had fortunately been left on him. He opened it. But at the same time, a cry of despair rent his throat.

"Oh, the brutes! The brutes!"

"Who?"

"The agents! Those wretches took hold of me last night with such violence that they've broken my ampoule!"

"That's regrettable…but you must have others?"

The question reanimated Mirande. In order to enquire about the serum, the medical examiner must believe him. At least his skepticism must be shaken.

In fact, Brimmel was in doubt again. All things considered, if the prisoner's affirmations were implausible, they were not impossible. Brion had a brain so fecund, so powerful! Twenty years ago, who would not have considered as a madman someone who promised to fly in an apparatus heavier than air, to telephone wirelessly or photograph a skeleton through the opacity of the flesh? Furthermore, prudence had become Brimmel's dominant virtue.

"Certainly I have others," replied Mirande. "I possess a whole set, which you'll discover easily, as well as the formula and the physiological observations of the serum, in a safe in my private laboratory."

"Rue Méchain, I know. And the safe?"

"Oh, there's no mistaking it. It's sealed into the wall, lacquered in white, near the chimney-breast. It's there that my master kept his toxins. I haven't changed

220

the custom." And, taking a key from his bunch, he said: "Here's the key."

Before handing it over, he hesitated again for a second He wanted to sound the physician's soul with his gaze. He thought he discovered frank honesty there.

"This key," he repeated, emotionally, "I swore never to separate from my person. But circumstances have overtaken me, and I have confidence in you, Doctor, I have confidence that no one but you will open that safe…and that once your investigation is finished…"

"You have my word," the alienist affirmed.

He slipped the little key into his fob pocket. Closing his register, he added: "Out of consideration for you, I'll postpone my report until later. I hope that it will be favorable, but as I can't conclude it, you'll allow me to keep you at my disposal pending the complete truth."

"If necessary…"

Brimmel left the room.

"Well, what are you doing about that poor Mirande?" Castillan asked him, as the automobile bore them away.

"Mirande. Oh, I'm very perplexed." And Brimmel related the resumption of the interrogation, the extraordinary confession, the entire history of the key the serum and the safe in the laboratory…

Castillan listened avidly. What a revelation! What a flash of enlightenment! That explained Mirande's attitude, his accusations. How had he been able to know the truth about Simone, about Gagny, if not in a supernatural fashion? Oh, he, Castillan believed them, all those affirmations that Brimmel, perhaps out of false shame, reported in a skeptical tone.

While speaking, with an instinctive gesture, the alienist had taken the key out of his fob pocket and showed it, in support of his story.

"That's the key of the famous safe?" asked Castillan.

"It's the one he's just given me, at least."

"Let me see…"

He seized it, tossed it into the air, caught it, and tossed it up again.

And that fashion of juggling, at such a grave moment painted the man in his entirety. He juggled with events. With his shirt-front thrust out, a smile on his lips, he followed them in their flight, and then took then in hand with an insolent pleasure.

However, he admitted that the game was new, this time. For this splendid coup, he would need all his dexterity. But if he succeeded, oh, what a future! What might that little key not open to him! If he could keep it for the space of one evening, time to penetrate into the deserted laboratory, open the safe, take out the ampoules and the formula…and that was, in fact, Mirande disarmed forever, incapable of proving his lucidity, incapable of getting out of his padded cell, incapable of pursuing his work of justice. Better still, it was to acquire at the same stroke the formidable power that the wretched chemist had only devoted to the triumph of a miserable cause. Oh, if he possessed it, that sovereign power! If he held it in his audacious hands! And he sensed that he would rule the world.

Still playing with the key, tossing it up and catching it in flight, he spoke, in a simultaneously coaxing and grave manner. He ended up demolishing, sentence by sentence, the already shaky faith of his colleague. What was Brimmel going to do in the laboratory?? Verify the delirium of a maniac? Waste an hour of precious time in that pleasantry? But Mirande was mad, mad enough to be locked up. The accusations he had made against Castillan were the striking proof of it.

He slid the ring on the key on to his little finger with a kind of voluptuousness.

"I don't have to tell you, my dear, that alongside the insane, properly speaking, there's an entire category of the mentally ill who carry their delirium through the world. Inoffensive as long as circumstances lend themselves to it, they're capable, at a given moment, of a morbid impulsion that renders them dangerous to society. They're the patients that one doesn't punish, but one cares for. One cares for them by keeping them safe. Well, I imagine that Mirande must be classified in their ranks. You ought to intern him, this Mirande. You'd be protecting society, and me!"

"But Brion's work, though!" said the alienist, hesitantly.

"Brion was one of those superior degenerates, in whom genius and dementia shared the brain. And Mirande is only imitating his master! Have you not yourself, in your latest treatise, envisaged the phenomena of alienation, contagious in a way, of *folie à deux*?"

He had touched the right spot. That allusion to his work flattered Brimmel. He swelled internally. He thought about his imminent candidature for the Académie de Médecine. Castillan took advantage of that agreeable reverie to dissimulate the key completely in his hand. Then he led the dialogue on to pathological considerations borrowed from his colleague's book. It was an important work, and such a fine literary quality!

"I'm glad of your opinion," replied Brimmel. "But to get back to Mirande, I'm wondering whether it's not a duty of conscience for me to take the investigation to the ends..."

"Your conscience? Oh, I approve of your inspiring it...but all the same, my dear, it's necessary also to listen to the fear of ridicule,"

"Ridicule?"

"Well, yes. Do you think that the press...?"

"The press? Who would inform them about my investigation?"

"Brion's pupils, Mirande's comrades, of course! That event, if you divulge it by delving into it uselessly, will become the news of the day! People will talk about it! Above all, they'll write about it. Can you see all those eager throats, thirsty for scandal? You know something about that! Be careful, Brimmel—the end of the year reviewers are watching out for you. Seriously, one last piece of advice: before pursing your investigation, keep Mirande under observation for a few days."

The auto had come to a stop. Brimmel stepped out of the limousine, thanked him, said adieu, and went under the porch of his house.

"Home!" Castillan ordered the chauffeur,

The vehicle pulled away. He threw himself violently back into the depths, his heart dilated, clutching the liberating key tightly in his hand.

"I have it! I have it! I have them all!" he breathed, in an intoxication. Then he sniggered. "Poor Brimmel! You'll be lucky if you can find me today!"

But what was happening? The auto, scarcely having drawn away, was braking, stopping, Castillan leaned out—and he perceived Brimmel running after it, his arms raised.

"The key! You haven't given me back my key."

"Oh, forgive me...here it is."

And the alienist apologized. "You understand that it's necessary for me to return it in a few days to the poor fellow, if I decide to renounce the investigation."

"Indeed...but what will you tell him?"

"Well...that I didn't find anything."

"Obviously."

The vehicle pulled away, Oh, the worthy Brimmel never spoke a truer word. Indeed, in a few days, he would not find anything. For already, Castillan, disarmed but ready for the revenge, was imagining the formidable pincers of the pirate, Le Crabe, forcing the safe....

PART FIVE

I

At the entrance gate, Jeanne rang. She had feared the bleakness of the place. On the contrary, it was quite cheerful. From the road that bordered the Seine, the park rose up in a gentle slope, extending its pathways of blond gravel in elegant curves. On the lawns, still green, the small trees were carefully packed with straw for the winter. The larger trees extended their leafless branches with a protective gesture. To the right and the left, the bright hedges masked the coquettish architecture of little pavilions in brick and stone. At the top, the principal building, framed by bushes, displayed its neo-Greek style. Over that décor, a chilly sun poured a pale light that the delighted birds saluted noisily.

Jeanne imagined the charm, the seduction of the sojourn under the adornment of spring, in the splendor of summer. Alas, why did it have to be profaned by the inscription displayed in golden letters on the fronton of the gate: *Sanitarium*. A place of health! A refuge for brains devoured by the fire of civilization, a tomb before death!

It was there that her brother had been imprisoned since the previous day. In what torments, poor fellow! In what delirium! She dared not think about it. She had not seen him since the evening when he had left for the fête at the Ministry of Foreign Affairs. He had kissed her tenderly, as always. She had scarcely noticed his distant, absent air. For some time, she had observed that absorbed preoccupation, but she had attributed it to the cares of the task he had undertaken, Might she be mistaken? Was it not a symptom of one of his fits? Had he fled to hide it from her?

He had, however, promised to return early. He wanted to be at the laboratory early, where a certain microbial culture demanded his matinal attention. So, what a surprise when she had discovered his bedroom empty! Distressed, stirring hypotheses, she had waited all morning, telephoned the Rue Méchain ten times to ask for her brother—in vain. At midday, she had resolved to set out on campaign. She would knock on the doors of friends, run to the commissariats, the bureaux...

But as she was about to set out, a note from the Prefecture of Police summoned her to the Boulevard du Palais. There, after peregrinations through the maze of corridors, mistaken doors and a nervous wait in a dirty room, she finally learned about her brother's adventure, his dementia, doubtless confirmed by a medico-legal examination, and his probable internment. She had emerged heart-broken, her legs unsteady, quivering from the obligation to remain inactive.

Visits, approaches, supplications: nothing could bend the order that isolated Gabriel. It was necessary to wait for the unfortunate to the transported to a sanitarium. They had, however, left the choice of refuge to her, provided that she bore the expense. She had accepted immediately, and indicated this suburban establishment, whose medical director she knew slightly. Finally authorized to see him, she was running to him, at the peak of anguish and the limit of her strength.

A concierge appeared, more akin to a gardener. His face was plump and cheerful. He took off his cap and asked what she wanted. Then he opened a small door in the gate and announced the visit by ringing a bell.

"I ought to warn Madame that she must see Monsieur le Directeur first."

"Yes, I know. Take me to him."

They headed toward the imposing façade. On the way she enquired: "Do you know anything about the inmates. My brother came here yesterday."

"The new one? Yes, I know."

"How is he? Better? Is he calmer?"

"Probably. He's allowed out alone in the park. He seems very gentle, the poor fellow."

He could go out alone! Jeanne breathed out, relieved. She went past patients. They seemed inoffensive, although male nurses kept them company. They look at her tranquilly. Some were chatting in placid voices. No spectacle of shackles, no terrors, no frantic cries, but rather an impression of docile idleness. Nothing of what she had feared.

The concierge climbed a perron, traversed a vestibule whose floor was covered with a brightly-colored mosaic. Then he stood aside at the threshold of a room whose modern furniture and carefully-chosen trinkets banished any idea of sadness.

"Monsieur le Directeur won't be long," he affirmed, with a broad smile. Then, with an engaging gesture, he designated the newspapers accumulated on a table,

Newspapers? No, Jeanne did not open them. She had retained a horror of them since the note—fortunately brief and imprecise—relating the incident in the Place Vendôme. She still trembled to discover new information, more precise and more extensive. Impatiently, she went back and forth between her chair and the window. Minutes passed. Finally, the director appeared.

"My dear Mademoiselle, excuse me. I was just retained with your brother."

"Is he worse?"

"Not at all," the doctor replied. "I merely find him very downcast. I've tried in vain to interest him in work. I've put my books at his disposal…wasted effort. To justify himself and leave, that's his obsession. Apart from that he maintains a resolute silence. Perhaps you'll have more luck than me, Mademoiselle."

"I can see him, can't I?"

"Certainly. I'll even leave you alone with him. Always stay within reach of the bell—for one never knows. In spite of their apparent calm, these invalids are sometimes subject to sudden impulsions."

"You're frightening me, Doctor!" Jeanne examined. "You're frightening me! Not that I have any fear for myself…but him, poor fellow! Oh, I beg you, tell me the truth. Don't hide anything from me. I'm strong. But I need to know, you understand. What's wrong with him? What is this illness, so sudden and unexpected? Can he be cured? Will he have to stay here for a long time?"

Under that avalanche of questions the director showed even more reserve.

"Wait, wait, Mademoiselle! I don't know yet. I'm studying him at the moment. Cerebral pathology is so complicated, so obscure. Give me a few days to form an opinion. I'll tell you frankly then, I swear to you." And he added: "Would you care to follow me?"

He preceded her. They went along a gallery on to which rooms opened, disposed in such a way that a single guardian could watch its entire extent: in sum, a banal hotel corridor. Having knocked on one of the doors, the director went in, and then reappeared almost immediately.

"I've told him that you've come," he said. "He's waiting for you. I'll give you half an hour, at the most. I'll come to collect you."

Without hesitation and without fear, but not without emotion, the young woman went in. Gabriel held out his arms to her.

"Jeannot! Finally! My Jeannot!"

"You! You!"

They were pressed heart to heart, with their arms around one another. She huddled against him, stammering her affection, caressing his cheek with the same gesture that one uses to calm the fear of a child.

"Jeanne!" he said. "My sister! My little one! I knew that there would be no obstacles for you! I was so sure that I would see you today! Oh, how I was waiting for you!" Then he recoiled. "At least you don't suspect…you…you're certain of my reason?"

"Yes, my dear, yes..."

He must have perceived her doubt, though, for, with a sudden, almost abrupt energy, he said: "Sit down. Your visit has doubtless been limited? Yes, they fear tiring me out. How much time can you spend with me?"

"Half an hour."

"That's sufficient for a man who can still coordinate his ideas, no matter what they claim. Listen to me, carefully."

And neatly, precisely, logically, he revealed the whole truth. Since he had been obliged to confess to Brimmel, what was the point henceforth in concealing it from his sister? He recounted his life since the night when he had exhumed Simone until the evening when he had been thrown into a cell at the remand center.

What a devastating revelation for Jeanne! The certain innocence of her fiancé…the unfathomable evil of

231

Castillan…so many crimes made manifest, mysteries clarified, hopes authorized. She felt dizzy.

She was afraid. Wall all that not the dream of a sick imagination? Then, with all rigor, all the clarity of her solid reason, she examined the facts. Evidently, only the marvelous could explain them.

Without a prodigious divination, how had Gabriel heard Simone through so many obstacles? How had he discovered the crimes that Castillan alone knew? And incessantly, reality came to confirm and certify the miracle. They were not chimeras, then, the existence of the pirate, the gambling win, the machinations deployed against Quatrefin, against the country itself?

But in her mind, avid for logic and evidence, an objection suddenly arose. She shook her head.

Already, Mirande was crying: "You don't believe me either?"

"Yes, yes, I believe you, I swear to you. But help me to dissipate one last doubt. This project, recalled in the ambassador's thought—why hasn't it been realized? Why has his sovereign not already disembarked in Africa?"

Immediately, however, he replied: "Yes, I've often thought about that. It hasn't been my least anguish for two days. There's no mention of anything, is there? No threat of war? No black sign?"

"None."

"I hoped so," he said. "First of all, as I said, I confided that project of disembarkation to the Commissaire. He didn't believe it, true—but he must have reported it anyway to his superiors, and, by virtue of that, set our diplomacy in motion. What about the newspapers? Have they related…the incident in the Place Vendôme?"

A brief article in the stop press—a veiled allusion to insensate words, a provocation by the Triplice."

"That's sufficient. Regarding the Italian ambassador, they must have read between the lines; they would have believed in an indiscretion, a treason, a skillful ruse of espionage. In brief, the bomb has been disarmed. It has been abandoned. Are you convinced now?"

With a passionate ardor, she said: "Yes, yes. I have faith in you, an absolute faith. I understand everything. For me, everything is illuminated, Now, time's pressing. Speak, order…what must I do?"

Oh, the delight for him of hearing, after those three days of torture, a voice of affection and confidence: someone, finally, who did not think him mad!

"You need to help me escape from here as quickly as possible. If we wait for the investigation, if we follow the legal pathways, it will be too late. My task isn't finished. Castillan is free; he's alert, active. I'm astonished that he hasn't yet tracked me down here, to tighten my bonds if possible. I sense him clearly behind all my defeats!"

"Speak," she said, resolutely. "Order." She had not forgotten that the salvation of her brother was also that of her fiancé.

He took her hand. "Go and find Quatrefin. He alone is capable of getting me out of here. He's an energetic man. He's richer and more powerful than ever. I've just told you how I've saved him from ruin, and perhaps suicide. He's seeking to prove his gratitude. He'll seize the opportunity. Then again, I'm something of a good luck charm, and, by virtue of a gambler's superstition, he'll want to hang on to me. Go find him. Tell him that he must get me out as soon as possible. Let him plan the most romantic, the most insensate abduction…it's all the same to me, provided that he acts quickly. With energy, decision, and above all with money, he'll succeed..."

At that moment, a ringing bell announced a new visitor. Instinctively, Mirande glanced out of the window. Immediately, he exclaimed in rage and fear: "Castillan!"

In fact, the physician was slowly coming up the path through the park.

He meditated, gazing at the floor. "You see," he said. "I suspected as much,. Evidently, he's following me step by step. His presence can't be explained otherwise. He's going to work on the director's mind, make him suspicious of me. Remember that he already treated me as a madman when I flung his crimes in his face. He has a strong hand. Oh, Jeanne, Jeanne, you have to get me out of here as quickly as possible. You have to see Quatrefin today, at his bank, his domicile, the Bourse, no matter where. Anyway, the half hour is up. The director will come to fetch you as soon as he's received Castillan..."

A new doubt traversed him.

"Unless they present themselves together, and the bandit has the audacity to harass me even here. With him, anything is possible. Listen—I have a key on me that I confided to Brimmel, the medical examiner, at the remand center. He returned it to me. He didn't want to use it. I'll tell you about that later. Only know that the key opens the safe that contains the serum, in the laboratory. I think it prudent not to keep it on me. Yes— because of Castillan. Who can tell? Take it, then. Never let go of it. You hear, never, at any price..."

He seized Jeanne's hand. The thought of the enemy nearby, a few paces away, stimulated his clairvoyance.

"One more thing. Castillan will certainly try to approach you…he'll enquire about me, express compassion for me, offer you his services. Oh, don't trust him! Mistrust anything he asks of you, and above all, be careful what you reply to him. Don't yield to indignation or disgust. Be much stronger than I've been. If he talks about my madness, agree with him. Declare that you're resigned to letting me remain here. Try, on the other hand, to discover what he's plotting. But above all, be careful…be careful…"

The young woman acquiesced with a nod of the head to the fraternal recommendations. Her energetic face and resolute expression rendered the unfortunate confidence. But footsteps were resounding in the corridor.

"Oh, I thought so," he said. "You know that I pressed Raucourt for the investigation. If the pirate is discovered before my release.....if you need men of law, go find Dutoit…"

That wretch!" she exclaimed. "Our worst enemy during the trial! You can't think so!"

"Yes, yes. I've thought about it a great deal. At the Foreign Affairs the other evening I read his mind again. Above all, he's avid for prestige. If Lacaze's innocence becomes evident, he'll serve you. It's a stain on his record. He'll have more interest than anyone else in effacing it. Go, go, believe me…"

The director came in. He was alone.

"It's time to go," he said to Jeanne. "We've passed the time."

One last time, the two young people hugged. Then, playing her role, Jeanne said: "*Au revoir*, then. Look after yourself. Rest. See you soon."

Gabriel's presentiment was not mistaken. As soon as she was outside she saw Castillan on watch in the corridor. He bowed, with a broad sweep of the hat that barred her path. She pretended not to divine his intention, replied with a nod of the head and continued on her way.

But the director had rejoined them.

"What? You don't know one another?" he said, introducing them.

"Indeed," said Castillan, "we don't know one another yet—but my wife has often talked about you, Mademoiselle, and we were bound to encounter one another someday. I express all my regret and all my chagrin that it should be in such painful circumstances."

Had she not been forewarned, Jeanne would have allowed herself to be taken in by the sadness of the voice and the attitude of respectful compassion. She remained silent, quivering with indignant scorn.

"Isn't it heartbreaking?" he went on. "That fine brain, so precious to science, suddenly sunk! And the suddenness of the attack! How can it be explained?"

"We've gone through a great deal," Jeanne said. "You know about our cares, or chagrins..."

"Enough to share them, Mademoiselle.

"Then you must understand," she said, "that all those ordeals have taken their toll on his intelligence, alas. Will he ever be cured?"

"Certainly," the two men assured her.

She applauded herself for having deceived them. On the perron, however, Castillan deliberately took his leave of the director, waiting to accompany her.

"Let's leave it there. I'll escort Mademoiselle to the gate."

She was tempted to run away, but she felt strong. In those few steps, perhaps she could perceive the wretch's intentions. She went with him.

"I've just heard you doubt your brother's cure, Mademoiselle," Castillan insinuated. "I'm less pessimistic than you. Are you so convinced of his madness?"

"Alas. Just now he said the most incoherent things to me...."

"Oh! What?"

But the young woman did not reply. She bowed her head, as if absorbed by painful memories of the conversation."

He persisted, more directly: "He must have talked to you…about the famous serum?"

"You know, then?" said Jeanne alarmed. What? Castillan knew about Brion's discovery! That, Gabriel did not know. He had only confided his secret to the medical examiner. She feared having allowed too much emotion to show. Mastering herself, she said: "It's Monsieur Brimmel, then?"

Castillan acquiesced, casually. "It is, indeed, Brimmel who informed me. I wouldn't have attached any importance to the words if I hadn't been struck, very struck, by the revelation of that discovery. It interests me personally."

"Personally?"

"Of course. Have you forgotten the circumstances surrounding Simone's unexpected resurrection? Haven't you wondered, as I have, by what prodigy your brother divined her in the tomb through so many obstacles. That phenomenon, inexplicable without a mysterious influence, troubles me, and leaves me in doubt regarding your brother's dementia."

Jeanne shook her head, incredulously.

More ardently, Castillan went on: "I too, at first, denied the miracle, but on reflection, I've changed my mind. I wonder whether it isn't my turn to save your brother, as he saved Simone..."

She did not look at him. She divined him leaning toward her, persuasive and compassionate. She felt that if she raised her eyes toward him she would be unable to resist the temptation to cry: "You're lying! You're lying again, still! You're preparing I don't know what new infamy..."

But she exhorted herself to prudence. She waited for him to unmask himself more overtly.

He went on: "I believe the moment has come to acquit that debt of gratitude. I think that Brimmel acted very lightly in refusing to check your brother's affirmations, and this is my plan: to recover the serum, experiment with it in the presence of a few serious, notorious colleagues, in sum, to reveal his unpardonable error..."

"Oh, there's no hope of that," Jeanne murmured.

"You can help me, Mademoiselle!"

"How?"

"By enabling me to attempt the experiment. I need the serum. Certainly, your brother must have hidden it carefully, locked it up—but perhaps you know what has become of the key?"

"No, no, I don't know."

Disappointed, Castillan stopped. With all his ascendancy, he ordered: "Well, go back to him. Question him cleverly. Try to procure that key. But be careful of allowing him to suspect your plan, for, haunted by persecution, in which he'll mistrust those who want to save him..."

"Alas, Monsieur, he's even more suspicious of me than all the others," Jeanne sighed.

238

In order better to lead him astray, she was bold enough to raise an afflicted gaze toward him. In any case, they had reached the gate.

"And then," she concluded, "how can I disentangle the truth in the midst of s much incoherence? Believe me, his dementia is unfortunately certain, and your generous project can't save him. It remains for me to thank you nevertheless. Adieu, Monsieur."

She bowed, opened the little door in the gate, and launched herself into the road. She had the sensation of escaping from a wild beast. Oh, how had she found the strength not to spit her hatred and disgust at him? But she knew now what the monster coveted: the prey for which he was lying in wait was the serum locked in the laboratory safe. Surely he would try to take possession of it. How? Alone? With the aid of an accomplice? Oh, she would find out…she would find out...

II

"Is that you, my prince?" breathed a voice in the shadow of the porch.

"It's me."

"Come."

"Where? I can't see clearly..."

"Straight ahead. I've opened the door, quietly."

"You don't have a hooded lantern?"

"Yes, in my bag...to do what?"

"To provide light, of course!"

"Better not, my prince. Better not, because of the concierge, who's in his hovel. He's dozing, warm in his pit...necessary not to disturb him. One would be obliged to ice him...best to avoid that, when one can do otherwise. Are you there?"

"I'm here."

"No noise, then. Duck down when you go past the lodge. It's straight ahead. No mistake."

Holding their breath, bodies crouching like wild beasts lying in ambush, Castillan and Forteau crept through the total darkness of the vault. An auto vibrating on the cobbles of the Rue Méchain held them in suspense for a few seconds, but the rumbling died away.

When they reached the concierge's lodge another alarm immobilized them. The burglar's tools that Le Crabe was carrying slung over his shoulder shifted and bumped into the wall with a metallic clink. The echo of the corridor amplified the sound. The man stifled an oath and felt for his knife.

Not no—nothing. The placid concierge continued dozing. They covered a few more meters.

"Keep still. We're at the end. I'm opening..."

Le Crabe straightened up. Groping his way he found the lock. When he had the handle in his hand, he turned it with infinite precaution. In any case, the door did not squeak. It had been greased sufficiently to facilitate their expedition.

"Nice! Not locked, this one. We're in clover...all good."

A faint light falling from the distant fiery sky that Paris spreads out in winter permitted them to glimpse the central pathway of the garden. It was bordered by trees from which melting snow was dripping. At the back, the laboratory buildings raised their brighter silhouette. They almost ran there, following the damp and shiny gravel.

"Let's take a breather," Castillan proposed.

He sat down n a step of the perron. Le Crabe sat down beside him, familiarly. It was the pause before the assault, the moment propitious for effusions.

"I see," he said, smiling. "Don't have the habit. True that burglary's a work that isn't for everyone. Needs heart. Me, I have it, my prince. I never forget those who've been good to me. I'm Le Crabe. I can twist a ten-sou piece like a meatball. Le Crabe is as if one were saying honor and gratitude. You cured me of my liver, I'm your mate for life. You've see that, eh, to-night? I've come. Didn't hesitate."

So saying, he displayed his pincers, then withdrew them. They could be divined, in the darkness, resolute and murderous.

"When did you receive me letter, then?" Castillan asked. "For two days I've been waiting to meet you at the entrance."

"Your letter? That was unlucky. I hadn't been to my bistro in Charenton for a week, because it reeked of cops, and I don't like that odor. But I told Asticot, a mate of mine, that if a pullet came, it was necessary to grab it. So, he brought your writing machine paper this morning. I ran to get my tools and came on the Metro…a fine invention…and here I am."

"How did you get in?"

"Though the door—it was easy. I opened it while waiting for you. It's child's play, a lock like that…and I nipped into the corridor. Tell me now what we have to do? I'm waiting for the program. I presuppose it's for burglary, since you told me to bring my tools?"

"Yes, yes," said the physician, hastily. "Enough blood."

"Oh, the fellow in a nightshirt, out there in the Avenue Raphael? And the kid at Billancourt? Hardly worth talking about. Nothing at all. Can ask anything of your mate. And then, they're good and cold—never be saying anything."

He spat in satisfaction. It was good work, well done. He experienced the profound peace that irreproachable and definitive work leaves.

Castillan shivered—and it was not with cold, even though the dampness of his improvised seat was reaching him. He tucked the fabric of the light overcoat that he had put on in order to be free of his movement underneath him.

"No," he said, "this time it's a matter of a game for you: opening a strong-box from which I have to take something."

"Money?"

"No…a chemical product I need, which only exists there."

"Poison, then," affirmed Le Crabe, ingenuously.

"Not that either...a medicament. But your help is as precious to me as if it were a matter of digging up a treasure. It's only just that I reward you. Here, take this..."

He rummaged in his pocket. In the great calm, the rustle of a banknote was audible.

"Nice!" mumble Forteau. "It's for me that you brought that fine paper?"

"Us. Take it."

"Necessary to know who I am!"

"You're refusing?"

"Until death! I'm Le Crabe. That's like saying honor and gratitude. No cash. For you, it's a favor!"

"Truly, you're refusing? In truth, I don't understand you. Why don't you take up another métier, then?"

"Probable that I'd have done something else if I hadn't been born under a bridge," sighed Forteau, in his hoarse voice.

That superhuman gratitude surpassed the physician's understanding. That rabble was refusing a thousand francs! But a thousand francs for Le Crabe was a million for him, Castillan! And he couldn't see himself refusing a windfall like that.

"All right, I won't insist," he said, putting the banknote away.

He reserved the possibility of offering it to him later, on a day of absolute poverty—unless the hazard of a brawl, or a return of malady rid him of his accomplice definitively. Forteau wouldn't always find a good physician to care of him!

Again, he deplored this expedition in the brute's company. But what could he do? He could not break into the safe on his own, and Forteau, left to himself, would never have discovered the ampoules of serum and Brion's notes among the flasks...

"Let's get on, now," he said, getting up.

The laboratory door loomed up before them. Already, Le Crabe was ferreting in his bag. He took out a lock-pick, slid it into the keyhole, sounded it with the delicacy of a surgeon, then pushed. The door opened. Forteau went through first and closed the door behind Castillan.

"Necessary to know if there's anyone in the shop?" he whispered.

"No one, except for an old maidservant who sleeps on the second floor."

"If she gets up, we'll stick her in a corner. Bring on the light!"

He lit his lantern and projected the glare into the vestibule. A vestry where the pupils' white smocks were hanging, a table, and the staircase at the back emerged from the darkness.

"Where are we going?"

"The second door after the steps.

"It's not even locked! That's lucky."

They were finally in Mirande's private laboratory. Castillan recognized it. The day before, on the pretext of asking for a product, he had studied its disposition. In the narrow beam of the projector, the place seemed more solemn than in broad daylight. The instruments, microscopes, test-tubes, Bunsen burners and retorts—all the engines of modern sorcery—disturbed in their slumber, send back bright reflections, like keen gazes. Nothing was alive, however, except for the regular tick-tock of the clock. In the great curtains of the table that were hanging down to the ground, not a flutter. In the vast fireplace, where the screen stood inert, not a breath of wind.

"Let's see—let me get my bearings," Castillan murmured. "The safe's near the fireplace, on the right, sealed into the wall, lacquered in white. It's this way."

He drew Forteau along. Then, taking possession of the lantern, he raised it to head height and paraded it over the wall. "Here it is." Turning toward his accomplice, delighted by the facility of the expedition, he said: "That's what it's necessary to open. Can you?"

"Oh la la! Necessary to know me. I'm Le Crabe. I..."

"I know, I know!" Castillan cut in. "Let's go. Open it. I'll hold the light."

Glorious, the scoundrel spat into his hands. He put his bag on the ground. He rummaged in it, and brought out a crowbar, a drill, a stout hammer, a long chisel and a screwdriver. With a sharp rap he tested the sonority of the safe.

"It's iron," he affirmed. "Doesn't matter. There's plenty of time."

Taking back the lantern, he examined the lock profoundly. Then he set to work. He deployed, contracted and rotted his crustacean appendices. Sometimes, he paused. He listened. The clock chimed the half hour, holding him alert for a moment. Then he recommenced, with a more prudent tenacity, attacking the hinges.

"Don't hurry...don't make a noise...we have all night," Castillan advised him, striving to project the light usefully.

He was stiff with impatience, though. Every movement of his accomplice, every new bite of the file brought the possession of the world closer. Oh, that serum, how he could profit from it! With its aid, he would

245

become the first among kings, the master of the world. Neither the armies and fleets of a bellicose potentate, nor the billons of a Vanderbilt, nor the domination of a pope would equal his power and glory! With its aid, above all—yes, above all—he would finally hold Lambrine captive, subservient, a prisoner in a cage of gold and diamonds...

"Ha!" said Le Crabe, with a final contraction of his pincers.

The door had just given way. They had to combine their efforts to prevent it from falling. They caught it, and laid it carefully on the ground.

"Well? Is that tidy?" said Forteau, proudly, wiping his face with the back of his sleeve.

"Perfect! You're a master!"

Feverishly, Castillan illuminated the interior of the cupboard. Rows of flasks labeled in red displayed their unequal silhouettes. He seized one and drew it toward his eyes. A subtle perfume of bitter almonds emerged from it.

"Prussic acid," he read, in a low voice.

He replaced the redoubtable bottle.

"No, the flasks only contain toxins. The serum is definitely distributed in ampoules, contained in a box. Let's look on the upper shelf."

He raised himself up on tiptoe, moved other bottles aide, and scrutinized the depths of the safe.

Suddenly exultant, he exclaimed: "A box! That's the serum! Yes, it's labeled. The notes now…the formula." Drunk with the imminent possession, he added: "Pass me a stool!"

What? Why was Forteau delayed in advancing him a seat? Why was he digging his pincers into his arm and squeezing, squeezing as if to crush him?"

"Don't move! There's someone…close the lamp…"

Castillan did not have the time.

The electricity, turned on full, abruptly illuminated the laboratory. From the vast chimney-breast, where she had been hiding behind the fire-screen, a woman emerged.

"Casque de Lune!" bellowed Forteau.

"Yes, my mate, it's Casque de Lune!"

Very pale beneath the streaks of soot that were staining her face, but pert even so, Francette turned to the physician.

"Yes, M'sieur Castillan, it's your chambermaid, resuscitated to take a look at your fine work." A loud burst of laughter uncovered her teeth. Then folding her arms, her eyebrows furrowed, suddenly furious she went on: "It's stronger than mêlé-cass, eh? You weren't expecting to see me play Santa Claus, emerging from the chimney? You were saying: 'Emptied, Francette, dead and gone.' But no! When Le Crabe planted his shiv in my heart…you remember, my mate?…I certainly thought I wouldn't be opening my poor peepers again. But M'sieur le Docteur, it's not only you who has science and skill! There's another, who saved me, by taking out three ribs! And they were prime ribs, too!"

Again she burst out laughing—a slightly too strident laughter, which still had a hint of fever. Then she looked at the two men. Motionless, in the attitude in which she had frozen them with stupor, they were rolling their eyes like hunted beasts. And Forteau was caressing the knife in his pocket.

"Let me talk, my mate…there's no point in you preparing your blade. I'm armored…I'm unsplittable. I'll tell you who fixed me up. It's Doisteau, M'sieur le Docteur—a true one, a pure one, that one. But less my ribs, I wasn't content, as you might think. I needed my revenge. Especially since Mademoiselle Jeanne, my *petite patronne*, suspected that the good doctor was planning a new scheme around the safe, with his mate, So, hup! Out of bed. One ditched the convalescence. And do you know who told me that you were working in the Rue Méchain this evening, my old Crabe? Do you know? Shall I tell you? It's your mate Asticot, my lover. Or rather, it's the good doctor's letter that I read in passing, before he gave it to you..."

But Forteau had brought his knife into the open. Terrible, his face contracted, with the drool of a mad dog on his lips, he pounced upon Francette, his arm raised, in a formidable surge. Briskly, she leapt sideways.

"What a greedyguts! He wants second helpings!"

She had leapt toward the window. With a gesture, she raised the long blind that was hanging down to the floor. Four agents, revolvers in hand, a Commissaire de Police and Monsieur Dutoit appeared.

"Pinched, Le Crabe!" cried Francette.

The revolvers were aimed at him.

"In the name of the law, I arrest you!" declare the Commissaire.

"All right! I'm done!" groaned the brute, dropping his knife. He held out his pincers for the handcuffs.

Castillan, livid, his eyes bulging, watched that *coup de théâtre* with his entire being in disarray. He calculated his disaster. What a downfall, at the very moment of triumph, at the very moment when his hand had taken possession of the serum! What a collapse of his dreams of domination! It was all over. No escape, no explanation was possible. For those witnesses, hidden behind the curtains, the complicity was undeniable. They would delve into the past. They would demand that he pay for his crimes. What a scandal....

Castillan caught *in flagrante delicto* committing burglary, accused of murder, dragged to the court of assizes. And Lambrine, who had led him to the crime, Lambrine would pass into other arms, Lambrine was lost forever...

No, no, not that. Better to finish it immediately. Come on, courage! Stick out the shirt-front, one last time...

They were completing the shackling of his accomplice. They were about to turn toward him. He stiffened, stuck out his chest, raised his handsome lustrous head, Rapidly, he seized the bottle whose red label he had read from the safe, uncorked it, recognized the subtle perfume of bitter almonds. For a second, he raised it in front of him, in the elegant gesture of a toast. Then, enveloping the audience with a look of disdain, he put it to his lips before anyone could leap upon him.

They ran forward. He was already nothing more than an inert mass.

"Pig-headed, to the last!" reflected Dutoit, addressing the Commissaire.

"Oh, Monsieur le Consciller," the latter replied, "let's not complain about that! It saves us work!"

Francette, however, was holding on to the curtain with her hand clenched. Her strength had abandoned her. She had wanted to come out too soon, in spite of the worthy Doisteau, for her *petit patrons*. Her heart was still hurting. She had to sit down.

Gamine to the end, however, she murmured, while they led Forteau away and picked up Castillan's cadaver:

"All that doesn't get me my prime ribs back."

III

On the morning that followed that tragic night, Mirande crossed the threshold of the sanitarium. Jeanne had got him released without difficulty. The attempted burglary, followed by Castillan's suicide, testified that the young scientist had not departed from the truth, prodigious and implausible as it seemed. Brimmel, the medical examiner, was forced to recognize his error and hastened to repair it.

Furthermore, without even waiting for the presence of an advocate, Forteau had talked, before the examining magistrate. Certainly, he was a man to keep his word, to protect his accomplice, to maintain a grim silence regarding the murder in the Avenue Raphael, even though he was henceforth convicted of being its author—but with Castillan dead, there was no need to shield him. And he did not hesitate, in order to attenuate his culpability, to demonstrate that he had only been an instrument in the doctor's hands.

Those confessions simplified Mirande's task, for he intended to use his liberty, above all, to obtain that of his friend. When Jeanne told him about the night's events, he did not abandon himself to triumph, to the great satisfaction of seeing an obscure justice repair so many iniquities at a stroke, nor even to the hopes awakened to him by the sudden widowhood of Simone. He wanted an immediate grace to open the prison gates before Lacaze, while awaiting a certain revision.

Thus far, Raucourt had only had one opportunity to testify his benevolence, by postponing the prisoner's departure for Guyana. Evidently, he would be favorable to a prompt release. But Mirande was apprehensive of bureaucratic slowness, of the instinctive reluctance of men of law to let go of their prey. He therefore resolved to request a new audience with the Minister and to put himself in possession beforehand of his power of divination.

Since the ordeal from which he had scarcely emerged, the serum inspired a kind of terror and repulsion in him, but he had need of it, in that supreme encounter with Raucourt, to assure himself of a superiority over his adversary.

Already, under the action of the injection, he had presented himself at the Ministry at the same time as the previous occasion. Castillan's suicide and the confessions of his accomplice were certainly known to Raucourt. He hoped, therefore, to be received without delay, even though he had made no arrangement in advance.

An unexpected hitch, however, derailed his project. The minister was absent, the two sphinxes in the vestibule assured him. On his insistence, a young attaché intervened. He certified that Raucourt was in the Chambre, retained by the budget debate. The session might last a long time; it was impossible to reach him as long as he was on the benches.

Mirande only obtained the meager satisfaction—ordinarily refused to the visitor who finds a door closed—of knowing that the Minister really was absent. The young attaché was speaking as he thought.

Disappointed, he briefly explained the urgency of the matter. In his own interest, Raucourt ought not to leave Lacaze in prison any longer. He was assured that the minister would receive his request as soon as he returned from the Chambre. Mirande would be summoned that evening, as soon as possible, by a telephone call.

He returned, therefore, to the Rue Monge. Jeanne was absent. He was ready to enjoy the repose of solitude, the mental silence whose release was so precious when he exercised his power, but the telephone rang.

What? He was being summoned to the Justice already? Had the Minister returned prematurely? As long as an unexpected fall had not deprived him of that support on the eve of success.

In a glad surprise, however, an expansion of his entire being, he recognized Simone's voice.

Oh, how he would have liked to read within her, after Castellan's tragic death, the revelation of the frightful past! Did she miss him after all? Or was she, on the contrary, congratulating herself on being free, on belonging to herself? And, in her most secret self, was she turning toward her childhood friend?

Alas, she was far away. To listen to the sound of her soul, he would have required the radiance of her presence.

And it was a new, irritating sensation, while being in possession of his power, to hear a voice and not to be able to perceive the thought...

His chagrin was brief, however. Simone wanted to see them—him and his sister. She was making sure of their presence.

He replied that she would find him at home, and that Jeanne would soon return. He did not have the courage to pronounce banal condolences. In any case, she was leaving. In ten minutes, she would be there.

To distract his impatience, he sought an explanation for Simone's visit. Doubtless, in the disturbance into which the tragic disappearance of her husband had cast her, alone and without support, she was taking refuge, on an instinctive impulse, with the companions of her childhood...

And indeed, as soon as he had welcomed her and taken her into the little drawing room, she confessed her solitude and her distress, but also her shame at having been mixed up, involuntarily, in the odious machination, of having drawn to herself the heritage reserved for Lacaze. Although innocent, she wanted to beg Jeanne's pardon for all that she must have suffered...

She avoided talking about her husband, but every time her thought was brought back to him, she drew away immediately, with a repulsion, horror and alarm that did not escape Mirande's clairvoyance.

She did not know—and must remain unaware of it forever—that Castillan had wanted to put her in the tomb alive, and that, but for a miracle, she would have counted among the number of his victims.

He tried to soothe her. The entire frightful past ought to be no more than a fever dream, a vision of delirium. Henceforth, she needed calm and quietude, in the interest of her health. At that price, and only at that price, she could avoid a recurrence of the terrible attack that had laid her low and left her for dead. Persuasive and pressing, he begged her to attempt the cure of forgetfulness.

"How good you are," she murmured.

Then she let herself go, overwhelmed by lassitude.

"Forget...but can one forget? Oh, so it's true that everything must be paid for, or at least that everything holds one, enchains one? Why did I not find the strength within me to rest all the voices that pushed me toward that marriage, in the name of custom, of convention? All that I could have avoided..."

Softly, he said to her: "But after that frightful detour, you're returned to yourself. You've become once again the Simone of old, the Simone of Chatigny."

Oh, how he would have liked to complete his thought! But the mourning of the day before...one scorns a living man, but one respects a dead one. And then, the disproportion of fortunes, although attenuated, continued to separate them. Once again, he was a slave to his scruples.

It was her who loosened them. She sighed, gently, seductively: "But those who surrounded me then, they haven't changed?"

An, overwhelmed by joy, he perceived, prolonging the sentence, the mute, sweet appeal of tenderness that encouraged him.

He put his hands together in a kind of ecstasy. "Oh, Simone, I loved you then, but you're even dearer to me now."

Then she murmured, so quietly that the words and the thought were confounded: "Well, we'll begin our life again..."

He kissed her forehead. So many dramas and alarms, so much blackness, ha brief sojourn among the mad...and that heroic Francette, who had been sent to finish her convalescence in the sun of the Midi, but who, well recompensed with an annual pension, would carry away the bruise of her excessively humble heart, and also the mourning of her ribs, removed from precisely where that heart beat to powerfully for the *petit patron*...! Yes, so many frightful events, and suddenly, this gift of Simone, his dazzling promise, this splendid dawn! He wondered whether he was living in reality, if that abrupt passage from darkness to light had not blinded his reason.

He stammered: "Is that true? Is that really true?"

But at the same time, his powerful clairvoyance reassured him. He only savored the sweet accord, the delicious harmony of speech and thought. Now, in the meditative silence, he fooled Simone in her joyful reverie. He heard the voice of the heart, the mute prayer, the hymn of delight that sang the praise of the beloved, the hope of happiness, faith in the future: everything that words translate so poorly, all that they submerge, all that they diminish; everything that freezes and condenses on the lips.

Divinely privileged, he respired directly the incense that rose from the altar, before the exquisite vapor dispersed in the chilly air of the vaults...

Oh, if only he could communicate his power momentarily to Simone! How she would have been able to hear, in her turn, without the tiresome assistance of words, the explosion of gratitude and joy that was bursting forth within him.

He had drawn closer to her, in adoration.

"I wish I could express all that I'm experiencing, all that I feel. There's such a fête within me...but I can't talk. If you knew..."

She smile, full of tender and sincere indulgence. "It doesn't matter. I know, in myself..."

But at that moment, a fatal comparison imposed itself on Simone's mind. Oh, it was only a flash of memory—but it had the clear, luminous, brutal precision of a snapshot. Her memory evoked, in her parents' drawing room, in the lamplight, Castillan's first declaration...his abundant and gilded speech, his easy gesture, his flavorsome accent, his solid smile, his lustrous beard, his firm self-confidence...

A fleeting impression, which Simone was already chasing away in disgust—but Mirande had received it with a cruel rigidity. A fiery point, drilling into his brain, could not have inflicted a more frightful torture on him.

Had he had strength to suppress a cry, but he stood up, all the blood flowing away from his heart, in a heavy mass.

She saw his gesture, his pallor, and, more alarmed than if he had acted of his own accord, she said: "What's wrong?"

"Nothing, nothing."

"But..."

"I beg you..."

She reproached him, bluntly piqued: "Do you already have secrets for me?"

Unwitting irony, alas. She could not have any for him.

But Jeanne came in. The two friends embraced. For a moment, they remained in a hug, without words. Then, holding hands, sitting side by side, mingling the bittersweetness of their tears, they exhorted one another to forget past troubles in the hope of joys to come.

After having acquainted his sister with the results of his attempt to see Raucourt, Mirande watched their effusions from a distance, pensively, When Simone had gone, after asking that they inform her of Lacaze's return, he was still meditating, having retired to his study.

A capital debate was agitating within him, but he could not succeed in making a resolution. No, decidedly, he deemed the verdict too serious to leave to himself alone. He needed a second judge.

He got up and rejoined Jeanne in her room. In sum, she alone had recognized the existence of the serum. For Brimmel, a doubt still subsisted.

He said to her, almost solemnly: "Jeanne, do you believe in Brion's discovery?"

"Certainly."

"He checked her frankness, because he was still under the influence of the magical elixir. He went on: "You know that Brion demanded secrecy from me. Events have proven his wisdom only too well. At any rate, I have spoken. It is known, it can be known, that the serum exists. In my place, what would you do with it?"

And as she wanted to interrogate him in her turn, he added: "No, no, I want to know your opinion. Suppose you held this discovery in your hands. What would you decide, at the present moment?"

While she meditated her response, he followed the labor of her thought, which examined, rejected and returned to each hypothesis. Her choice made, she pronounced:

"In my opinion, you ought to keep it entirely to yourself. Perhaps Brion didn't have the time, or the strength, to explain himself, Perhaps he only wanted to engage you to prudence. For me, you ought to convince yourself slowly, by experiment, initiate, put it the proof, around you, in your scientific milieu. And gradually, extend and expand the power that way, until it becomes a new faculty, within the range of everyone."

Then he cried, with a violence that surprised him: "Well, personally, I think that it ought to be suppressed, and suppressed absolutely..."

He stopped, for he had just perceived doubt in Jeanne, horrible doubt. She too, for a second, had wondered whether he was mad…and the injurious thought, in that fraternal heart, reinforced his resolution.

"Yes, I think it's necessary to suppress it, to break the full ampoules, burn the formula—in sum, send all of that to oblivion.

She did not allow all the anguish she was experiencing to show. It was, however, in an anxious voice that she replied: "How? Why? But first of all, you don't have the right. What about Brion, whose supreme discovery it was? Brion, who confided it to you as to a son..."

He shook his head. "It's to give proof of filial respect, it's also to serve his memory, not to charge him with that false benefit, a baneful work..."

She exclaimed, in increasing amazement: "What! It's you, Gabriel, you who are talking about destroying his discovery, today? Have you thought about what you owe to it? Has it not snatched Simone from the tomb? Has it not returned my fiancé to me? Not to mention all that I only glimpsed...the resources that permitted you to act quickly...the influence that earned you Quatrefin's gratitude, Raucourt's benevolence. Without that miraculous aid, where would we be today? Castillan would have triumphed. His crimes would remain unknown, unpunished. Henri would already have departed for Guyana, where I would have followed him. It's impossible that you haven't thought about all the good that might be done with such a power. What then, can you throw into the other side of the balance, which can prevail over such benefits?"

He recoiled before the admission, the absolute confession. He hedged: "Is it nothing, then, to lose an illusion, to darken thus the spectacle of life? For a few consoling revelations, for a few harmonious accords, how much disgust, how much pestilence! Can you imagine what it is to plunge into that sewer, into that cloaca, into

258

that base retreat where everyone believes that he alone can penetrate, where so much egotism, stupidity and turpitude is elaborated?"

Jeanne shook her head. "No, it's not that. All of that you expected. You knew full well that we aren't perfect, that we're subject to moral infirmities as well as physical infirmities. Those fortunate impressions to which you refer ought to have rendered you indulgent to abjections. The beauties ought to have compensated for the flaws. No, no, it's not that..."

He had to surrender more:

"You don't sense the necessity, then, of an inviolable refuge, where one can have one's thoughts to oneself, to oneself alone, in order to live in peace, in happiness, with one's neighbors? If this power were spread, as you wish, don't you sense, then, that existence would become abominable, impossible, between individuals linked by interest, by affection, who respire under the same roof? To be spied, on, discovered, at every moment...but you, even you, just now, when I violently affirmed my intention to destroy the serum, didn't you suspect me of madness? Haven't I surprised your insulting doubt? And yet, we love one another dearly, the two of us. We've climbed the rudest calvary side by side. But what tenderness can resist such a solvent, if its action were incessantly repeated? Yes, a solvent, a poison, and the deadliest..."

She did not give in yet.

"But isn't it a poison that bears its own antidote? Isn't it a weapon that curies the wounds it inflicts? How do you know that we won't become better, healthier, if we knew that we were observed, at the mercy of a nearby lucidity, if we knew that we had forehead of glass? The crimes of a Castillan would become impossible, for we would read the confession in him. Finally, how do you know that we wouldn't have a coquetry of thought, as we have a coquetry of costume because it's offered to our gaze? Our entire life is founded on lies—so be it. But why shouldn't it be founded on sincerity?"

For a moment, he was troubled by that distant vision of an ameliorated future. But there, beneath his skull, in the delicate substance of his brain, the fiery point had left its ardent and profound trace.

He smiled sadly.

"All right. I admit that the relations of amity and interest might adapt to that constant investigation. But isn't there a more fragile, more precious, more sacred bond than all those? Is it necessary to remind you of it? There's amour..."

He looked at her fixedly, and read within her. Jeanne had immediately glimpsed the truth. She had understood that he was speaking under the empire of a disappointment, and that he must have experienced it while he was alone with Simone.

He dispensed with a more direct confession.

"Do you believe," he asked, "that a couple united by love could resist that absolute clairvoyance? Seizing on the wing all the little lies, all the little regrets, all the little ironies, all the little ruses, all the little trivialities that escape the purest and most tender heart? Being peppered by those paltry and venomous darts in the most sacred, the most pathetic moments? Imagine them, those two infatuated individuals...do you understand now, for each of them, the necessity of a secret life, of an inviolable refuge in which to isolate oneself, to conceal from the other everything that might offend them, wound them, afflict and diminish their passion? Can you see that it's necessary to retain a modesty of the soul?"

She did not reply. She imaged her life alongside the man she had chosen, that she had joined, with an impulsion increased by the frightful ordeal. With a sincere effort, she evoked that absolute frankness, without veils...those penetrating gazes that nothing arrested, which would not respect anything...and entire labor of termites, scrupulous and imperceptible, and which, however, would ruin the beautiful edifice...

Yes, perhaps he was right.

But again, the bell of the telephone vibrated. This time, the communication did come from the Ministry of Justice. Miranda was awaited.

He had not been deceived in his anticipations. He had been right to count on the benevolence of the Incorruptible. Raucourt was one of those people who await events, and then, seeing them in motion, place themselves at their head with the appearance of a drum-major, in order to appear to be directing them.

His reports certified Lacaze's innocence. He assured Mirande that the prisoner, already notified of the abrupt *coup de théâtre*, would be treated with all the respect due to his misfortune. Quite sincerely, he promised to reduce the formalities to the strict minimum, to present, perhaps as soon as the next day, a decree of grace for the signature of the Head of State.

He kept his word.

Yes, Jeanne was right. It was thanks to Brion that the following evening, the two engaged couples were reunited in the small drawing room in the Rue Monge, in order to savor, amid the indescribable delight of deliverance, all the promises of happiness.

And yet, Mirande did not regret having realized the project that a night of meditation had further affirmed in him. That same morning, oppressed but resolute, he had gone into the laboratory where Brion had died and where Castillan had committed suicide, and there, without hesitation, he had broken the ampoules that were still full; he had held out to the flame of the Bunsen burner the pages of the notebook in which the master had minutely recorded the method of the preparation of the serum. Of the prodigious discovery, nothing subsisted but a pinch of ash and some broken glass.

No, he did not regret it. What good would it have done to give themselves to one another if, tempted by the magic power, they had poisoned all their joys with it? At that very moment, would they be savoring, two by two, the ineffable delights of presence, if they had not been able to throw the light veil of mystery over their hearts? And of how many other reckless couples, all over the world, would it have troubled the ecstasy?

No, he did not regret it, for all the benefits of clairvoyance are not worth as much as the benefit of amour.

Afterword by the Translator

As I pointed out in the introduction to this translation, *Le Lynx* seems to be a deliberate attempt to fuse a
conte philosophique with a popular melodrama, in order
to make an interesting hypothetical question more interesting for general readers, and perhaps obtain a success
that had previously evaded the more serious work of
both writers. It failed, but one can hardly blame them for
trying, and the failure was not so much down to them as
to the stubborn stupidity of the readers of the day, the
majority of whom did not want to be asked to think, and
were resentful of any such invitation. Things have not
changed in the intervening century, of course—if anything, they have got worse—but for the sake of the mi-
nority who are, in fact, interested in this sort of thing, it
might be worth taking a closer look at what they did and
why.

Why does the story end in the way it does? Why
does Gabriel make the decision to destroy Brion's formula, thus taking it upon himself to deny humankind a
great scientific asset, only consulting one other person
before doing so, and then ignoring her perfectly justified
argument in favor of his own ridiculous conviction?

The simple answer, of course, is that he does it because he is a coward and an idiot, as the story has proven
abundantly. Given that even Jeanne wimps out at the
end, the story has only one hero, in Francette, and it is
perhaps worth considering what her reaction would have
been to Gabriel's appalling treason. She, of course,
knows far more about amour than he does, having been
unwise enough to love him—even heroes are not im-

mune to falling for the worst possible member of the opposite sex—so she would know better than anyone whether amour is so precious as to outweigh everything else that Jeanne puts in the balance against it.

Where has amour got Francette? Stabbed in the heart—which is in essence, where it gets everyone, metaphorically if not literally speaking. It has got her so nearly killed that only a miracle can save her—but miracles are easy to contrive in fiction, where an author simply has to write that "and then there was a miracle." Even so, she is maimed for life—and for what? So that she can be packed off to the south of France with utter contempt, in order that her continued presence in her loved one's proximity will not be an embarrassment to him. If she had had the use of the serum, of course, she could have identified Le Crabe without exposing herself to any danger, but her employer, having exploited her affection ruthlessly in order to send her into the jaws of death, did not even think of offering it to her, nor suffer an instant's regret over the fact that he could have saved her from being stabbed in the heart. Of course, if she had had it, and had been able to read Gabriel's mind, she might have been very rapidly cured of her infatuation, having seen him for what he really is—but that would only have worked to her advantage, not his, so the repulsive egomaniac does not even consider it.

In reality, of course, Gabriel would not even have had the chance to favor his own silly oversensitivity over the good of the human race, because Simone would never have given him a second look. She would have married Quatrefin instead, he being by far the better catch and by far the better man. But this is fiction—and that, really, is the whole point. In fiction, the protagonist has to get the girl, and in fiction, amorous servants don't matter. All that matters is that the rules of fiction are observed, and the rules of fiction say that what qualifies as an ending for a story is that the protagonist gets the girl and that the world is restored to the condition it was in at the beginning of the story: the known, familiar situation, which, however putrid an disgusting it might be, is the way things are and therefore (in fiction) the way things ought to be. Endings are normalizing, because that is what qualifies as an ending, in popular fiction. Innovations have to be eliminated, and the protagonist's amour, however sick it is, must conquer all, whereas the amour of minor characters can go to hell, which is where minor characters belong, simply for being minor characters, and hence cannon fodder. That is what popular fiction is all about.

Did Michel Corday and André Couvreur believe what they made Gabriel say at the end of the story? Everything about their previous works implies that they did not, that they made him say it because they were trying to write popular fiction, and because the rules of popular demanded that he say it. Were they being sarcastic? Almost certainly. Did they secretly hope that the reader's reaction to the ending would be to vomit in disgust? Probably. Did it actually have that effect? Who can tell—but if they did, they shot themselves in the foot, success-wise. Did they ever do it again? Yes. If at first you don't succeed...

Writing serious speculative fiction is a thankless task, but some people try to do it anyway. Sometimes, they try to sneak seriousness in by the back door, using cunning and trickery.

Does it ever work?

Well, does it?

SF & FANTASY

Adolphe Alhaiza. *Cybele*
Alphonse Allais. *The Adventures of Captain Cap*
Henri Allorge. *The Great Cataclysm*
Guy d'Armen. *Doc Ardan: The City of Gold and Lepers; The Troglodytes of Mount Everest/The Giants of Black Lake*
G.-J. Arnaud. *The Ice Company*
André Arnyvelde. *The Ark; The Mutilated Bacchus*
Charles Asselineau. *The Double Life*
Henri Austruy. *The Eupantophone; The Olotelepan; The Petitpaon Era*
Honoré de Balzac. *The Last Fay*
Barillet-Lagargousse. *The Final War*
Cyprien Bérard. *The Vampire Lord Ruthwen*
S. Henry Berthoud. *Martyrs of Science*
Aloysius Bertrand. *Gaspard de la Nuit*
Richard Bessière. *The Gardens of the Apocalypse; The Masters of Silence*
Chevalier de Béthune. *The World of Mercury*
Albert Bleunard. *Ever Smaller*
Félix Bodin. *The Novel of the Future*
Pierre Boitard. *Journey to the Sun*
Louis Boussenard. *Monsieur Synthesis*
Alphonse Brown. *City of Glass; The Conquest of the Air*
Émile Calvet. *In a Thousand Years*
André Caroff. *The Terror of Madame Atomos; Miss Atomos; The Return of Madame Atomos; The Mistake of Madame Atomos; The Monsters of Madame Atomos; The Revenge of Madame Atomos; The Resurrection of Madame Atomos; The Mark of Madame Atomos; The Spheres of Madame Atomos; The Wrath of Madame Atomos* (w/M. & Sylvie Stéphan)
Félicien Champsaur. *Homo-Deus; The Human Arrow; Nora, The Ape-Woman; Ouha, King of the Apes; Pharaoh's Wife*
Didier de Chousy. *Ignis*
Jules Clarétie. *Obsession*

Jacques Collin de Plancy. *Voyage to the Center of the Earth*
Michel Corday. *The Eternal Flame*
André Couvreur. *Caresco, Superman; The Exploits of Professor Tornada* (3 vols.); *The Necessary Evil*
Camille Debans. *The Misfortunes of John Bull*
Captain Danrit. *Undersea Odyssey*
C. I. Defontenay. *Star (Psi Cassiopeia)*
Charles Derennes. *The People of the Pole*
Georges Dodds (anthologist). *The Missing Link*
Charles Dodeman. *The Silent Bomb*
Harry Dickson. *The Heir of Dracula; Harry Dickson vs. The Spider*
Jules Dornay. *Lord Ruthven Begins*
Alfred Driou. *The Adventures of a Parisian Aeronaut*
Odette Dulac. *The War of the Sexes*
Alexandre Dumas. *The Return of Lord Ruthven*
Renée Dunan. *Baal; The Ultimate Pleasure*
J.-C. Dunyach. *The Night Orchid; The Thieves of Silence*
Henri Duvernois. *The Man Who Found Himself*
Achille Eyraud. *Voyage to Venus*
Henri Falk. *The Age of Lead*
Paul Féval. *Anne of the Isles; Knightshade; Revenants; Vampire City; The Vampire Countess; The Wandering Jew's Daughter*
Paul Féval, *fils. Felifax, the Tiger-Man*
Charles de Fieux. *Lamékis*
Fernand Fleuret. *Jim Click*
Louis Forest. *Someone is Stealing Children in Paris*
Arnould Galopin. *Doctor Omega; Doctor Omega and the Shadowmen* (anthology); *Harry Dickson: The Man in Grey; Harry Dickson: Tenebras*
Judith Gautier. *Isoline and the Serpent-Flower*
H. Gayar. *The Marvelous Adventures of Serge Myrandhal on Mars*
G.L. Gick. *Harry Dickson and the Werewolf of Rutherford Grange*
Raoul Gineste. *The Second Life of Doctor Albin*

Delphine de Girardin. *Balzac's Cane*

Léon Gozlan. *The Vampire of the Val-de-Grâce*

Jules Gros. *The Fossil Man*

Jimmy Guieu. *The Polarian-Denebian War* (2 vols.)

Edmond Haraucourt. *Daah, the First Human; Illusions of Immortality*

Nathalie Henneberg. *The Green Gods*

Eugène Hennebert. *The Enchanted City*

Jules Hoche. *The Maker of Men and His Formula*

V. Hugo, P. Foucher & P. Meurice. *The Hunchback of Notre-Dame*

Romain d'Huissier. *Hexagon: Dark Matter*

Jules Janin. *The Magnetized Corpse*

Michel Jeury. *Chronolysis*

Gustave Kahn. *The Tale of Gold and Silence*

Gérard Klein. *The Mote in Time's Eye*

Fernand Kolney. *Love in 5000 Years*

Paul Lacroix. *Danse Macabre*

Louis-Guillaume de La Follie. *The Unpretentious Philosopher*

Jean de La Hire. *The Fiery Wheel; Enter the Nyctalope; The Nyctalope on Mars; The Nyctalope vs. Lucifer; The Nyctalope Steps In; Night of the Nyctalope; Return of the Nyctalope*

Etienne-Léon de Lamothe-Langon. *The Virgin Vampire*

André Laurie. *Spiridon*

Gabriel de Lautrec. *The Vengeance of the Oval Portrait*

Alain le Drimeur. *The Future City*

Georges Le Faure & Henri de Graffigny. *The Extraordinary Adventures of a Russian Scientist Across the Solar System* (2 vols.)

Gustave Le Rouge. *The Dominion of the World* (w/Gustave Guitton) (4 vols.); *The Mysterious Doctor Cornelius* (3 vols.); *The Vampires of Mars*

Jules Lermina. *The Battle of Strasbourg; Mysteryville; Panic in Paris; The Secret of Zippelius; To-Ho and the Gold Destroyers*

André Lichtenberger. *The Centaurs; The Children of the Crab*

Maurice Limat. *Mephista*

Listonai. *The Philosophical Voyager*
Jean-Marc & Randy Lofficier. *Edgar Allan Poe on Mars; The Katrina Protocol; Pacifica 1, 2; Robonocchio; Return of the Nyctalope;* (anthologists) *Tales of the Shadowmen 1-12; The Vampire Almanac* (2 vols.); *The French Fantasy Treasury* (3 vols.)
Ch. Lomon & P.-B. Gheuzi. *The Last Days of Atlantis*
Camille Mauclair. *The Virgin Orient*
Xavier Mauméjean. *The League of Heroes*
Joseph Méry. *The Tower of Destiny*
Hippolyte Mettais. *Paris Before the Deluge; The Year 5865*
Louise Michel. *The Human Microbes; The New World*
Tony Moilin. *Paris in the Year 2000*
José Moselli. *Illa's End*
John-Antoine Nau. *Enemy Force*
Marie Nizet. *Captain Vampire*
Charles Nodier. *Trilby and The Crumb Fairy*
C. Nodier, A. Beraud & Toussaint-Merle. *Frankenstein*
Henri de Parville. *An Inhabitant of the Planet Mars*
Gaston de Pawlowski. *Journey to the Land of the 4th Dimension*
Georges Pellerin. *The World in 2000 Years*
Ernest Pérochon. *The Frenetic People*
Pierre Pelot. *The Child Who Walked on the Sky*
Jean Petithuguenin. *An International Mission to the Moon*
J. Polidori, C. Nodier, E. Scribe. *Lord Ruthven the Vampire*
P.-A. Ponson du Terrail. *The Immortal Woman; The Vampire and the Devil's Son*
Georges Price. *The Missing Men of the Sirius*
René Pujol. *The Chimerical Quest*
Edgar Quinet. *Ahasuerus; The Enchanter Merlin*
Henri de Régnier. *A Surfeit of Mirrors*
Maurice Renard. *The Blue Peril; Doctor Lerne; The Doctored Man; A Man Among the Microbes; The Master of Light*
Restif de la Bretonne. *The Discovery of the Austral Continent by a Flying Man; Posthumous Correspondence* (3 vols.)
Jean Richepin. *The Crazy Corner; The Wing*

Albert Robida. *The Adventures of Saturnin Farandoul; Chalet in the Sky; The Clock of the Centuries; The Electric Life; The Engineer Von Satanas*

J.-H. Rosny Aîné. *Helgvor of the Blue River; The Givreuse Enigma; The Mysterious Force; The Navigators of Space; Vamireh; The World of the Variants; The Young Vampire*

Marcel Rouff. *Journey to the Inverted World*

Marie-Anne de Roumier-Robert. *The Voyage of Lord Seaton to the Seven Planets*

Léonie Rouzade. *The World Turned Upside Down*

Han Ryner. *The Human Ant; The Superhumans; The Son of Silence*

Frank Schildiner. *The Quest of Frankenstein*

Pierre de Selenes: *An Unknown World*

Norbert Sevestre. *Sâr Dubnotal: Vs. Jack the Ripper; The Astral Trail*

Angelo de Sorr. *The Vampires of London*

Brian Stableford. *The Empire of the Necromancers (1. The Shadow of Frankenstein; 2. Frankenstein and the Vampire Countess; 3. Frankenstein in London); Eurydice's Lament; The New Faust at the Tragicomique; Sherlock Holmes and The Vampires of Eternity; The Stones of Camelot; The Wayward Muse.* (anthologist) *News from the Moon; The Germans on Venus; The Supreme Progress; The World Above the World; Nemoville; Investigations of the Future; The Conqueror of Death; The Revolt of the Machines; The Man With the Blue Face; The Aerial Valley; The New Moon; The Nickel Man; On the Brink of the World's End; The Mirror of Present Events; The Humanishere*

Jacques Spitz. *The Eye of Purgatory*

Kurt Steiner. *Ortog*

Eugène Thébault. *Radio-Terror*

C.-F. Tiphaigne de La Roche. *Amilec*

Simon Tyssot de Patot. *The Strange Voyages of Jacques Massé and Pierre de Mésange*

Louis Ulbach. *Prince Bonifacio*

Théo Varlet. *The Castaways of Eros; The Golden Rock.; The Martian Epic* (w/Octave Joncquel); *Timeslip Troopers* (w/André Blandin); *The Xenobiotic Invasion*
Pierre Véron. *The Merchants of Health*
Paul Vibert. *The Mysterious Fluid*
Villiers de l'Isle-Adam. *The Scaffold; The Vampire Soul*
Gaston de Wailly. *The Murderer of the World*
Philippe Ward. *Artahe; Manhattan Ghost* (w/Mickael Laguerre); *The Song of Montségur* (w/Sylvie Miller)
Willy. *Astral Amour*

Victor Margueritte. *The Bacheloress; The Companion; The Couple*

NON-FICTION

Stephen R. Bissette. *Blur 1-5. Green Mountain Cinema 1; Teen Angels*
Win Scott Eckert. *Crossovers* (2 vols.)
Georges Grison. *The Heads that Fell in Paris*
Jean-Marc & Randy Lofficier. *Shadowmen* (2 vols.)
Randy Lofficier. *Over Here*
Brian Stableford. *The Plurality of Imaginary Worlds*